1ext Classics

AMY WITTING was the pen name of Joan Austral Fraser, born on 26 January 1918 in the inner-Sydney suburb of Annandale. After attending Fort Street Girls' High School she studied arts at the University of Sydney.

She married Les Levick, a teacher, in 1948 and they had a son. Witting spent her working life teaching, but began writing seriously while recovering from tuberculosis in the 1950s.

Two stories appeared in the *New Yorker* in the mid-1960s, leading to *The Visit* (1977), an acclaimed novel about small-town life in New South Wales. Two years later Witting completed her masterpiece, *I for Isobel*, which was rejected by publishers troubled by its depiction of a mother tormenting her child.

When *I for Isobel* was eventually published, in 1989, it became a bestseller. Witting was lauded for the power and acuity of her portrait of the artist as a young woman. In 1993 she won the Patrick White Award.

Witting published prolifically in her final decade. After two more novels, her *Collected Poems* appeared in 1998 and her collected stories, *Faces and Voices*, in 2000.

Between these volumes came *Isobel on the Way to the Corner Shop*, the sequel to *I for Isobel*. Both *Isobel* novels were shortlisted for the Miles Franklin Award; the latter was the 2000 *Age* Book of the Year.

Amy Witting died in 2001, weeks before her novel *After Cynthia* was published and while she was in the early stages of writing the third *Isobel* book. She was made a Member of the Order of Australia and a street in Canberra bears her name.

MARIA TAKOLANDER is the author of a collection of short stories, *The Double*, as well as three books of poetry and a work of literary criticism. Her poems have appeared in annual best-of anthologies since 2005. Maria is a senior lecturer at Deakin University in Geelong and is currently working on a novel, *Transit*.

ALSO BY AMY WITTING

The Visit
I for Isobel
Marriages (stories)
A Change in the Lighting
In and Out the Window (stories)
Maria's War
Faces and Voices (stories)
After Cynthia

Isobel on the Way to the Corner Shop
Amy Witting

Text Publishing Melbourne Australia

textclassics.com.au
textpublishing.com.au

The Text Publishing Company
Swann House
22 William Street
Melbourne Victoria 3000
Australia

First published by Penguin Books Australia 1999
This edition published by The Text Publishing Company 2015

Extracts from John Donne's 'A Feaver' appear on pages 163 and 211, extracts
from Gerald Manley Hopkins' 'Heaven-Haven' (*Poems*, 1918) appear on pages
171 and 173, and an extract from Hilaire Belloc's 'Juliet' (*Complete Verse*,
1954) appears on page 212.

Cover design by WH Chong
Page design by Text
Typeset by Midland Typesetters

Printed in Australia by Griffin Press, an Accredited ISO AS/NZS 14001:2004
Environmental Management System printer

Primary print ISBN: 9781922182715
Ebook ISBN: 9781925095647
Author: Witting, Amy, 1918–2001.
Title: Isobel on the way to the corner shop / by Amy Witting ; introduced by
Maria Takolander.
Series: Text classics.
Dewey Number: A823.3

CONTENTS

The Walking Wounded
by Maria Takolander

'THE world is full of walking wounded.' This is how Amy Witting accounted for the breakthrough success of her bestselling 1989 novel, *I for Isobel*. That book—republished as a Text Classic in 2014—introduces us to Isobel Callaghan, the victim of an abusive mother. It begins with the child Isobel masochistically anticipating her birthday, knowing that her mother will once again withhold gifts. It ends with Isobel as a young adult, resolving to forge an independent life for herself as a writer.

I for Isobel, as Witting recognised, resonated with readers familiar with the wounds of childhood, wounds that often endure unseen into adulthood, wounds that can be secretly undressed—and redressed—in the private infirmary of reading. I was one of those readers. When I first encountered the novel, as a young adult, I was stunned by Witting's insight. As is often the case with great books,

I felt as if the writer had discovered my secrets, though I also knew that she was securely on my side.

If I initially avoided *Isobel on the Way to the Corner Shop*, the sequel to *I for Isobel* published in 1999, it was because I felt a cowardly—and misplaced—sense of trepidation. While Witting's insights are fierce, her writing is always humane. *Isobel on the Way to the Corner Shop* is as devastating and as enriching as its predecessor.

In the second Isobel novel our protagonist still finds refuge in reading and has achieved some success as a writer. Yet she is troubled by poverty, hunger, isolation and, moreover, what she describes as the 'dead country' in her heart: 'not a matter to brood on.' Upon trying to write a romantic scene and confronting writer's block, she must admit her tragic inexperience in love. Her identity has been defined by her mother's hatred.

Among a group of writers in the pub, Isobel comes close to losing her cultivated façade of invulnerability and self-sufficiency.

> 'If you knew what it was like to be mad,' said a loud, angry voice that brought sudden silence. 'If you knew what it was like, not being able to say, "I am I." Being taken over, that's it. The other, the secret thing using your mouth to speak through.'
>
> 'I say, calm down,' said a voice beside her.
>
> She knew then that it was herself speaking but she didn't care. Let them find out. What joy, what marvellous relief it was to say the words.
>
> 'It's no help to set your teeth and fight it. It's smarter than you. Bigger and stronger. And it's

everything you hate. But you're there. That's what they don't see, that you're there. You're watching and you can't do anything. A fly on the wall, that's what you are.'

Soon after, Isobel attempts a journey from her writer's garret, a shabby attic in a Sydney boarding house, to the corner shop. On the way she experiences a breakdown and is transported to hospital, where she is diagnosed with tuberculosis and institutionalised for treatment.

Far from being alarmed, Isobel is relieved to 'have all horrors assembled under the name of an illness, represented by a baby's hand-print on her lung'. As the infant metaphor suggests, she remains afflicted by more than tuberculosis. Among the eccentric staff and patients of the sanatorium, Isobel finds treatment for both disease and childhood injury.

It is impossible to believe that Amy Witting could write so powerfully about such matters without first-hand knowledge of them. She once said that she would rather 'dive stark naked into a barrel of rattlesnakes' than write her autobiography. However, we know that Witting spent five months in a tuberculosis sanatorium in the Blue Mountains. And her literary obsessions suggest that she survived a traumatic childhood. In fact, she confessed that the Isobel novels were autobiographical, that it was the 'terrible truth of fiction' which helped her 'to conquer the truth of that situation'.

Witting was fifty-nine when her first novel appeared, and most of her life's work—which includes other novels, and short stories and poetry—was published when she was in her seventies. Before that, Witting worked as a teacher; she married and had a son. She may well have spent these years coping with the demands of the present and overcoming the damage of the past. 'I really was a very disturbed person,' she said late in her life. 'I don't like to look back on it.'

Witting's habit of using pseudonyms for her writing similarly communicates a desire to hide, although it also reveals an Isobel-like rebellious intelligence. Born Joan Austral Fraser in 1918, Witting published her first poem as a teenager under a pen name. As a student at the University of Sydney she hoaxed James McAuley with a mock avant-garde poem allegedly written by Sun-Setna—and this was before McAuley and Harold Stewart invented the infamous poet Ern Malley to hoax Max Harris.

Witting also published a parodic work of short fiction that exposed the sexism of a pair of stories by Frank Moorhouse and Michael Wilding about the rape of an unconscious woman. 'A Piece of the Puzzle Is Missing', attributed to the androgynously named Chris Willoughby, gives that unconscious woman a voice.

Her final pseudonym announces a commitment to policing the unconscious ideologies and behaviours not only of others, but also of herself. As a junior teacher in rural New South Wales, Witting worked for a sadistic headmistress named Amy Wicht, whom Witting surmised was inflicting suffering on others because of her own unacknowledged pain. Witting resolved that she would never be 'unwitting' in that way. This resolve is shared by Isobel, who learns in the sanatorium to self-consciously guard against her cruel past when interacting with fellow patients.

Witting's choice of pen name thus attests to her concern with morality—not in an abstract sense, but as it is enacted in our day-to-day behaviour. Morality is not a sentimental concept for Witting; neither is it given by religion. It is hard won.

Individuality is another concern of Witting's. *I for Isobel* highlights that interest in its very title. *Isobel on the Way to the Corner Shop* continues the author's exploration of social conformity, of how unconventionality is often feared and attacked. In an interview Witting referred to 'the cage where you can neither sit nor stand nor lie'. Isobel rattles that cage by reading, despite others around her feeling threatened by this transgressively intellectual and individualistic activity.

Kafka famously wrote that 'a book must be the axe for the frozen sea within us.' It is unsurprising that Isobel reads *The Metamorphosis* in the sanatorium, for Witting is Kafkaesque in her savage commitment to shattering our illusions and exposing our vulnerabilities, in provoking us to question our complacent understanding of ourselves and our relationships.

Despite its comparable tale of claustrophobic personal distress, *Isobel on the Way to the Corner Shop* is less like *The Metamorphosis* and more like Charlotte Brontë's *Jane Eyre*. In that novel, Jane finds refuge in a mansion where she is haunted by the madness of the past, before finding peace. Witting's novel, in which Isobel recovers from her terrible past in a grand sanatorium, is similarly uplifting in its conclusion. Witting does not want to destroy; like Brontë, she wants to recreate. The impetus for both women's resurrection is love. It is a love stripped of romance and religion; it is love restored to the simple fact of its necessity and therefore its true potency.

Ultimately *Isobel on the Way to the Corner Shop* speaks even more urgently than its predecessor. The novel is compelling—a true page-turner—while maintaining the complexity we expect of great literature. It is a tragedy that Witting, whose writing has been acclaimed internationally yet remains undervalued in Australia, died before she completed the third and final Isobel book.

An unconventional obituary in the *Guardian* described Witting as a 'freak', remarking on her 'strange juxtaposition of a raw history with a playful, merciless, fastidious mind'. The same can be said of her unforgettable doppelgänger, Isobel Callaghan. 'Freak' is a term that Amy Witting might have embraced, given her empathy for the walking wounded, those individuals who are often given such labels and to whom Isobel so unforgettably speaks.

Isobel on the Way to the Corner Shop

PROLOGUE
CONCERNING LOVE
AND PARANOIA

'How can I write about love,' Isobel asked herself, 'when I don't know the first thing about it?'

She sat at the typewriter staring at the blank page where George should hours ago have made his delicate, sensitive approach to Anna.

Since she had rolled that sheet into the machine, she had played a dozen games of patience, stared out from her attic window at the view of the houses across the street, eaten a baked bean sandwich, chewed a fingernail painfully down to the quick, keeping at bay the thought that the whole enterprise had been a mistake, that perhaps she couldn't write at all.

Two successful stories and a rave note from an editor and she was off. Living in an attic, how childish. Had she really supposed that three and a half flights of stairs would take her halfway up Parnassus?

She would not get up from the typewriter. She could not give up, she must not fail. She had burnt her boats, thrown up her job...

Now, don't dodge.

You told Mr Richard to fuck off.

She had screamed at Mr Richard to fuck off. She had screamed in a rage, a flash of red lightning frightening to remember.

I'm not mad, no, not mad. Frank always said that one day I would explode, and so I did. Told him to go and find something useful to do, instead of peering over my shoulder clucking like a bloody half-witted hen. Get the fuck off and let me get on with my work in peace, will you?

He had fucked off, all right, and after a moment of shock and horror, so had she, cleared her desk in a frantic hurry and run, run all the way back to Glebe, bawling. Too ashamed to go back, ever. Run through the front door of the rooming house and up the stairs to her room without for the first time pausing to look for mail in her letter box, where Fenwick's letter had been waiting to change her life.

Fenwick's praise had been warming, but it was no help to her now.

'Oh, come on, George. There you are, in front of Anna, and you have to indicate a certain special interest. The thing exists, doesn't it? At the least it's a kind of pairing device. Not very reliable, in my opinion. But that's beside the point.'

It was not at all beside the point.

This was the final resort. She would not budge from her chair until George had declared himself to Anna.

'Oh, do come on, George. Spit it out. You can blush and stammer all you like, but get it said. You have plenty to say on other subjects. On politics, I can't shut you up.'

Nervous, articulate, vain, dyspeptic George was in trouble at the school where he taught History, suspect because of his regrettably left-wing opinions. A parent had complained to the headmaster about his indoctrination of his pupils.

George had had plenty to say to the headmaster. Why couldn't he speak his heart to Anna?

What was love anyhow?

Her own researches into the matter had been disastrous. One didn't learn about love in one night stands.

It puzzled her still that an activity which had such a long, extensively documented connection with human love, was regarded indeed as its expression, could be performed with such indifference to the partner and even with dislike and contempt.

'*You can just piss off now.*'

That had been an extreme example but not, she understood, an exception. At least the young man's frankness had given her an opening also.

'I thought I was doing you a favour. Is this how you react when someone does you a favour?'

'You were ready enough.'

'Well, yes. That's the favour I was speaking of.'

'Oh, thank you very much. Now piss off.'

5

She had dressed in silence. Sitting on the edge of the bed to pull on her stockings, she had expressed the idea she had been considering as she had stepped into pants and skirt.

'Look at it this way. There's a general tradition that sex is connected with...well, with friendly feelings. You seem to see it differently. I was just wondering why.'

He had groaned, seized a clump of his hair in each fist and tugged.

'A clever bitch. Just what I was needing!'

'But that's the point. What do you need? Apart, that is, from the physical thing?'

'Nothing you've got.'

'I wasn't thinking about meeting your needs. I just wanted to know what they were. Matter of interest.'

This polite inquiry had seemed to be a very satisfactory reprisal for his insults, though she had not meant it so. She had stooped to put on her shoes; she looked up to find him staring at her white-faced, in baffled fury.

'Oh, get out!'

She had gone taking with her the honours of war, but why had it been war in the first place?

She could cope with the difficulties of promiscuous women—after all, she was one, had been one. The difficulties of promiscuous men were beyond her.

One thing was established: one didn't go looking for love in strange beds. She hadn't found much physical pleasure there either. The whole procedure had been much overrated.

So what was love?

A truce? A temporary suspension of the normal state of hostility between the sexes? That was a bit savage. Shared personal fiction. She knew about that. She had been essential to Mr Richard's personal fiction, which was that he was gainfully employed at Lingard Brothers, where it was Isobel's duty to translate the German mail. Mr Richard's share in the task was to select a letter, probably at random, since he knew no German, to commend it to Isobel's attention as urgent, to disappear for five minutes or so into his cubbyhole, to dash out and ask her if she hadn't finished it yet, then to stand behind her clucking, twitching and sighing, until the letter was finished and he could perform the important task of carrying it to Mr Walter, his elder brother and boss.

Mr Richard's personal fiction was essential to his self-respect. She had worked that out the day Olive had said, 'Mr Richard, Isobel would get on much faster if you didn't interrupt her.'

And Mr Richard's reaction had been not indignation but fear.

Seeing the dread in his eyes before he turned and walked away, she had resolved on tolerance. 'Let him have his little dream of importance. I can afford it, now that I know the fear behind it.'

According to her theory of shared personal fiction, she had been having a love affair with Mr Richard. Scrub that definition.

Tolerance had failed, after all.

Well, she had had a headache. The German words had been drifting and eluding her, trying her temper already.

Truly, she had seen red, the flash of lightning which had seemed to split her skull had been bright scarlet. So she had stripped poor big, flabby Mr Richard to his small, cowering soul. Not pretty.

No use expecting a reference, either. She had slammed that door behind her, all right.

It had been a matter of timing. Fenwick's letter had seemed like a directive. If the letter hadn't come that very day, found her jobless, without prospects, frightened, too, by that flash of red lightning...

A place to hide. A signpost to the future and a place to hide. It was timing not only to the day but to the hour. She had stopped crying, had washed her face, combed her hair and discovered that she was hungry. She had decided then to defy fate and brace herself for the ordeal of breaking the news to Aunt Noelene with cinnamon toast and real coffee at Repin's. She had found Fenwick's letter in her box on the way out, had noted with a lift of the spirits that it was a thin one, promising acceptance, and had put it in her bag unread. It would be an extra treat with the cinnamon toast. So it was in the cheerful and reassuring atmosphere of the crowded café that she had read it at last.

> Dear Miss Callaghan,
> Thank you for sending us 'Meet me there'. It is a most impressive story and I'll be happy to publish it in our April issue.
> I do want to tell you how much I like your work. It is just the sort of thing I am anxious to find for *Seminal*.

I think you have the gift of universal acceptance. In your first story, 'Perhaps they were dancing', the Lesbian embrace the girl surprises is shown with sympathy and respect, while the comments of the schoolgirls in the discussion which follows are extremely funny, yet touched with the same sympathetic acceptance. That last comment, 'Well, if they were dancing, Miss Weatherby was the man,' I thought a stunner.

From that to a suicide pact is a long step and a bold one, but you bring it off very well. Apparently it is established fact that intending suicides experience an improvement in mood once the decision is made. Observers often remark that the victim 'had seemed so much better lately'—I don't know if you had known this, or were simply going on writer's intuition. You seem to have that in abundance.

I am looking forward to seeing more of your work.

Sincerely,
Tom Fenwick

Why not? she had thought, reading and rereading the letter. She had savings, all of fifty-six pounds in the bank, a typewriter and—it had seemed at that moment—an infinite capacity for fiction and, perhaps, talent. Fenwick thought so.

The attic too had seemed part of a grand plan. The tall, shabby rooming house would, she had told herself, be full of stories. But in that house there seemed to be one story only,

9

and the people she passed on the stairs lived it in the privacy of misery, the last stand of human dignity. The odd old lady alone, mumbling, shuffling along the street in slippers with her few provisions in her string bag, the single mother with the two whining children, tired, harassed and sullen— they had closed upon their fate, their looks said, 'Keep away.'

And Mr Lynch.

She averted her thoughts from Mr Lynch and fixed them on the uncooperative George.

So you know nothing about love. You write about plenty of things you know nothing about. What do you know about people in a suicide pact? Fenwick had said it was writer's intuition.

It didn't work with love.

Right. If intuition won't work, and you don't have experience to guide you, and this is one you can't get from observation, use your intelligence, use what you do know.

She typed.

'"Anna," said George. "I love you." '

No. Apart from being absolute corn, and out of context, it doesn't leave George a retreat. Being George, he'll be tentative, testing the water.

'"Anna, do you know you have beautiful eyes?" '

So Anna, being Anna, will answer, 'All the better to see you with.'

It has to be more than a compliment, a suggestion of good faith and serious intentions.

A way of retreat for George, a promise of commitment for Anna.

Oh, the hell with the pair of you. George can be a crusty old bachelor, Anna can wither on the stem.

She pulled the sheet out of the typewriter, crumpled it and tossed it into the basket at her feet.

It was worse than lack of experience, or lack of imagination. This was the dead country, the airless space where she could not breathe nor move nor speak.

It was not a matter to brood on.

That settled it. She would go out this evening after all. She would go to the McIvors'.

She hadn't meant to go to the McIvors', having a suspicion that she had worn out her welcome. Liza had said, last Friday evening, without warmth, 'You're getting to be quite a regular.'

What had she meant by that? Had she meant 'quite a pest' or 'quite a freeloader'?

Duncan's letter had been warm enough. Her first fan letter ever, it was another she knew by heart:

Dear Miss Callaghan,
I am writing to tell you how impressed I am by your story 'Meet me there'. It was a brave subject to tackle and I think you brought it off wonderfully well.

My wife Liza and I both enjoyed 'Perhaps they were dancing' and we are looking forward to reading your next story.

We should very much like to make your acquaintance. Friday nights we have a few friends in, mostly people with an interest in writing, or at least in reading.

You will find some admirers among them, too.

We both hope you will drop in, any Friday evening from 7.30 on.

Sincerely,
Duncan McIvor

Any Friday evening didn't mean every Friday evening.

There was another reason for avoiding the McIvors. The trouble with success was that it roused expectations. Questions like, 'What are you working on now?' That was not a question one welcomed when one was spending hours staring at a blank sheet of paper in a typewriter.

She couldn't stay alone with it all evening. It would have to be the McIvors'.

If she went to the McIvors', she must take a contribution. That might be what Liza had been hinting, that she was freeloading. Other people brought flagons of wine, and sometimes bottles. A bottle might be insufficient. One problem about being poor was that one couldn't afford to look poor.

She went across to the bed and rolled back the mattress to reach the copies of the *Sydney Morning Herald* which served as insulation against the cold. She groped under the top copy and brought out a large envelope. She replaced the mattress, straightened the bedclothes and emptied the envelope onto the quilt.

Two pounds four and fivepence.

She had a week's work in prospect from Secretary Girls Friday, which found short-term employment for office workers (five pounds joining fee and ten per cent of the first fourteen days' pay).

At the agency she had got over the lack of a reference very neatly. Looking sideways and downwards, she had said, 'I left without notice. I had some trouble with one of the partners. A personal matter.'

Mrs Martin's cosy, plump face had tightened. She had clicked her tongue in sympathy and said indignantly, 'Men! I shan't ring them up then, dear, if you'd rather I didn't. I'll just give you a little test in typing and shorthand. I have to be sure of your efficiency, you know.'

The thought of Mr Walter or Mr Richard in the grip of lust could brighten the gloomiest moment. She dismissed that entertaining image in order to concentrate on practical matters.

The job wouldn't start till next Friday. Eight shillings for next week's rent. Fares and lunches for the week at the office.

She certainly didn't want to go to the bank, where the account was at danger level.

She opened the food cupboard, which had begun life as a washstand: tin of powdered milk, sliced bread still in its waxed wrapper, four tins of soup, three of baked beans, one of Spam, two (small) of spaghetti in tomato sauce—it would be tight, but she could make it.

The thing to take was a bottle of whisky, a personal present for Duncan and Liza. She didn't see herself lugging a flagon; besides, she had seen Duncan accepting a bottle

13

of whisky with gratifying enthusiasm. It would need to be a good brand, too.

Think of it as an investment in the future.

She could do without dinner tonight and hold out for supper—one of Liza's wonderful suppers, savoury mixtures wrapped in fragile pancakes, leek and mushroom pie... meanwhile she could stave off hunger by grazing with discretion on the savouries. There was always plenty to eat at the McIvors'.

She put the cover on the typewriter. Perhaps George and Anna might get together overnight.

Now for the expedition to the bathroom. This was not a simple affair. She got her duffle bag and a bath towel from the store cupboard, added soap and washer from the corner basin and clean underwear from the suitcase under the bed.

With all personal items concealed in the duffle bag, her door locked, the key in the pocket of her slacks, she moved quietly down the five steps that took her to the half-landing above the staircase, moved even more quietly down six steps and craned to look at the door of Mr Lynch's room.

If it was ajar, Mr Lynch would hear her step, no matter how lightly she tried to move. He would come out of his room to watch her pass. The bathroom was a flight further down; even if she got past before he came out, he would wait, patiently, for her return. He did not speak. At first she had nodded to him, but he had made no response. He seemed only to want to watch her go past.

He was a small, pastel-coloured man with silver hair and pink-rimmed pale blue eyes. His gaze was steady; his

14

mouth on the other hand moved with the shiftiness one expects of eyes.

He frightened Isobel very much. If his door had been ajar, she would have retreated to her attic and made do with ablutions at the washbasin.

She had asked Mrs Foster the manageress if that old gentleman in 14A was all right in the head.

'Old Charlie Lynch? There's no harm in Charlie. He wouldn't hurt a fly.'

Which did not answer the question.

Isobel waited. Mrs Foster yielded, grudgingly.

'What's he doing anyhow?'

'He just watches me all the time. Whenever I go downstairs, he comes out of his room and watches me. I tried to speak to him but he didn't answer me. It's a bit creepy, that's all.'

'A cat can look at a king, I suppose.'

The look she directed at Isobel had nothing to do with cats and kings. It said clearly, 'And if you think yourself too good for the company, you can take yourself off.' Mrs Foster hadn't wanted Isobel as a tenant. She had looked with meaning at her office clothes and said, 'It's three floors up. A bit of a climb.'

Isobel in her turn studied Mrs Foster, an ageing woman with faded red hair, a puckered mouth and cold, pale, desolate eyes. She was neatly dressed, appearing slatternly only because she wore the remains of beauty like a dilapidated model gown.

'That's all right. I like to be high up.'

Mrs Foster had stared again, more searchingly.

15

'You're not on the game, are you? I won't have that.'

'What game?'

The quirk of the mouth which was possibly a smile did not soften the woman's countenance.

'No, I can see that you're not. All right then. Have a look at it. Here's the key. Eight shillings a week, including gas and electricity, gas used for cooking only, rent payable in advance Monday morning. No incoming phone calls and no men.'

The attic had appealed at once. It was spacious. The sloping outer wall was masked by a partition in which a central door opened on storage space, room to hang washing to dry or to keep unwanted articles out of sight.

All the furniture was shabby but came of two different species: the narrow iron bedstead with its thin mattress (certain to discourage illicit sex), the bedside cabinet, the table and the straight chair were utilitarian, but odd pieces seemed to have come down in the world as they migrated upwards—the heavy glass-fronted bookcase, with a large crack across one door, the marble-topped washstand, the chest of drawers with one drawer broken-fronted, and most of all the table under the gas ring, with its curved legs and its two carved drawers seeming to protest against the sheet of tin nailed to its upper surface, had all begun their lives in better circumstances.

The chamberpot in the cabinet had obviously belonged to an old-fashioned set of bedroom china, being decorated with roses in oval embossed frames. She had been amused by that discovery but the article had soon become functional, supplemented by a lidded enamel bucket which spared her embarrassment on her way down to the lavatory.

She hadn't known then about Mr Lynch; as she had arranged her crockery, her cooking utensils and her few books on the shelves of the cabinet, she felt that she was taking possession of her kingdom.

Today he must be out in the park feeding crumbs to birds. That was his other occupation.

Probably his observation of Isobel was just as harmless. No harm in old Charlie. Reason could not prevail against the queasiness of her stomach. Her usual homemade prayer for universal acceptance, her invocation of Saint Thomas More, 'Both must ye die, both be ye in the cart carrying forward', did not help either. She just wanted the cart carrying Mr Lynch to go a whole lot faster.

This time she was lucky. His door was still shut when she came out of the bathroom. She got back to her attic without experiencing that lurch of disgust that the sight of him caused her.

Going without dinner meant time to spare. She went out to buy her present of whisky before the pub shut at six, then feeling disinclined to go back to her room, she set off to walk downtown.

Though she had spent an hour window-shopping before she took the tram in King Street, she arrived too early at the McIvors'. It was past half past seven but the front door was shut and she had to ring the bell. She was hoping to give the bottle of whisky to Duncan, but it was Liza who came to the door, pale and fair as Hans Andersen's ice maiden in lime-green tunic and loose dark green trousers.

Isobel held out the bottle, knowing at once that it was a mistake. Liza was looking at it consideringly, as if she had forgotten that whisky could be drunk. Perhaps only Duncan drank whisky.

She looked sharply and intently at Isobel as if she were trying to place her, knew she had met her somewhere but couldn't recall her name.

'Come in. They're in the living room.'

She turned and Isobel followed her down the hall, pondering this behaviour. Its openness was somewhat reassuring. Though she might be too frequent a visitor— there was no longer much doubt about that—she was no gatecrasher, nor did her presence cause Liza any real inconvenience. Liza tended to vagueness; she must have something on her mind that had nothing to do with Isobel's arrival.

In the living room there were only Ray and Joel, the long and the short of it, sitting side by side in the best armchairs. They looked at her warily, as if she were a traveller getting into their compartment, certainly a nuisance, possibly a bore...

Now don't start imagining things.

After a brief nod, the two went back to their conversation, leaving her exposed to attack from the furniture: nothing as vulgar as a lounge suite, but deep armchairs upholstered in olive green corduroy, one sofa in tan leather, the big divan in beige velvet, cushions a controlled riot of colour, leaf brown carpet, cream linen curtains. You don't

18

belong here, it said. You belong elsewhere. In a room where everything is battered, broken, nakedly utilitarian, with newspaper stuffed under the mattress and a slop bucket hidden behind a partition.

Well, nobody knows that. Furniture can't talk.

Then Duncan was beside her. Duncan and Liza demonstrated one theory of love: the attraction of opposites. While she was tall, fair and aloof, he was stocky, dark and eager to please.

'What do you think of our new hanging, Isobel?'

He drew her towards the side wall where a large square of batik hung above the big divan.

'Interesting, isn't it? We picked it up at the exhibition of Eastern art and craft in Canberra. Do you see the motorbike?'

He pointed. On the red-brown background straw-coloured lines drew shoulders hunched over handlebars, a helmet aslant above then, a wheel roaring forward.

'Among the traditional motifs. Fascinating. A marriage of cultures.'

His tone, apologising for the cliché, was faintly amused.

Better than any motorbike you'll ever draw.

A warm breath of sympathy stirred as she thought of the artist, vague and brown-skinned, innocently in love with the motorbike, making himself an object of amusement to the sophisticated.

'I like it very much.'

'But you don't have a drink. What can I get you?'

'Oh, later!'

She had in fact let herself get too hungry. It would be dangerous to drink on an empty stomach.

'I'll get something later. I know where it is.'

Was there a flicker there in Duncan's eyes? Was he thinking, 'Too right you know where it is'?

Had Liza told him about the whisky? Had they condemned her as a freeloader?

Well, she wouldn't be coming again, not for some time at least.

Other people had come in and Duncan went to greet them. She looked round: some of the University mob, dull clothes and vivid faces. No Robbie.

She went on looking at the motorbike, thinking how the artist had exposed his childishness, drawing newness and astonishment into shoulders and wheel, pretending nothing.

That's right, she thought. You have to. Let them laugh if they like. You have to.

Since the hanging had become an object of interest, Joel had come to stand beside her. He was the long one, the two-syllable one.

She pointed out the motorbike.

'Like drawing the excitement of being a child, don't you think? Not just drawing a motorbike, but drawing the first one ever.'

Joel raised his eyebrows.

She had meant the comment sincerely, but now it seemed forced and pretentious. Without waiting for an answer, she sat down on the divan and slid along to the end of it, out of range of his scorn.

What was she doing here? Hours till supper, an empty stomach and the prospect of making conversation with cold, tedious, arrogant people…and beautiful girls who gave her heartburn and young men who seemed like Martians— or perhaps it was the planet Venus that they all came from, and she was the alien—why couldn't she have stayed safe at home?

Both must ye die. Both be ye in the cart carrying forward. In that we are companions.

The sensible thing would be to go and get something to eat. There would be savouries on the dining-room table. She had better get a glass of wine for protective colouration.

In the dining room a boy and a girl were standing at the table, she waiting as he poured a glass of red wine from a flagon. The sight of her in her pliant, forward-stooping attitude sent Isobel into a crimson-wattled rage. What bloody affectation! Who does she think she is, tricked out like a goddamn priestess?

The boy turned towards Isobel.

'Red?' he asked, holding out the glass.

She accepted it, thinking remorsefully that there was nothing odd about the dress. All the girls were wearing them. She would wear one herself if she could afford one.

No she wouldn't. She wouldn't be game.

Look at Isobel! Take a dekko at Isobel in that dress! Making a real effort! Poor old Isobel, pretending to be a girl.

The prison of other people's eyes. No prison narrower.

The nearer half of the dining-room table was devoted to drink, the further half to food. Not much of a spread, for the McIvors.

21

She sidled towards a tray of cracker biscuits concentric round a bowl of dip. Now she could see into the kitchen, where Liza was standing facing Duncan, her back to the stove, his to the open door.

There was something odd about the way Liza was standing, the contrast between the rigidity of her figure and her meek, placid expression—mulish was the word. Duncan too seemed to be standing rigid, so that Isobel fancied that the same invisible chains which the young couple wore looped about them in joy had tightened round Liza and Duncan and were tightening further as they pulled against them.

All at once she knew. She knew what Liza was saying to Duncan.

'Get rid of that awful girl. I won't go out there till she's gone.'

Duncan would be pleading embarrassment and social conscience, but in vain. He would come, apologetically, and ask her to go.

Liza hated her. She didn't know why. It had happened before and she never did know why.

Don't invent life, she told herself firmly. Let it happen. Wait at least till it happens.

But she heard those words so clearly that her heart thudded in her uneasy body as she forced herself to go back to the living room.

Ray was now standing beside Joel in front of the batik hanging.

22

'See the motorbike?' Joel was saying. 'You can imagine that it's the first motorbike he'd ever seen. Like drawing the excitement of childhood, wouldn't you say?'

I did say, thought Isobel, and felt better. Laughter was the bones of the mind, or its carapace.

'I don't read emotion into graphics myself,' said Ray.

Serve you right, thought Isobel.

There were more people in the room now, standing in groups, heads lifted above the taut, shining net of conversation. She stood watching, drinking her wine, taking comfort from the sound. She didn't want to be in there helping to weave the net. She would tear it, tear some great, jagged hole in it.

She said to herself, 'I'm seeing them from the middle distance.'

The middle distance was the most favourable range for viewing the human race. Usually she saw them too close, or too far away.

The girl in the Indian dress and her companion had come back. She was sitting on the divan and he on his heels on the floor beside her, silent, looking at nothing. She didn't see them in the middle distance. They were far away, in another world. Or maybe not; in another world all right, but close, too close.

'Want a refill there?' asked a middle-aged man with silvered black hair and a shadowy jaw.

It seemed that she did.

He tilted the jug he was carrying and filled her glass.

'What are you dreaming about?'

'Looking at the batik hanging. Do you like it?'

23

'Charming. Indonesian, isn't it? Have you been to Indonesia?'

'No.'

All my journeys are inward.

The man moved on.

I hate them for taking it for granted, like people born rich. Staring into space, but each knowing the other is there and feeling the better for it. If they feel just one fraction of an inch the better for it, then the thing exists; even as a delusion, the thing exists.

Now she bends down and feels in her sandal and he looks down too. She takes off the sandal and he feels inside it. A nail, a rough place. No words. A private patch of sunlight. Their small candle. How did they manage to open their mouths and speak without blowing it out?

She had forgotten her uneasiness about Liza. She went back to the dining room to fill her glass. There were two couples there now filling glasses. The kitchen door—odd again—was half closed. Because of the presence of the couples she took only one cracker biscuit, thinking that was a mistake, that it would only remind her stomach what food was like.

The couples departed. While she was filling her glass, Duncan came out of the kitchen, pulled the door to behind him as if there was something to be hidden, and walked past her set-faced, without speaking.

There was trouble all right, but it had nothing to do with her. Probably they were having a domestic row in the kitchen.

Suddenly she felt anxious. It wouldn't—it couldn't interfere with supper. They had to give you supper.

Wearing a serious and intent expression, as if she had been sent to fetch it, she took a bowl of cashew nuts and carried it back to the living room. She set it down on a small table where she could graze discreetly.

In the living room, Duncan was talking to the Fergusons and Barbara Smith, animated, laughing loudly.

She began to eat the nuts, quickly and privately. This was the third glass of wine. Dangerous on an empty stomach. Go easy.

'Isobel! There you are!'

Here came Robbie, beaming, his deepset eyes almost closed between the low forehead and the rounded cheekbones of his jolly-fat-boy face, such a contrast with his bony frame that he gave the false impression of having outgrown his clothes, of showing thin wrists and ankles, though they were covered by sober clothing of good quality.

She smiled at him, welcoming the safety of his simple view of the world. Robbie saw everything at the middle distance. When he looked at her, he saw a girl who lived in an attic and wrote—how romantic. How she would like to be the thing that Robbie saw.

'Will you come over? There's somebody who wants to meet you. Stephen Hines, he does some reviewing for the *Herald* besides lecturing in English.'

He took her arm and drew her away from the bowl of nuts. She came with her eyebrows raised in surprise. She did know of Stephen Hines. The name had a life of its own, and, crossing the room with Robbie, she was creating an image

25

to match it. The image deflated in a soft fizzle of laughter at the sight of him, a little slip of a man, so young in face and in figure that the even grey of his hair and his beard looked as if it had been applied from a bottle in an effort to achieve a mature and dignified appearance.

He was listening to an emphatic speech from a big, bony girl perched like a raven on the arm of a chair which was occupied by a smaller, more graceful girl who bent her neat ballerina head as she listened with attention to the pair.

'But Stephen, symbolism is acceptable when it is the only possible language to convey meaning. It isn't a mere enhancement of the commonplace. It's for something that can't be said in any other way.'

'You have something there.'

He paused as they came within speaking range.

'Here she is, then,' said Robbie. 'Isobel, this is Stephen Hines. Isobel Callaghan.'

Stephen Hines's deeply serious expression seemed, like the colour of his hair, to be an attempt at gravitas. In spite of it, he looked like a pixie.

'I was very impressed by a story of yours in *Seminal*. About the survivor of a suicide pact.'

She nodded.

'"Meet me there".'

'You write with great power.'

'Thank you.'

'What made you choose such a subject?'

Made fretful by hunger, she answered sharply, 'I don't choose subjects. They choose me.'

'That's an interesting observation. I suppose subjects do choose writers, but I wouldn't have expected a writer to say so. Do you think that is a good thing?'

'It's rather limiting. Depends on one's range, I suppose. I'd like to be able to venture outside my limitations.'

'If you can write about a suicide pact and make it so convincing—but so unexpected, the happiness of that pair constructing an afterlife that will give them everything the world has denied them, such an air of play about it—I don't think your limits are very narrow.'

Isobel said, 'Sometimes the extreme things are easier. Ordinary things can be most difficult.'

She looked across at the young couple on the divan, sitting now side by side, heads bent, talking quietly together.

'That boy and girl,' she said. 'I suppose they aren't planning suicide.'

'Not by the look of them, no.'

He gave up dignity at that and grinned a pixie grin.

'But...how do they...' she tried for a word, 'how do they communicate? That ought to be easy, but it isn't.'

The raven girl came to her help.

'You mean the love talk. I can see the difficulty. What one may say in life would sound pretty foolish in fiction.'

'It's for the moment only,' agreed Stephen.

'But if it's my business to catch the moment,' said Isobel.

'Yes, we can see the problem, but we can't solve it for you. It's unfortunate that it is when one is expressing one's sincerest feelings that one sounds most artificial.'

The ballerina girl spoke.

'The artificial can sound sincere enough. Remember Romeo and Juliet and the saints and palmers. That rings true, all right.'

'I think you may be right, Judith. Love seeks disguise. It is always literature.'

'One dresses the naked feeling in symbols.'

'What was that, Sybil, about enhancing the commonplace?'

'If you think it commonplace, Stephen, you have lived a very interesting life.'

'Touché!'

Stephen laughed very heartily.

Isobel had her mind on George and Anna.

'Everybody isn't up to thinking in symbols.'

'But a symbol can be a very simple thing. Everybody isn't an expert with words, either.'

'There's a lot to be said for body talk,' said a young man who had come to listen and was standing behind the armchair. 'But we have that sorted out back home. There's one creek called Today Creek, and another called Tomorrow Creek. So you ask a girl to go for a walk, a mile to Today Creek, and if you're looking for a wife, you stop at Today Creek and ask her if she wants to go any further. "How far?" she asks you. "As far as Tomorrow Creek?" If she says yes, you're engaged. Simple.'

'But suppose her feet are killing her?' asked Sybil.

'That's the beauty of it,' said the young man. 'Girls need stamina, where I come from.'

'Would you call that ritual, or symbol?'

'I call it a test of a girl's devotion, not to mention her stamina. How far is it to Tomorrow Creek?'

'If she asks that, she's not worth having.'

Judith said, leaning back to look up at him, 'It's very much the man's way, I think.'

'Well, we're the ones with the problem.'

Stephen Hines spoke to Isobel, taking his responsibility seriously.

'I do believe that there's always a little bit of theatre involved, whether it's ritual or symbolic act. If that is helpful. But as for the words, otherwise, I don't think there's anything special about them. They are the same words your mother used when you were a small child.'

And if you didn't hear them then, you'll never learn them.

All of them, young or old, short or tall, fat or thin— they talked about love as if they owned it, as if it was for everybody. How could they know?

She stared into her empty glass and felt her heart muscle straining in misery like a rudimentary animal shut in a casket, straining after air and circumstance.

'Good enough for Shakespeare,' said Sybil.

'Always a guarantee,' she agreed, thinking of getting away and finding something to eat. 'I'll work on those lines.'

She looked back from the dining-room door and saw them laughing together. Probably the young man from Tomorrow Creek was entertaining the group. She was sorry to be missing the conversation, but her need was urgent.

There was little food left. She took the last two biscuits and scraped the last of the dip from the bowl.

29

The kitchen door was open. She heard Liza saying, 'What about me?'

Were they still involved in that row? Wasn't it time they snapped out of it and set about getting the supper? What could they be thinking of?

Liza spoke again.

'What about me? What about me?'

She was repeating the phrase, tonelessly and without emotion, as if she had forgotten what the words meant.

'What about me?'

Duncan spoke, urgently.

'All right. All right. But pull yourself together, please. Don't make a scene.'

'Get rid of them. Tell them to go away.'

'Yes, but you stay here. Just try to relax. Keep calm.'

Isobel moved quickly, not wishing to meet Duncan.

Her fear of rejection was now superseded by her fear of going hungry.

They couldn't do this. They couldn't.

But Duncan had come in and was talking to the Gilberts, his particular friends; they began to move among the groups, explaining. People looking startled, nodding, women picking up handbags, knots of people moving towards the door.

Duncan spoke to the young couple. They looked at each other, nodded and got up, unaffected by the general unease. They walked out, the last to move except for the Gilberts, who must be intending to stay, Isobel, who did not know what to do, and Robbie, who was standing by the door and must be waiting for her.

30

Gratefully, she went to join him and they went out together.

'Liza's been taken ill. A few of us are going to Stephen's place. We'll get some food and drink and have supper there. It's rotten luck about Liza. Did you like Stephen?'

Since he seemed to want her to like Stephen, she was inclined to say no, out of peevishness over the lost supper, but there was something about Robbie—he was so guileless that it would be a mean trick. He made himself so open to attack that one was never inclined to attack him.

'Mmm.' She added fretfully, 'I'm starving.'

'Come on, then. I'll buy you a pie. There's bound to be something open along here. We'll eat a pie in the park.'

Robbie did not seem to be at all downcast by the failure of the party. He seemed oddly excited.

They had reached the main road, passed a few of the ejected guests waiting at the tram stop and went on till they found a lighted milk bar where Robbie paused to read the notice in the window.

'Fresh sandwiches, sausage rolls, hot pies. I should say the sandwiches are probably about as fresh as the notice. I think it had better be pies. Is that all right with you?'

She nodded, although the word 'pie' brought cold sweat to her forehead. She must discipline herself. Pies are food. I must eat. This is hunger, only hunger.

While Robbie was buying the pies, she leaned against the window, breathing deeply.

He came out carrying two paper bags. As he handed one of them to her, he bowed and said, with odd formality,

'Will you accept this pie as a token of my devotion?' He breathed deeply and said in a quick breath, 'Dearest Isobel!'

She knew at once, of course. She saw them laughing together after her departure; they must have been laughing at her. Never had heard love talk, poor girl. Have to do something about that. He wouldn't have thought of it by himself; they must have put him up to it, told him that it would be a service to literature.

'What sort of fool do you take me for?' she shouted. 'Do you think I don't know what you're at? Who put you up to this?'

His jaw sagged and he looked at her like a loon. When he had got his face under control, she saw a brief, dead sadness in it. She had done murder. Even if it was of a little thing like a light in the eye, death was still death, the irremediable absence. Nothing would bring that light back, ever again.

Thought and pain returned to his face. His lips trembled; he turned away quickly and hurried in the direction from which they had come.

She stood in an absolute blackness and bleakness, the pie in her hand like a warm little corpse growing colder. At last she thought with disgust, 'But I have to eat. Like a horse munching its way through a bunch of roses it doesn't know the meaning of, that would go on munching even if it knew, because horses must eat.'

In spite of the blackness and bleakness, she was relieved. They were safety. Better to lose now than to be always anxious, waiting for the blow to fall. Robbie was safe, too. Imagine Robbie's cheerful, direct gaze reaching into that black desert.

She couldn't finish the pie after all. She threw it into the gutter and walked on until light and the sound of known voices drew her through the open door of a pub lounge.

She bought a beer at the bar though her gorge rose at the smell of it. The lounge was a small room, nearly empty. Seven guests from the aborted party at the McIvors' were sitting round two small tables pushed together.

In spite of the empty spaces, two withered, brightly coloured old women were sitting sipping gin close by, as if they needed and got some comfort from the crowding.

She wanted after all to sit alone, but the group was moving chairs to let her in. They acknowledged her with brief smiles, then went back to the talk about Liza.

Was this a genuine breakdown, or a way of telling Duncan she was overworked? Why not both? Wasn't a breakdown always a way of telling somebody something?

'I feel so guilty,' said one of the women.

Perhaps Liza had had that in mind, too.

'But it was the standard she set,' said another. 'I never dared to offer help. It was Liza the perfect cook, Liza the perfect hostess.'

Isobel drank her beer. It was not too bad. At least it wasn't going to make her sick. Indeed, she was beginning to think that it was very good. It tasted of things as they were, strong, bitter, melancholy.

'But why hadn't Liza told Duncan, for heaven's sake, that the work was too much for her?'

'Perhaps she had, and he hadn't listened, so she was driven to this form of communication.'

Liza, Liza! Isobel was sick of the sound of her name.

'Well, perhaps it was a way of communicating, but not a very sane way, surely.'

If they knew what it was like to be mad...

'If you knew what it was like to be mad,' said a loud, angry voice that brought sudden silence. 'If you knew what it was like, not being able to say, "I am I." Being taken over, that's it. The other, the secret thing using your mouth to speak through.'

'I say, calm down,' said a voice beside her.

She knew then that it was herself speaking but she didn't care. Let them find out. What joy, what marvellous relief it was to say the words.

'It's no help to set your teeth and fight it. It's smarter than you. Bigger and stronger. And it's everything you hate. But you're there. That's what they don't see, that you're there. You're watching and you can't do anything. A fly on the wall, that's what you are.'

'Oh, for God's sake!'

'And the rest of it, the muddle. Walls around you that aren't walls, and what you think is a door is all the wall there is.'

She was proud of that, and was hurt when the man beside her said, 'I don't follow you. How about letting it go for the moment?'

She tried again, speaking to him particularly.

'It's being a situation, do you see? Not a live person, but a live situation that uses you—whatever you are—no, a

34

morality play. A morality play, you see, that uses everything that comes to act itself out. That you can't get away from by saying I, no use saying that.'

He opened his mouth and closed it again. The others had vanished into a sunken background from which voices came across an invisible barrier. A haha. That was just the name for it.

Oh, my God...what on earth...can't somebody?

She raised her voice at them, coldly.

'It's no use trying to beat madness with reason, either. Madness is reason, reason gone wild.'

The man beside her was nodding as if he was hypnotised.

'Now listen,' she said to him, and had to giggle, because it was like saying to a large, pale praying mantis, 'Now be eaten.'

'Now listen. I know you are alive like me. But it's a bab...It's abstract. I know by eye. I see you. I know by ear.'

'So do we know by ear. Do we ever!'

Trouble in the haha. She quelled it with a glance.

Now they were all visible, all staring. The two old women at the next table were staring too.

She must have fresh air at once.

Graciously, she said, 'Will you excuse me? I'm afraid...'

She did not stop to tell them what it was she feared. Outside in the cool air, the world swung heavily through a small arc and settled back into place.

An arm went round her and held her unpleasantly tight. She struggled against it.

35

A harsh voice said, 'Now then, lovey. You stick with me. Don't want to get yourself run over, do you?'

Whatever gave her that idea?

Protesting was too much trouble. She allowed herself to be led across the street to the park.

As soon as they had halted, the world swung again.

She leaned out of the woman's arms and vomited.

The woman thought that a clever, praiseworthy thing to do.

'That's right, lovey. You bring it up, my darling. Come on, that's it.'

She tried to get away, to plunge into the security of the grass.

The arms tightened.

'Not there, love. Come on, my little darling. My own little girl, you come and sit with me and hold your dear little head up. Now wait. I'll be back in a minute.'

She did not have enough energy to escape.

The woman came back with a wet handkerchief, wiped her mouth with it and held it against her forehead.

'There. You'll be right in a minute, love.'

Christ. This must be the comic hit of the evening. Miss Isobel Callaghan with unknown admirer.

She put the hand with the wet handkerchief away from her, saying coldly, 'I think you must be thinking of somebody else.'

The hand vanished.

The woman uttered a shocked, discordant laugh, then said bitterly, 'Who isn't, I should like to know?' She added stiffly, 'Sorry, I'm sure.'

Isobel said, 'Is that right?'

There was no answer.

'Thinking about somebody else—is that right?'

Again, there was no answer. Did she deserve one?

They sat on the bench silent and apart, birds of a feather.

The woman said at last, seeming casual, 'It's more your stomach than your head, I think. What did you have for tea? You didn't have anything much to bring up.'

'Half a bunch of roses.'

She wasn't as drunk as all that, not any more. She was trying to pass off that insult as a piece of drunken nonsense.

'You and your roses!'

The woman's voice was easier.

'Thank you very much. I'll be all right now.'

'Are you sure?' The woman hesitated, but she was eager to escape. 'You're not going to go to sleep here?'

'No. I'll start walking to the tram stop in a minute.'

She got up and stood steady.

'Well, if you're sure. I'll be off then.'

'And thanks a lot.'

'Don't mention it.'

As she watched the woman walk away, Isobel said to herself in astonishment, 'I know the words now. I know the words.'

She woke early next morning feeling well.

After all, she hadn't had so very much to drink. It had been the empty stomach and that last fatal beer that

37

had caused the trouble. After she had got rid of the beer in the park, she had recovered fairly quickly.

It was a pity about that scene in the pub, but she need never see those people again, and she could not bring herself to regret the outburst. Whatever she had said seemed to have cleared her mind. It had been like the bursting of a boil and the resultant stream of nasty matter. Pity about the spectators. Grandma used to say, 'Well, we all have to eat our peck of dirt.' That was part of theirs and she wished them better luck in future.

Meanwhile she had work to do.

She got up, had hurried recourse to the slop bucket and the washbasin, took her topcoat off the bed where it had been serving as an extra blanket, put it on over her nightdress and rolled a sheet of paper into the typewriter.

She began to type.

The other woman had moved away. Anna was standing alone. It was now or never for George. He took up the plate of sandwiches and crossed the room to stand before her.

'Anna,' he said, bowing with some formality, 'will you accept a sandwich as a token of my sincere devotion?'

Anna looked at him thoughtfully.

'What's in them?'

'Ham and cheese, I think.' He added boldly, 'I wish it could be larks' tongues.'

Anna's gaze had not wavered.

She said clearly and firmly, 'I am prepared to settle for what is there.'

'Well,' said George, 'that's that, then.'

They were both smiling wide, foolish smiles.

'Don't you think you'd better take a sandwich? I mean, as well as everything else.'

'Oh, yes. Of course.'

She took one, nodding and laughing.

'I'd better offer them round. But I'll be back,' said George.

And that was that.

That was that for George and Anna. Anna knew how. Anna was no Isobel.

In that dead centre there was after all a little movement, a stirring of breath like a sigh.

I
BUS STOP TO SAINT URSULA'S

On the third day of what she must now call the illness, she woke to the immediate knowledge of her problem.

She had no food left. Last night she had crumbled the last slice of bread into the last bowl of soup. At some time today, she had to get to that corner shop. No food left and no-one to send on an errand.

A difficult situation.

She was quite alone. How, in this world full of people, did one get to be quite alone? It wasn't a natural state of affairs. One had to work at it. She had been working at it for some time, it seemed, shutting doors behind her, one after another.

Slammed doors, panic flights, rejections...

One couldn't blame Aunt Noelene. Since the death of Mrs Callaghan, Aunt Noelene had given support, had paid her fees at Business College, helped her with money, meals and hand-me-down clothes. It could not be welcome news that she had left Lingards and meant to work part-time and try her hand at writing.

'You're no better than the rest of them,' she had said with contempt and disgust. 'Don't come running to me when you're in trouble, that's all.'

Well, this was trouble and she mustn't go running to Aunt Noelene. She wasn't going back until she had something to show for it, like a book with her name on the cover.

Certainly she had never meant to shut the door on Margaret. They had got on well enough, better than a lot of sisters, being too different ever to clash. It had been the wedding invitation, the impersonal printed invitation card to Margaret's wedding that had done the damage. Isobel had not even known that it was an insult until Aunt Noelene had told her so, reading it aloud and fuming:

'Mr and Mrs W.J. Campbell of
Whitefields, Melville Plains
have pleasure in announcing
the marriage of their niece
Margaret Anne

—not even Callaghan! Not even Callaghan! That shows you where we stand! And you ought to be a bridesmaid. Her only sister and you're not even invited to stay in the house!'

'A sister who isn't a bridesmaid would be a bit of an embarrassment staying in the house,' Isobel had said. 'And

41

you know, it wouldn't have been practical. I couldn't afford the time off work, let alone the dress. Margaret would know that.'

'It wouldn't have hurt Yvonne to give you the dress.' An odd turn of phrase, for Aunt Noelene knew that such an outlay would cause her sister considerable pain. 'But that's Yvonne for you. Spends money wherever it shows, and as mean as cat's meat everywhere else. And this is the first you've heard, even of Margaret being engaged?'

'Of course I'd have told you if I'd known. But I was the one who stopped writing, you know. There never seemed to be anything to say.'

Nothing to say in answer to Margaret's reports of her wonderful new life with Aunt Yvonne—tennis parties, picnics, dances, evening dresses, boyfriends...

'Not true,' she had added. 'I was plain damned jealous.'

Not so much jealous as conscious of an unhealthy hunger for a way of life she mustn't long for. She didn't think she grudged it to Margaret.

Aunt Noelene had said, with a heavy sigh, 'I know the feeling. It's winner take all, isn't it? Well, I'll send a cheque and you can just return the compliment. Send a card. Inability to accept. Tit for tat!'

So Isobel had sent the card and almost at once had regretted it. She could have written to Margaret and wished her well, she could even have packed up a heavy cut lead crystal flat cake plate, bought at staff discount from Lingard Brothers, and sent that with her best wishes. It would have been the correct response, even if the snub had been deliberate, as Isobel was sure it was not. There was no malice in Margaret. Finding the correct response at the correct moment was the problem. Too late Isobel understood that she and Margaret were being drawn into the long quarrel of their elders.

She hadn't expected to miss the people in the office so much, Frank and Olive, Nell and Sandra, the new girl. Isobel had found an unexpected satisfaction in being no longer the latest comer. She and Olive had become almost friends, and Frank had been a protector as well as an amusing companion. Of course they had thought her odd, translating German and reading poetry at lunch time, but they had accepted her with all her peculiarities. And now she understood the importance of being expected, having somewhere to go every day. Daily bread. It meant a little more than food for the belly.

She had slammed the door on that familiar world. She would be too embarrassed ever to go back.

It was no use appealing to Mrs Foster. Mrs Foster had a loyalty to misery which Isobel admired, but she never counted Isobel among its victims.

What about Mr Lynch? Could she crawl down and knock at his door and cry for help?

The thought would have made her laugh if laughter didn't hurt her head so much.

She had almost had her own lover. It had come close.

That was worse than a slammed door. A slammed door leaves live people behind it. She would write a poem one day, in Robbie's honour, though he would not know of it: An elegy for lovelight.

Oh, for God's sake! You've got no food and there you lie, thinking about writing a poem. You have to get up, and wash and dress, and what's more, there's that bucket to empty.

She hadn't emptied the bucket for two days. It would be too heavy to carry. That would mean a very careful operation, transferring urine from bucket to po to lighten the load, emptying bucket, returning to transfer urine from po to bucket...

She raised her head and hastily lowered it again to her pillow.

Aspirin. She did have aspirin. Within reach, in her handbag by the bed.

She groped, found the packet, swallowed two tablets dry, and waited.

She had read about an old Marquise who had starved to death in a garret in the Palace of Versailles. Nobody knew she was there.

Three old ladies locked in the lavatory...they were there from Monday to Saturday...The tune droned through her head.

Fear got her to her feet. Not so bad. Never so bad once you got to your feet.

She pulled on pants and sweater and tried to lift the bucket. It was, as she had expected, too heavy to lift. She assembled po, enamel mug and the cloth to cover her nose and mouth against the ammoniac stench, and set to work, moving with care. There was plenty of time. Even after that long lie-in and the retrospective, which had done little to cheer her, it was still only half past eight. Now the po was full and the bucket was manageable. She carried it down to the lavatory, used the lavatory and raised the seat to pour away the contents of the bucket, retching a little because she hadn't of course worn the protective cloth. Then back to the room, urine from po to bucket—that was the tricky bit, take it easy, plenty of time. Second trip done. Rest a bit.

Rinse bucket and po with water in mug from tap. We're getting there.

She decided she couldn't make it to the bathroom. Heat water on gas ring. Soap and washer job at the sink, do the worst spots, armpits, crotch and feet. Pants and sweater again. Shoes.

She was ready to go.

Just down three and a half flights of stairs, then a block and a half to the corner shop. Food, then back to hole up until she was better.

She sat on the edge of the bed for a while, practising minimal existence. This was a technique she had been using to gather the strength to get out of bed: perfectly still, breathing slow and shallow, not thinking, she waited for the moment. It came, she stood up and went out. When she locked the door behind her, she felt that she was at the end of the ordeal, not at its beginning.

The stairs were all right. She held the handrail and descended slowly to the hall.

She paused there. Come on, it was only a block and a half.

As soon as she got into the street, she knew that a block and a half was an impossible distance. There was the bus stop, just a few yards in the other direction. She could

45

make that, working her way along the front of the buildings—without support, she reeled like a drunk—and sit on the seat practising minimal living until she had gathered sufficient reserves to make the journey.

She sidled along to the bus-stop shelter and sat down.

Strength was returning. Soon she would get up and move.

Then a bus came and she got on the bus. She got on the bus because that is what people do at bus stops. She seemed to have forgotten her purpose in being there.

The conductor as he took her fare said, 'Are you all right, love?'

'Oh, yes. Thank you.'

'Well, you know best. You don't look all right to me.'

Though she had not meant to take the bus, it seemed after all not a bad idea. Riding in a bus was better than walking. She could get food at David Jones' basement just as easily and with less walking.

When the bus stopped at the top of Market Street, she tried to get up and knew that she was facing calamity. She tried again, succeeded and made her way handhold by handhold to the door, down the steps and into the street, where she stood reeling. She clutched at the shoulder of the man ahead of her and clung. He looked round, startled, then astonished and displeased.

She muttered, 'Sorry. Sorry. I slipped.'

'Starting a bit early, aren't you?'

That stiffened her spine. She let go and stood steady and measured the distance to what looked like safety, the footpath and the shop windows which would offer support

46

at need. She arrived without stumbling and stood looking through a shop window at the plastic reproduction of a gentleman who had never seen trouble in his life and was now ready to go skiing.

The main thing was to find shelter. She was abominably exposed, conscious even of her nakedness under the sweater and the slacks which had been adequate for that walk to the corner shop. Somewhere to hide maybe for an hour or two, while she got herself together.

There was the newsreel theatrette down at the George Street end of Market Street. Just about the same distance from this point as the corner shop from that stop where she had so foolishly taken the bus. That theatrette was the place to sit in a comfortable seat in the dark; a rest there would set her up, she would get the strength to come back to the food basement of David Jones, get her supplies—and then a financially ruinous taxi ride back to the building. The expense couldn't be helped. Survival was now the aim. Survival without disgrace.

This was going to take effort. She stared at the gentleman with the skis and willed herself into the image of one of those native women walking gracefully, carrying on her head a pitcher of water—though for Isobel the head itself would be the burden to be held upright.

Bringing that burden erect caused considerable pain, which was an advantage, another reason to hold it steady. She set off, head up. She used the sidling technique, easier with shop windows she could pretend to be studying, crossed Pitt Street as carefully as a tightrope walker, arrived without disaster at the foyer, fumbled stiff-necked for her change purse, bought her ticket while staring over the head of the ticket seller, and went in.

The usherette who tore her ticket in half looked at her with suspicion. She maintained her lofty stance.

Lady, I haven't touched a drop.

There were not many patrons in the little theatre. In the dark, she did lurch towards a seat in a back row, hoping that the usherette couldn't see her. She worked her way along the row and, thankfully, sat down.

She had to expect a reaction after that effort. It was cool in the theatre. She hadn't noticed the cold out in the street, but now shudders were running down her body, continuous as rain down a window pane, and she had to bite on her sleeve to keep her teeth from chattering. Her breathing came quick and shallow. In short pants. That was a joke from somewhere: her breath came in short pants. Not a bit funny when it happened to you. She was even sorrier now that she hadn't put more clothes on.

She stared at the screen. The sound didn't mean much. It simply hurt her head. There was a procession, people with banners, shouting, but whether in happiness or anger she could not tell. Probably anger. What could they have to complain about? But after all, there was plenty to complain about. One thing she could be sure of: she wasn't the only one in trouble in this world. She liked to watch, however. It was good to know that things were still going on.

There was something wrong with the back of the seat, some projection sticking into her below the right shoulder blade. She couldn't be bothered to change her seat. She wriggled into a more comfortable position and the pain disappeared.

Now the people on the screen were in Antarctica watching a lot of penguins waddle down to the sea like odd little manikins, then with a leap transform themselves into creatures of exquisite grace in the sea. A lesson there if she could think of it.

Then there was a woman launching a ship, having trouble with the champagne bottle, which refused to break. She never did discover if the woman had succeeded at last. She must have dozed off, for she opened her eyes to see the same procession, the multitude of people united in one emotion, whether it was joy or anger.

The sleep had done her good. She felt quite steady now, quite able to walk out and back to David Jones' food basement, buy her stores and go home. All problems were solved.

She got up and walked out into the night.

She stood in the dark street among the lights that shone from foyers, restaurants, shop windows and tried to make out what had happened. She had slept, not through one session, but through two. The shops were shut and she had still not bought food.

Why had she got on the bus? She could have sat at the bus stop long enough—she could have stayed longer in the attic practising minimal living and gathering strength... never mind all that. What could she do now to retrieve the situation?

Get something to eat, take a taxi home and try again tomorrow.

She walked to the corner, walking well now that it was of no use. Across the road in George Street light was coming from a doorway above which shone the name The Soup Kitchen. That would do.

Hunger wasn't a problem. It had been, but it had been balanced by a disgust of almost all food. Now getting food into her stomach was a mechanical act needed for survival. Soup would be easy.

She crossed the road, shivering in the cold night air, went down a short flight of stairs into a warm, bright room furnished with long tables flanked by benches. It was a cafeteria. There were a few people waiting in a queue at the serving area; she lined up, took a tray, moved along the display cases, ignored salads and desserts, took a bowl of minestrone and a glass of wine, paid at the cash register and walked to a table, quite elated by her competence. What a pity she hadn't thought to add to her tray one of those plates with a small pack of cracker biscuits and a foil-wrapped wedge of cheese. She could have taken it home; it would have done for the morning meal, till she got to the corner shop next day.

There were baskets on the tables full of hunks of bread. She took one, ate her soup without difficulty, chewed at a piece of bread and thought she would go back and get the cheese and biscuits. The problem was solved.

It was with the glass of wine that the muttering began. She did not know that the voice was her own until staring faces located it at her centre. This had happened somewhere before; she could not remember where or when. She felt sorry for the people who were looking at her with such embarrassment. She said punctiliously to the nearest diner, a few places down at the other side of the table, 'I am not drunk. I am strapped to the black horse of madness.'

The apology, which had been intended to smooth things over, seemed to have made them worse. The man had turned away. Everyone had turned away.

But I can't turn away, she thought. There was the whole terrifying problem in four words. I can't turn away.

One thing was certain. She had to get away from here, and at once. Unfortunately, the little spurt of energy which had carried her into the cafeteria was now exhausted.

She surveyed the situation with care. Exit: lighted, visible. One made for it, from table to table. No point in keeping up appearances now. Stairs: one climbed them, thankful for the handrail. Pavement: one followed it, but in which direction? Downward. That was the imperative. She took a few steps away from the lighted doorway, yielded to the invitation of the pavement and lay down.

She was not left in peace for long. A voice said, 'You disgusting. You get up from there and go away. You don't act like this in front of my restaurant, decent place. We don't want drunks. You get up, you hear? You want me to call the police?'

She did not answer.

The voice grew more agitated.

'I tell you. Get up! Is disgusting! Get up and go away!'

It was the voice that went away, which was a relief.

Then it returned.

'I tell you, officer, she was staggering drunk in the restaurant. We don't serve drunks there. Never sell a glass

51

of wine to anyone drinking. A good place, I run a good place, good food and a glass of wine, that's all. The girl says, she went out staggering, terrible. One glass of wine only in my restaurant. Came in drunk from somewhere else, cashier not notice.'

A deeper voice said, with contempt, 'Get up from there. You're a disgrace. Come on. Move.'

She did not stir.

A hand gripped her shoulder and shook it, jerking at the dagger which had lodged itself under her shoulderblade, so that she yelped with pain.

The hand moved from her shoulder to her forehead, the voice said in pity and astonishment, 'Why, you're not drunk. You're sick!'

She was lifted then and was leaning against a warm, solid body and discovering that perfect love was rough like serge and smelt of tobacco and sweat. There was an arm around her holding her steady.

'Get her a chair, will you? She's sick, I tell you.'

'She didn't get sick here. I don't want her here.'

'She is sick and the sooner you call an ambulance the sooner we'll be out of your way. Meanwhile you get her a chair and get to the telephone. If we're bad for your business, get moving.'

It was good to hear that contempt turned on the other.

She was sitting now on a chair in the doorway, still supported by serge and a column of muscle and living flesh and wonderful humanity. The best thing was his saying 'we'. She could love him for ever for that.

She whispered, 'Thank you. Thank you very much.'

52

'All in the day's work, love.' He sounded embarrassed, but tightened his arm about her for a moment. 'We'll have you in hospital soon. And here comes the ambulance.'

The urgent whine of the ambulance was the last thing she heard for some time.

After that it was darkness.

Voices began to come through the dark.

One of them said 'Isobel Callaghan', and she thought with relief that she hadn't lost her handbag. Didn't they say that it took a surgical operation to separate a woman from her handbag? Her honour is the second last thing to go. It's a surrogate womb. Some smart-arse had said that once. Why don't men carry them, then? That comment hadn't gone down so well.

She was handled, moved about, rolled over. She didn't like it.

'Beastly cold,' she grumbled. That must have been a stethoscope pressing on her bare chest. 'Beastly cold.'

They ignored her.

Somebody said, 'Better take it per rectum, Sister.'

What on earth? How dare you?

'Just keep still, will you?'

She kept still.

One voice said, 'I don't like the sound of it. I don't like the sound of it at all.'

She was a parcel. She didn't mind being a parcel. It was easy.

Someone was tapping most annoyingly on the bones of her ribcage, one after the other. It was too much. Then somebody rolled her over and the tapping began again on her back. She uttered a sharp protest, which was answered by an odd sound like the clucking of a subterranean fowl.

'What's she mumbling about?'

'Says she isn't a bloody xylophone, sir.'

'Oh. Well, it's still no laughing matter.'

'No, sir. Sorry.'

Then she woke up to morning light and found herself in a little tented room with walls of heavy white cloth. There was a nurse standing beside her bed.

'So you're with us, are you? About time, too.'

'How long?'

'How long have you been here? Just the neat forty hours. You came in on Wednesday night. If you call that coming in—not under your own steam, I assure you. What were you doing, wandering about town in a high fever?'

It was too difficult to explain.

'I just thought I had a bit of 'flu.'

'Well, I can't offer you anything to eat yet. Doctor wants a specimen of your sputum before you take anything by mouth. Want the pan?'

'Yes, please.'

One had to remember that one was only a parcel. Parcels can have no pride.

'Right. And I'll see about the jar for the sputum.'

What was sputum? The nurse departed. Something one spat, of course.

The nurse came back carrying a huge china shoe. She slipped it into the bed and sat Isobel on it and left again. Isobel considered her situation. She was clean and smelt of soap. She was wearing an extraordinary flowing garment of pink cotton which seemed to have no back to it. She investigated and found that it was fastened with tapes at the back from neck to waist. Below the waist it hung free. What an odd arrangement. Very convenient of course for sitting where she was sitting at the moment.

The nurse came back and set down on the cabinet beside the bed a small screw-top jar still warm and shining from the steriliser.

Bright and brisk, she said, 'Finished?' She removed the pan, peered at the contents and frowned. 'Doctor says you're to cough up from as deep as you can and close the jar straight away. Okay? After that I can get you something to eat.'

If I wasn't a parcel, thought Isobel, I'd be wondering what this was about. It was all too much trouble.

Coughing proved difficult, extremely painful and quite exhausting. She spat the small trophy into the jar, closed it as hastily as if she were trapping an insect and lay back on her pillow.

'You finished?'

The nurse must have been waiting outside.

'Yes.'

The nurse came in, picked up the jar, saying, 'Doctor's waiting for this,' put it in her pocket and departed.

She must have pulled a cord as she left, for the curtain walls rolled away and Isobel appeared as it were on centre stage to the sound of a cheer and gentle hand-clapping.

'She made it! She made it!'

'Good on you, kid!'

There were five other beds in the room, all of them occupied by women who were to Isobel voices rather than faces, though each face was turned towards her with a look of beaming goodwill.

'You were all very quiet,' she whispered. 'I didn't know there was anyone there.'

'We were afraid of disturbing you, love,' said her neighbour. 'Sister said this morning you were in a natural sleep and we didn't want to wake you.'

'That was very kind of you.'

'Did you know what was happening? They had a specialist come in from North Shore last night. Doctor told Sister that you were reacting and it looked like you were coming round.'

'I got bits and pieces,' she said.

'Well, you better keep quiet for a while. Don't tire yourself.'

There was a rumbling noise as a trolley approached, and appeared, pushed by a gangling, fair-haired young man in a white coat.

'Breakfast!'

He pushed the trolley into the centre of the room and began to distribute bowls of dry cereal.

He approached then with a large jug of milk and poised it above the bowl on the table which spanned Isobel's bed.

She looked at the bowl and shook her head.

'The sooner you eat, the sooner you're on your feet,' he said.

'Don't bully her, Eric. She can't eat what she doesn't fancy. What else have you got under those covers?'

'A nice bit of poached egg on toast.'

'Try her on that then. What about a bit of poached egg, love?'

Eric took away the bowl of cereal and replaced it with a poached egg on toast.

'The first mouthful's the worst. Give it a go.'

Isobel, feeling foolish, like an infant under the eyes of five anxious mothers, tried a mouthful and discovered that she was quite hungry. All the encouragement which accompanied her ingestion of the poached egg was unnecessary. She was relieved when the others withdrew their attention to their own meal.

Eric went away to distribute other breakfasts, came back to collect the used crockery and to pour tea.

'Milk for you,' he said to Isobel, handing her a plastic beaker. 'Seeing you didn't eat your cereal.'

'Bit of a boss cocky, aren't you, Eric?'

'Got to look after you all, haven't I? Now get on with it. I'm off.'

Isobel drank her milk and set the plastic beaker on the table.

'When they brought you in in your clothes, we thought, God forgive us, that you were drunk. In the DTs, like, because of the way you were talking. But Sister said straight, "Don't imagine that she's drunk. She's wandering a bit because she has a high fever." How come you were in your clothes?'

'I went out to buy food. I thought I had a touch of 'flu, that's all. I must have collapsed in the street. They did think I was drunk and somebody sent for a policeman. He sent for the ambulance. I don't remember much after that.'

'Don't worry her, Marj. Let her be.'

Marj nodded amiably.

In the ensuing silence Isobel slept again.

When she woke, the curtain was closed and a nurse stood beside the bed holding her sweater and her pants.

'Don't you have any underwear?'

'I was only going to the corner shop.'

The nurse raised her eyebrows in astonishment and disapproval.

'You'd better put these on then. You have to go down to X-ray after lunch. Bend forward, will you?'

She untied the tapes which held the indecent smock in place and hung it on the end of the bed.

Isobel pulled on pants and sweater, the nurse opened the curtains and departed.

There were gasps from the sympathetic audience when they saw Isobel dressed in outdoor clothes.

'They're not going to turn you out? In a bit of a hurry, aren't they?'

'Heartless, I call it.'

'No. I'm only going down to X-ray after lunch.'

She did not feel inclined to explain that it was for want of a pair of knickers that she was wearing outdoor clothes.

At the mention of X-ray the women had fallen silent. One or two of them exchanged glances, then looked hastily away, as if some secret was making them uneasy.

Eric wheeled in the lunch tray, six plates of salad, five of them on thick white china, the sixth on a paper plate. With a grimace of apology, he set the paper plate on Isobel's table.

Parcels do not ask questions. Isobel accepted the discrimination in silence under the eyes of the other five, in whose faces sadness had replaced unease.

She did not do well with the salad. Eric did not scold. He offered her a cup of tea, which came in a plastic beaker, and said, 'I'll be back for you in half an hour. Going to take a nice ride in a wheelchair.'

'That'll be fun.'

'That's the spirit, kid. Take it as it comes.'

Marj, blonde, bony and high-coloured—no doubt by her own hand—said, 'Are you on your own, kid? No Mum or Dad? We wondered when nobody came.'

'That's right,' said Isobel. 'Orphan child.'

She spoke flippantly, without knowing why. It might be in reaction to the solemnity which she sensed now in the air. She could not understand that either. She was still brooding over the humiliation of being without knickers. The best people wore knickers, even on a trip to a corner shop.

When Eric came back, he was pushing a wheelchair. He scooped Isobel out of bed and sat her in the chair with a smile, as if he were taking a small child on a treat.

Someone said, 'Best of luck, kid.'

This was getting really spooky.

They rolled along a corridor and into a lift which took them down to a basement. She was expected in the basement. Eric called out, 'Here she is,' and a voice answered, 'Right. Wheel her in, Eric. That'll do, thanks.'

Eric departed.

The speaker was another white coat, a brisk and stringy woman of commanding manner.

'Strip to the waist, please.'

Isobel had managed to wriggle into her two garments, lying exhausted on her bed after that effort. The upward heave required to take off the sweater was beyond her.

She shook her head.

'Sorry.'

The brisk woman hesitated. A radiographer left alone with a patient who could not take off her own clothes was, it seemed, a woman with a status problem.

She solved it with a reversal of attitude and came smiling to help as a gesture of friendship rather than a humiliating chore.

'You shouldn't be out of bed, but Doctor Hansen wants this as soon as possible, like yesterday. I'll get you as close as I can to the machine. Right, now? Rest your chin on this ledge, elbows here, lean forward, breathe in, hold, breathe away. There you are, all done.'

She helped Isobel back to the chair and into her sweater.

'You should have a blanket. Eric!' She opened the door and called, 'Eric! Go find a spare blanket, will you? You know you have to wait?'

There was a price to pay for friendship.

'Is that right? The police picked you up in the street and got an ambulance to bring you in? How come?'

What sort of plausible fiction could she invent to cover her situation? They didn't give her time to think up a story. It would need to be some story, at that.

'I just went out to buy food. Things sort of got out of hand.'

'Didn't know how sick you were. Wasn't anyone looking after you?'

Oh, it's a long story.

She shook her head, looking sad and sensitive.

The woman said no more.

Eric arrived with a blanket.

The radiographer wrapped it round her as a final gesture of friendship and resumed her official manner.

'Do you know you have to wait for doctor? They're developing straight away. Doctor Hansen will be down in a minute. You can wait outside till he arrives, I think.'

'Would somebody mind telling me what this is all about?' asked Isobel.

The woman looked at her and seemed about to speak, but changed her mind.

'Doctor will speak to you soon. I'll just see how Don's getting on with the developing.'

She disappeared. Eric wheeled Isobel out and they waited. Eric found nothing to say to lighten the atmosphere.

He said at last, with relief, 'Here comes the doc,' as a small, dark, rosy-cheeked young man in a white coat came hurrying down the corridor and into the room. Minutes passed. The young man reappeared. 'Wheel her in, will you, Eric?'

They followed him into the X-ray room, where the radiographer stood holding at arm's length a dripping X-ray suspended from a frame.

Doctor Hansen looked at it and nodded. He put his hand on Isobel's shoulder and said, 'Do you see that whitish blob on your right lung? Between the third rib and the fifth?'

Isobel looked at the white hand-print which had settled itself in her chest, thinking, 'So that's it. So there you are.' The source of it all, the red lightning of rage, the muttering madness, the scream of paranoia—it was like seeing the master criminal revealed, the evil spider in the centre of his web of mischief. The invader. Not I. The enemy within. Something that looked like a baby's hand-print.

'Well, we did think at first that you had pneumonia, but…we sent a specimen of your sputum down to the Tuberculosis Clinic and we can't say definitely till we get the results from them, but meanwhile…Combined with other indications, we can't ignore the possibility that you have tuberculosis.'

'I was beginning to get the message.'

'You mustn't panic. Even if it does turn out to be tuberculosis, remember that it is curable. It's not a death sentence any more, you know. Meanwhile, we have to take precautions for the sake of other patients, so we'll have to isolate you while we're waiting.'

'May I ask you for your own opinion?'

'I don't think there's much doubt about the diagnosis.'

'Thank you.'

'You're taking it very calmly.'

However, she was not taking it at all. She was suspended somewhere above reality.

62

'What to do with you now is the problem. We don't have a tuberculosis ward here. A pity,' he said to the radiographer, 'that she wasn't taken to North Shore in the first place.'

'The Registrar rang them and they said they didn't have a bed vacant.'

'If the ambulance had taken her there, they'd have had to find room.'

One was not only a parcel. One was a toxic, undesirable parcel.

'Room 207 is vacant, isn't it? Better take her up there, Eric. I'll fix it with Matron. She can't go back to the ward, of course.' Feeling a belated need to recognise Isobel's humanity, he said, 'Do you want us to notify anyone? Doctor Manning will ring your parents for you.'

'No parents.'

'Ah. Well, if you think of anyone…Well, Room 207, Eric. Better take her there straight away.'

'Oh, they're all heart, aren't they?' said Eric as he wheeled her away. 'But Hansen is a very decent sort and they do know their job. The doctor's right, you know. It's not what it used to be. They've got the drugs to deal with it now.'

'That's the first time anyone has said "the doctor" instead of "doctor".'

'It gets my goat, too. I feel like telling them sometimes, "There may be only one God, but there sure is more than one doctor." Well, you can even raise a laugh. That's the spirit.'

They rode in the lift to the second floor, along the corridor and into a small room bright with the light from a large window.

Here Eric lifted her into an armchair, saying cheerfully, 'Limp as a wet bath towel, you are. Just remember, kid, when you look at your dinner and you don't much feel like it, food is muscle. Just say to yourself, "Food is muscle."'

'And voice,' she whispered.

'Yes. Voice too. Only don't use it too much.'

'Say goodbye for me to the ladies in the ward.'

'I'll do that. They were really worried about you. They'll be sorry about this. I'll get your things and bring them down.'

'Find my handbag, will you? I need it. But I don't need that awful smock.'

'Got an alternative, love?'

She shook her head.

He went off grinning. Isobel sat on the bed and looked about her.

The diagnosis which had made her a social pariah had brought a great improvement in her material situation. This was a luxury room for one: one bed, an armchair, two straight chairs, a regulation side table, a reading light, a corner door which opened on a closet containing shower and lavatory. Beside the shower and the lavatory there were chrome bars fixed to the wall to provide handholds for the invalid. She made haste to use the lavatory before anyone arrived to forbid that freedom. She was glad of the hand-hold and glad to lie down on the bed.

She ought to be thinking about her situation. No use. Parcels don't think. Parcels are not required to think.

Eric came back with her handbag and the smock.

'Sorry. Sister says it's only until you can get someone to bring your own things. And you're to get into bed straight away.'

'Right.'

'Well, bear up, kid.'

'Shall do.'

'You haven't really taken it in yet, have you?' he asked with tenderness which embarrassed him into a hasty departure.

She opened her handbag and considered her resources. A pocket comb, which she put to use at once, with relief—what a pity that she didn't carry a toothbrush—two handkerchiefs, both crumpled, one soiled, money: four pounds in notes, seven and fivepence, a bankbook with a balance of forty-two pounds ten—but how was she to get to the bank?—the letter from *Seminal*, fountain pen, notebook, two pencils, pencil sharpener and the key to her room. The key set her thinking. Would she ever see that room again? Certainly, she had no sentimental attachment to it. She tried the pen. It still had ink. Well, she was equipped for something, if not for what lay ahead. She put all the contents back except the comb, which she put on the bedside table, by way of moving in. This is now my territory.

She took off her two garments and entered the smock—one couldn't say that one put it on—managed with difficulty to tie the tapes and got into bed.

That was, she had to admit, a relief.

A young woman in mufti, a plaid skirt and a scarlet sweater, tapped at the open door and came in. She was carrying a clipboard and a pen. She brought a straight chair to the bed and sat down.

'Isobel Callaghan? I need a few details for our records. Up till now you've been too ill for us to get your admission form filled in.'

While she was prepared to forgive this social lapse, she made it clear that the inconvenience had been serious.

Isobel forbore to apologise.

'Full name?'

'Isobel Catherine Callaghan.'

'Date of birth?'

Isobel supplied it.

'Religion?'

'I don't have a religion.'

'Look.' The young woman spoke slowly and firmly. 'We are filling in a form. I am not asking if you go to church on Sunday. Everyone has a religion.'

'Is that right?' Isobel reflected. 'I think I'll be a Buddhist. I've always liked the idea. You just write OD,' she said helpfully.

The young woman wrote 'OD'. Think you're funny, said her expression.

'Next of kin?'

Isobel was sorry at once that she had made herself conspicuous in the matter of religion. She said, 'I'm an orphan,' in a tone which she hoped would discourage questioning.

That was servile. It did not solve her problem, either. The young woman said, 'Just give me the name of a close relative.'

Isobel paused. Not Aunt Noelene. *Don't come running to me when you're in trouble*. Well, this was trouble, all right, so she mustn't go running. Margaret? She could not remember Margaret's new surname. Bruce Edgar, son of... no use. She tried to visualise that wedding invitation but could get no further.

'Look, we need this information for your protection,' said the young woman. 'There's no need for you to be obstructive.'

Of course a parcel must have a return address.

'I'm sorry. I was trying to think.'

She gave the name 'Margaret Callaghan' and the address of Whitefields.

She was indeed sorry. The young woman was softened by her apologetic tone.

'That's fine then. I have the date of admission.'

She left, mollified.

A nurse brought a cup of tea and biscuits on a paper plate. She asked if it was true that Isobel had collapsed in the street and been brought in in her clothes.

Isobel said yes.

The nurse asked, 'How come?'

Isobel shook her head and the nurse went away. Doctor Hansen came in, accompanied by a tall, stately woman of disagreeable aspect.

67

'Well, here she is, Matron. We've come to talk about the future, if you feel up to it. How are you feeling? I know it's going to take some time to adjust.'

'I think I'm relieved, really, to know the enemy's name.'

Ignorance had not been bliss.

'That's the idea. Now that we know the enemy, we can fight it.'

He gave her a genuine smile, which was heartening. Matron had no time for niceties of feeling.

'You must understand, doctor, that we are not equipped to handle the case here. I must insist...'

'It won't be for long, Matron. They've rung through from the Clinic that Doctor Stannard will be there on Thursday. They're getting him to drop in.' He said as an afterthought to Isobel, 'Doctor Stannard is the medical superintendent of Mornington Sanatorium. We think that it might be the place for you.'

There were limits to passivity even for a parcel. Was nobody going to ask for her consent to this arrangement? No use protesting, since in reality she had no choice, but it would have been nice to be asked.

Matron said, 'Are there no beds at the Clinic?'

'No. It is outpatients only.' His tone suggested that Matron must know that very well. 'In any case, I cannot take the responsibility of moving her before Doctor Stannard sees her on Thursday.'

'I have to go home some time,' said Isobel. 'I have to give up my room and pack my things.'

'Can't you get a friend to do that for you?'

It was Return to Sender again. No religion, no knickers, no next of kin, no friends.

She shook her head.

Doctor Hansen was looking at Matron.

'I'll get Mrs Mills to talk to her.' He turned to Isobel. 'Mrs Mills is our social worker. She'll find a volunteer to look after you. One of our wonderful Pink Ladies. Till Thursday then, Matron. And I shall be wanting to talk about a special diet for her.'

Put that in your pipe and smoke it, Matron.

Isobel was beginning to be fond of Doctor Hansen.

'The best you can do for yourself now,' he said, 'is keep quiet, keep warm, eat your food and keep up your spirits. Mrs Mills will be along to see you later. Oh, and a nurse will be along with some tissues. Make sure that you cover your mouth when you cough. That's about it, I think.'

Isobel nodded and lay back, hoping that there would be no further demands on her attention.

The next visitor was a nurse carrying towels, a box of tissues and a small lidded pan of white enamel. She was wearing a face mask above which she winked at Isobel.

'Matron's orders,' she said in a tone that dismissed them with amused contempt.

She put the tissues and the pan on the bedside table.

'Cover up each cough and sneeze. Place all used tissues in the receptacle provided. You're allowed to get up to go to the loo and to have a shower if you feel up to it. If you don't feel up to it, you can ask for a bed bath, but I wouldn't if I were you. See how you feel tomorrow, anyhow. I'll just get your pulse and your temperature and you can settle down till dinner time. You've had enough for one day, you poor kid.'

Isobel, sucking obediently at the thermometer and extending her wrist on request, was quite of the same opinion.

She dozed until dinner time. The dinner trolley was wheeled in by another young orderly, less forthcoming than Eric.

'Doctor says if you can't manage anything else, eat the icecream. But he wants you to eat the lot.'

She nibbled some ham. It wasn't so much that she wasn't hungry. The effort of chewing was just too much. The icecream was a commercial paper tub with a wooden paddle for a spoon. That must be part of the special diet.

To her horror, she began to cry. About the icecream, not about having tuberculosis. It was the small things that affected her most, the humiliation of being helped out of her sweater, the tenderness in Eric's voice and now a tub of icecream. She would be humiliated enough if anyone saw her crying. What she needed was a visit from Matron. That would be bracing. She mopped her eyes and blew her nose on a tissue, which she put into the enamel pan. Then she finished the icecream. If anyone brought me a toothbrush, I'd break my heart.

There was salt on the tray. She shook some of it into a tissue, thinking she could scrub her teeth with salt on a finger—better than nothing.

However, she didn't get her teeth cleaned that night. As soon as the young man had taken away the tray, she fell asleep and slept seriously until morning.

*

The hospital woke early. Isobel woke to the sound of trolleys rolling over linoleum and the morning light which came through the large window.

She enquired of her body how it felt. The headache was gone and so were the other pains, even the dagger under the shoulderblade. She was weak, but weakness without pain was a rather enjoyable sensation. She must get up soon and have a shower. It was the familiar problem of accumulating enough strength to perform the task ahead, but how much easier that would be lying comfortably in bed.

She was getting a lot of sympathy she didn't deserve. People generally expected her to be overcome by the news. They could not know how happy she was to have all horrors assembled under the name of an illness, represented by a baby's hand-print on her lung. This thing is not I. This thing is visible and can be fought.

What better news could one have, than the hope of a future without madness?

She would do everything they told her, she would eat whatever they gave her, beginning with breakfast.

A new orderly appeared at the door, this time an older man, short, sturdy and grey-haired. He looked to be one of the kind ones.

'Want a cup of tea?'

'Yes, please. No milk or sugar.'

This time the tea came in a cup.

'Is it all right for me to use the china?'

'Special issue. You have your own. No need to take too much notice of her.' He didn't have to identify the woman

71

behind the pronoun. 'We don't mind looking after you. Keeping the china separate is no trouble.'

Isobel smiled at him and accepted the tea, which came with two biscuits. She would eat them both.

'Is that right, the police picked you up in the street and got the ambulance?'

She nodded. There was always the same price for kindness.

'How did that happen?'

'I live by myself. I ran out of food. I went out to buy some. I don't,' she said boldly, 'really remember much more.'

That would be it from now on. I don't know. I must have passed out.

He nodded sympathetically and left her to her tea and biscuits.

The story would not cover the absence of knickers but it would do for most occasions.

After breakfast—she managed half the cereal and most of the milk it swam in, being determined to drown that hand-print in milk—she showered, clinging to the chrome bar, and managed to scrub some of the hoarded salt along her teeth. She walked back into the smock and collapsed again. How odd to be inhabiting this flaccid body. It sprawled limp on the bed and she had the greatest trouble in urging it under the covers.

The blonde nurse who had winked at her came in, pulling on a face mask.

'It's just while I make the bed, dear. Rules from the TB Clinic this time. That's when the bugs fly, apparently. Matron's been on the phone to them, carrying on, asking what measures she should take to protect her staff. Honestly! You don't want to pay too much attention to Matron. We all think you are marvellous to be so game. Eric said you even raised a laugh when he was wheeling you back. Could be shock, of course. But you're just as good this morning. Hanged if I could take it like that.'

Meanwhile she had hoisted Isobel's limp body out of bed, had sat it in the armchair and was making the bed.

How could she explain the relief she felt at learning that this thing had a name and a location, that there were people whose business it was to deal with it? That she was no longer alone in the grip of something she could not understand? That there was even hope for the future? Her troubles were embarrassments only, bodily weakness, lack of knickers and kin; they could not dim her joy.

'Do you think somebody could get me a toothbrush and some toothpaste?'

The nurse looked startled.

'Somebody should have thought of that. You've set us all on our ears. Real tragedy queen, you are.'

'I'd better make the most of it. It's not likely to happen again.'

'That's the spirit!'

The nurse helped her back into bed.

She produced the thermometer from her breast pocket, saying, 'Put it under your tongue and keep your mouth closed. And what on earth are you grinning about?'

Impossible to explain while she was keeping her lips closed on a thermometer, that a memory had returned with enlightenment.

The nurse shook her head in bewilderment while she pressed fingertips to a vein in Isobel's wrist and counted seconds.

She removed the thermometer, checked temperature, made a note on the chart hooked to the end of Isobel's bed and said, 'Now what was that about?'

'Per rectum. I just remembered, somebody said, "Better take it per rectum, Sister." I just realised, she must have been taking my temperature. But I didn't know what "per rectum" meant.'

'You found out!'

The nurse was laughing, too.

'And I was most indignant! I thought I was being got at in a very nasty way. I'd forgotten it until this minute.'

'You weren't right out to it, then?'

'Not all the time. Things kept getting through.'

'Like saying you weren't a bloody xylophone.'

Isobel groaned.

'Did I really say that?'

'Yes. You got Doc Hansen into trouble for laughing. He said he couldn't help himself. It just took him by surprise. Well, it'll certainly take a lot to get you down. I'd better get on or Her Nibs will be on my back. I'll see one of the orderlies about the toothbrush and anything else you want from the shop. Bye.' She said from the doorway, 'My name's Bernie, by the way.'

I like you, Bernie. And you didn't ask me, 'How come?'

The chat had been enlivening, but tiring. She lay back and dozed, thinking she could do this for ever, just lie passive and let the time pass.

Her next visitor came after lunch, a small slight woman, black-haired and black-eyed, quick in movement, earnest in manner.

'Hullo. You're Isobel? I'm Roberta Mills. Doctor Hansen thought we should have a talk. About things in general. Facing up to tuberculosis is a big thing. I'm not talking about the cure, that's for the doctors and they know what they are doing. You can be sure of that. There may be other things you would like to talk about. Doctor Hansen said you haven't asked to have anyone notified?'

'My parents are dead.'

That wasn't going to satisfy Mrs Mills.

'No other family?'

'I have a sister who lives in the country. We had lost touch.'

'Any family problems I can help with? Anyone you would like me to approach on your behalf?'

'No thank you.'

Mrs Mills wasn't going to give up easily.

'Tell me something about yourself. When did you and your sister part?'

You couldn't tell Mrs Mills to mind her own business. This was her business. This was all part of being a parcel. Parcels can be opened and inspected.

'After my mother died, an aunt took Margaret to live with her in the country.'

Mrs Mills became alert.

'Did you feel rejected, that your sister was chosen? Were you invited to join them?'

How to keep Aunt Noelene out of this? If Mrs Mills discovered the existence of Aunt Noelene, she would be making an approach there, whether Isobel liked it or not.

'No. I didn't want to go to the country. And I wanted to be independent.'

'At what stage were you when your mother died?'

'I'd just finished the Leaving. Margaret was working in an office. She is two years older than I am.'

'And you didn't think it odd, that the younger sister should be left alone in the city, while the other was taken into a family?'

'It was what I wanted.'

Mrs Mills nodded.

'How did you do at school?'

Pretty well. Dux, actually.

Truly, the question was impertinent.

'All right.'

'What about your pass in the Leaving? Were you happy with it?'

'First class Honours in English and German, As in French and History, Bs in Maths I and Chemistry. I suppose I wasn't too happy about those.'

Mrs Mills looked at her steadily and earnestly.

What's a nice girl like you doing in a plight like this?

Just lucky, I guess.

No use trying dirty jokes on Mrs Mills.

'Isobel, are you sure there is nothing you want to talk to me about? No trouble you want to discuss?'

Drink, drugs, kleptomania, men?

Only the Muse. And what a tyrannical, possessive, secretive old witch she is.

She must somehow get control of this conversation, find a sop or two to throw to this earnest, well-meaning Cerberus.

'I was working in an importer's, doing office work and translating the German mail.'

Mrs Mills approved.

Isobel assumed a frank and confiding expression.

'I don't know really how things went wrong. Everything seemed to weigh on me. I lost my temper and I lost my job. Things just went downhill from there...I don't know how to explain. I felt wretched...Everything seemed to slip away from me.'

Mrs Mills was sympathetic.

'You didn't think that you were ill?'

'Not seriously, no. I just seemed to be depressed, and I couldn't make the effort to get in touch with anyone...'

She hoped she wasn't overdoing the pathos.

'Perhaps it's all for the best. We'll find people to help you now. I've asked Mrs Delaney to look after you. You'll like her, I'm sure. She's one of our volunteers and a truly lovely person. And you're quite sure that there's nothing I can do for you?'

Isobel smiled gratefully and shook her head.

You can just go away.

'I'll leave you then. Rose—Mrs Delaney—will be in to see you tomorrow.'

*

77

When Mrs Mills had left, Isobel lay back on her pillows, feeling ashamed. That pathetic expression! That soapy voice! Was that me?

This sort of thing is not at all good for the character.

She was cheered by the reappearance of Eric.

'Bernie says you want some shopping done.' He added, 'This isn't my area, but I took the chance to come and see how you were making out.'

'All right. Bernie is a dear. It was good of you to come. Will you hand me my purse? I want a toothbrush and some toothpaste.'

'Right, love. Any preferences?'

'Not a hard toothbrush, please. Any toothpaste will do.'

'Right. Everybody in the ward is asking about you.'

Isobel remembered the muted cheer and the soft clapping and smiled without pathos.

'Tell them I'm fine. Living in the lap of luxury and loving every minute.'

'That's the style. Enjoy it while it's on. I'll be back with this as soon as I get a break.'

That, Isobel decided, was enough traffic for one day. She closed her eyes and played possum. The effect of that was to send her to sleep, which passed the time.

When she woke, she found toothbrush, toothpaste and change of a pound on the side table. It was disappointing to have missed Eric's return visit. Funny, that, to become attached in so short a time. It was like clutching at people as one drifted past, going where?

The evening meal arrived: runny scrambled egg. Don't think of it as food, think of it as fuel or muscle. One couldn't live for ever in a body that flopped about like a dead jellyfish. She worked her way through half of it.

Lights out. Morning. Tea, shower, breakfast, Bernie and bed-making.

'Thanks for getting Eric to shop for me.'

'He didn't mind. Said you were asleep when he got back. Found the things and your change all right?'

'Yes. I never dreamed I could sleep so much.'

'Best thing for you. I do believe you're looking a bit better. Feel any better?'

'Kind of boneless, that's all. All right otherwise.'

'Well, it's to be expected.'

Bernie took her temperature, counted her pulse-beats, made notes on the chart and departed.

That was another one she wanted to cling to, absurdly, crying, 'Don't leave me!'

Jellyfish body, jellyfish mind.

The woman who arrived that afternoon, announcing herself as Rose Delaney, was middle-aged yet looked girlish. This was not, Isobel saw at once, the effect of vanity, a desperate clinging to youth, but indifference to the passing of time, as if the curling brown hair had been greying and the flesh of her neck and her body loosening while she was thinking of other things. Age had lined the skin about her beautiful blue eyes but had left the wide mouth untouched. She had about her an air of privilege which she owed as much to her casual manner as to her expensive silk shirt and loose-fitting but well-cut suit of burgundy red wool. Her handbag and her low heeled shoes were made from the skin of a reptile. She wore wealth as carelessly as she wore age.

'Hullo. I'm Rose Delaney and I've come to be your friend in need. I've heard you could use one. What can I do for you?'

She took a small notebook and a slender silver pencil out of the reptilian handbag and sat waiting.

'It's a lot to ask.'

'It's what I'm here for. Speak up.'

'Well, I need someone to pack my belongings and close my room for me. The rent's paid to the end of the week. I don't think they'll worry about short notice.'

'Address?'

She wrote down the stark address without raising her eyebrows.

'Got any idea how much stuff you have to move? And how much luggage do you have?'

'The things that really matter are my typewriter, my folders, any pages with writing on them, my books. Oh, and a shoebox with my embroidery. And my topcoat and my suit. They're hanging in the corner behind the curtain.'

Thank Heaven she had emptied that bucket. How close she had come to utter degradation!

She had, on the contrary, achieved esteem. Mrs Delaney had detected the presence of the Muse, and was smiling as she nodded in understanding.

'What about luggage?'

'A suitcase and a duffle bag. It won't be enough. I can buy something. I do have some savings. If you could go to the bank for me. I have forty pounds.'

'We'll make the money go as far as we can. There'll be things to buy if you go into the sanatorium, which looks likely.'

'Do I have any choice about this? I mean, nobody's asked me.'

Mrs Delaney considered this.

'In theory I suppose you have, but in practice, no. You would have to prove that you were living in conditions that didn't endanger others, I think. There would be so many difficulties that in the long run you would have to agree. But they are being a bit highhanded, I suppose.'

'It would be nice sometimes to be included in the conversation. I feel like a parcel being handed around.'

Mrs Delaney laughed.

'You're not the only one. I always feel like that if I'm unlucky enough to fall into their hands, believe me. Is there anything from the room you want straight away?'

'Some knickers and my nightdress, please. And, if you wouldn't mind, there are three paperback books of poetry, Auden and Donne and Gerard Manley Hopkins.'

'You're just like my daughter Sara. She loves poetry too. I'll get them for you. Now you'll have to give me a letter of authority to show to the manager. I didn't think of that. Um. I'll go and get some notepaper from the desk. I'll probably have to buy an old tin trunk or some such, for storage. I'll look around the secondhand shops if I can't scrounge one somewhere. I'll scrounge what I can.'

At the prospect of scrounging she brightened and looked more juvenile than ever.

She added as an afterthought, 'You don't mind, do you? You don't object to taking handouts?'

'Am I in a position to mind?' asked Isobel, but she was grateful for the courtesy.

'Well, I'll fetch the notepaper, you can give me the authority, and we'll be in business.'

After her departure, Isobel thought how painful this conversation might have been, and how comfortable she had found it. What a rare talent, to give charity without giving offence.

Mrs Delaney returned with a writing pad of small pages bearing the printed name and address of Saint Ursula's Hospital. Isobel wrote to her dictation:

> I give authority to the bearer Mrs Rose Delaney to remove my possessions from Room 14B and to bring them to me at the above address.
>
> Isobel Callaghan

'And I'll want your key, of course.'

Isobel handed it over, knowing for certain now that she would never see the room again.

'Thank you, my dear. I'll be back with your things tomorrow and we can talk some more about the situation when I've seen what we have to do. Goodbye now.'

No doubt about it, the room seemed dimmer without her. Mrs Delaney radiated.

*

She looked even more radiant when she returned, late in the next afternoon, carrying Isobel's duffle bag.

'I've scrounged a suitcase! I knew I probably could. People don't throw out luggage. It's an old expandable leather bag, heavy as lead and it looks like a dead dinosaur, but it will do. And I've got a little grant for you. Five pounds. The Auxiliary has a fund. I think I can stretch it. I'll get pyjamas straight off. SSW, are you? I thought so.'

Isobel smiled at her enthusiasm and whispered, 'Do you enjoy vicarious poverty?'

'Oh, dear, does it show so much? Yes, I do rather. I grew up during the Depression. Of course it was a terrible time. I always think of it when I smell soup. Mum used to start the soup pot in the morning, meat stock she saved from everything, chopped vegetables and barley. That was for the people who came to the door selling bootlaces and such. We were better off than most. Dad stayed in work and though we were poor it was, as Mum used to say, enough for ourselves and a bit over. And she was a marvel at managing, making something out of nothing. I went to my first dance with an evening coat, a pretty olive green bolero, they were all the rage, and nobody knew that mine was made out of the best bits of an old velvet curtain. I can see her now, holding the cut-out pieces to steam over a kettle. She was a wonderful person. Scrounging and managing for somebody else just takes me back, I suppose. Well, so long as you don't mind it...'

'It's a whole lot better than someone doing her duty without a smile, I assure you.'

'I'll tell that to Sara, the next time she tells me I'm just enjoying myself instead of tackling the serious issues of society. Now I'm making you talk too much and I've been told not to. Not another word from you. I'll unpack for you and be off. Don't expect me till you see me. I don't know how long things will take.'

She put Isobel's nightdress and her two singlets and three pairs of knickers—all, Isobel noticed, newly washed and ironed—into her cabinet, the books of poems on its top, soap, toothbrush and toothpaste into the small bathroom, put her finger to her lips and departed.

Nostalgic about poverty, thought Isobel. How nice to be so rich. But the thought was affectionate, not critical.

'Well, today's the day,' said Bernie on Thursday morning.

Today Isobel's fate was to be decided—or rather, the decision was to be made official, for it seemed to have been decided already.

After she had put Isobel back to bed, remarking cheerfully that she was getting stronger, she said, 'I don't think the great man can be here before eleven. I'll be in to tidy up later.'

However, it was a strange nurse who arrived before lunch. She nodded briskly, looked about her, set the chairs straight against the wall, put the books of poems and the pocket comb out of sight into drawers, checked the bathroom, sat Isobel upright while she straightened her pillows, stretched the quilt to absolute smoothness and told Isobel firmly to keep it that way and not go wriggling about and

84

disturbing it. There was no doubt that a person of very great importance was expected.

'You'll have to wait for your lunch till Doctor's been.'

Isobel sat up, awed into immobility. Would the great man say with a scowl, 'There's a wrinkle in that quilt, nurse'?

No, of course. Only Matron inspired such dread.

A long hour later an orderly arrived carrying a large buff envelope which he laid at the foot of Isobel's unwrinkled bed. He nodded and left.

She waited again.

At last the party arrived: Doctor Hansen, accompanied as she had expected by Matron, and by a tall, broad-shouldered figure who was quite the handsomest man she had yet seen. Chieftain of the eagle tribe, she thought, though there was nothing beaklike about the straight nose, the firm, beautifully shaped mouth and the quite adequate chin.

'This is Doctor Stannard, the medical superintendent of Mornington Sanatorium,' said Doctor Hansen.

Lucky he took to tuberculosis, thought Isobel. You wouldn't want that one examining your haemorrhoids.

Her nod went unnoticed. Perhaps it had not been required.

She was introduced too. Doctor Stannard acknowledged the introduction by nodding to the X-ray he had taken from the buff envelope and was holding to the light.

'Yes,' he said. 'Yes, I see. That bit of clouding in the corner—that's your machine, is it?'

'Yes.' Doctor Hansen was apologetic. 'Our machine isn't quite...'

85

'We simply aren't equipped to handle a case of this kind,' said Matron.

Doctor Stannard was rubbing his exquisite nose between thumb and forefinger as he studied Isobel's chart.

'No BSR? No, of course not. Um.'

'We had to send the specimen down to the Clinic by taxi,' said Doctor Hansen. He forestalled Matron. 'I didn't think it would be safe to move her.'

'No.' Doctor Stannard stared at the chart. 'So I see. Pity it wasn't North Shore in the first place. How did she get here?'

Matron said coldly, 'She collapsed in the street and was picked up by the police. The ambulance brought her here. I suppose it was the nearest hospital.'

Indignation forced Isobel's whisper to a furious croak.

'I went out to buy food. I was only going to the corner shop. Things just…got out of hand.'

She was panting from the effort of speech. She thought, It was a beautiful moment, beautiful. Never forget that.

'Such things do occur,' said Doctor Stannard. His words were for Isobel, but his gaze was on Matron. 'This isn't the bubonic plague, Matron.' His voice was gentle, apologetic and only faintly amused, the voice of a man accustomed to defusing situations. 'The precautions are few and simple. You've had advice from the Clinic about that, I'm told.'

His charm had as much effect on Matron as a sunlit wave washing against a granite crag. It seemed however to be supported by authority, for she made no answer.

'How to get her up to us is the problem. We have an ambulance coming from North Shore on Tuesday. It can take her as well.'

'Tuesday?' asked Matron without enthusiasm.

'Tuesday. Can't manage it before. Would you give them a call and let them know you have a passenger for the ambulance? And Peter...' he looked at his watch. 'I'm sorry, but I do have this meeting...'

He looked at Isobel and said, 'At Mornington, we cure people. We'll cure you. You're going to get better. Remember that.'

She nodded, the croak of indignation having left her speechless.

Bernie came in with a late lunch of sandwiches and coffee.

'Coffee's off the menu for you but I thought you could do with a cup. You're off to see the Wizard, are you?'

'Yes. Tuesday.'

'Was that him I saw walking down the corridor with Doc Hansen? Holy gee, what a looker! I thought Hollywood had come to town!'

Isobel offered her thought about haemorrhoids, which fetched a giggle.

'You're a card. Better not be talking. You haven't got much voice left. I'll leave you to it.'

One could almost forget Doctor Stannard's looks at moments: when he managed to convey to Matron that he knew some very nice people who had fallen down in the street and been picked up by the police. Serge, sweat and tobacco in a column of warmth and strength—there was

87

nothing wrong with it, she would never think there was anything wrong with it. And when he had said, 'You're going to get better. Remember that!'

The memory encouraged her to tackle a second sandwich.

Doctor Hansen came in to visit, to tell her what a wonderful place Mornington was and what a brilliant doctor Doctor Stannard.

'I'm sorry he was a bit rushed today. He has a very busy schedule.'

'I can see that.'

'Believe me, you couldn't be in safer hands.'

Isobel nodded and smiled, registering gratitude. She was thinking only that she could keep her luxury accommodation until Tuesday, with the added satisfaction of annoying a very unpleasant woman. This living for the moment was new, not a resolution but a physical change, as if the moment was all she had strength for.

'How are you getting on with Mrs Delaney?'

'Love her.'

'Yes. She's a very rare person. We're lucky to have her.' Doctor Hansen left and Isobel retired to her voluntary coma. Enough for today.

'So it's fixed, is it?' said Mrs Delaney. 'Off on Tuesday, they tell me.'

Isobel nodded.

'I'd better hurry up with your shopping, then.' She took the armchair, set a carrier bag down by her side, rummaged in the handbag for a sheet of paper which she handed to Isobel.

'Now I've packed the dinosaur and these are the things in it, so far. Check it and see if you want anything that's there.'

'You didn't have to worry about the china and the saucepans.'

'You'll be setting up for yourself again later.'

How much later? Neither of them lingered over that thought.

'I'd better store the big case for you. There's my address and my signature on the back. A kind of receipt, you know. Well, don't laugh. You never can tell what may happen and you need some kind of evidence that you own the things. Particularly your typewriter. I've packed all the manuscripts except one exercise book that seems to have bits and pieces in it. I thought I might put that in the small case. I have a list from the sanatorium. Two pairs of pyjamas, hot water bottle, winter dressing gown, summer dressing gown, slippers...Oh, about the dressing gowns. This is Sara's old winter gown. The satin is frayed round the cuffs but I've darned it in. I hope it will do.'

Sara's old gown was of rose-coloured wool, trimmed with quilted pale pink satin. Mrs Delaney had darned the cuffs very neatly. Isobel stroked the darned surface with a smile.

'And here—oh, it's a bit conspicuous, I'm afraid. Souvenir of Hong Kong. One buys these things because they are there and when you come home you can't imagine

89

what came over you. But it would do for a summer dressing gown over pyjamas.'

She was holding out for display a long jacket of dark blue cotton, bound and belted in scarlet. Across its back sprawled a magnificent dragon embroidered in brilliant colours.

'As I said, it does stand out a bit.'

'I think it's beautiful.'

'They call them happy coats. I hope that's a good sign.' Overcome by this outburst, Mrs Delaney bent her head to rummage further in the bag.

'Same with the slippers. If they fit you and you think they'll do. Don't try them on now. Wait till you get up to go to the bathroom.'

The slippers were Turkish, with pointed, beaded toes. Isobel picked one up, slipped it onto her hand and looked at it with admiration.

'You can always say they were a present. Well, I'm inside my five pounds and I'll have a bit over for a few little things. Like a pack of solitaire cards. Do you play Patience?'

'How can I ever pay you back?'

'You don't pay it back, my dear. You hand it on. Some day you'll meet somebody in trouble and that's the time to think of paying back. And some day, Isobel, you're going to have a lot to give.'

'What makes you think that?'

'Just a feeling I have. Right, if you're happy with this lot, I'll finish the shopping and pack the small bag for you. You tuck that list away safely in your bag. I'll be in with it on Monday so that we can check through but I'll come to see you off on Tuesday. Keep the slippers to try on. That's it, then.'

It was lucky that Mrs Delaney was finding it all such fun. That eased the burden of gratitude.

Mrs Delaney arrived on Monday afternoon with Isobel's suitcase and brought with her, in spite of her cheerful manner, a sense of unease with the approach of the unknown.

'You didn't get all this for five pounds,' said Isobel, observing the two pairs of pyjamas, one frilly, one tailored, the new knickers, the toilet bag with soap and talcum, the pretty handkerchiefs and the Patience cards.

Her own two summer dresses, her blouse and skirt had been washed and ironed and it seemed that the winter coat which Mrs Delaney carried over her arm had been to the cleaners.

'I shan't lie about the handkerchiefs and the toilet bag, dear. Everything else. I do think, you know, that you should dump that hairbrush.'

'It doesn't do much for my social standing, I agree.'

'I've bought one of those little plastic gadgets that will do instead. Out with the hairbrush.'

She put it into her carrier bag. Even in the waste bin, it would not have done much for Isobel's social standing.

Out of the carrier bag she brought three paperbacks.

'You can't always be reading poetry. These are from home. You can hand them on when you've finished them.'

'Do you do this sort of thing all the time?' asked Isobel.

'No, I don't. I'm not as admirable as the people who turn up every day and do a dreary chore out of the goodness of their hearts. I'm emergency help. Maybe next week or next month they'll call me in, maybe not for months. But when I'm at it, I do concentrate on the job.'

'Lucky for me.'

She was already feeling jealous of the unknowns who would claim Mrs Delaney's attention. This would not do. Charity must not be confused with friendship.

The ambulance was to arrive at two o'clock on Tuesday. Mrs Delaney arrived at twenty past one to help Isobel to dress and to see to the luggage.

'You had better put a pair of pyjamas in your duffle bag, dear, in case you can't get at your suitcase.' Mrs Delaney was in a last-minute fuss which made the situation seem quite domestic. 'Soap, washer. Have you finished with your toothbrush? Right. Now you pop into the shower and I'll get out your clothes.'

'Pop' was hardly the word, thought Isobel, as she crept to the bathroom supported by Mrs Delaney.

She came out wrapped in her bathtowel and sat with relief on the bed as she dried herself. Modesty was long gone.

'Isobel, where are your socks?'

'Socks?'

'Yes, dear. Those things you put on your feet so you don't freeze to death. Don't you have any socks?'

'Yes. Two pairs of socks. But I wasn't wearing any socks, I think. You see, I was just...'

'Going to the corner shop. Yes, I know. Well, I didn't see them when I packed up. They must be still in the room somewhere and I missed them. If only I'd thought. I could easily have bought socks. Oh, dear. What do we do now?'

'I could wrap my feet in bandages.'

Mrs Delaney gave her a quick, impatient look which she resented. There was a limit even to Mrs Delaney's patience.

'So would I as a last resort. How long do we have?' She looked at her watch and answered herself. 'Thirty-five minutes. I just have an idea. I'll be back.'

Isobel was glad of privacy after all to make her slow way into knickers, slacks and sweater and to lie down for a minute or two to recover some strength.

Mrs Delaney came back with four nylon stockings draped over her arm, her good humour restored.

'There's a box of them in our office. One of the Auxiliary collects them to crochet into bath mats. Cuts them into strips.'

'Are you going to crochet a pair of socks in twenty minutes?'

'If you keep on like that, I am going to forget that you are a sick girl.'

'Sorry.'

'Forgiven.'

Mrs Delaney had taken a pair of scissors from her bag and was cutting the stockings into long socks.

'You'll have to put them on, two to each foot. Should give a bit of warmth. Better than nothing. I'll roll them down and stitch a hem.'

She worked fast, rolling two layers of nylon leg together down to the ankle and stitching a hem.

'Your Mum would be proud of you,' said Isobel. 'Do you carry needle and thread about with you?'

'It was all down in our office. Do keep still, dear.'

She finished one hem and turned to the other.

'How's the time?'

'Ten to two.'

'I'll do it with five minutes to spare. So long as the ambulance isn't early. Well, there we are.'

'Positively stylish.'

Isobel lifted one foot to admire the neat little nylon sock with its rolled hem sitting snug above her ankle.

'Hurry up, now. Get your shoes on. Ready! They can come when they like.'

They came at half past four.

'This is terrible,' said Isobel. 'You really must go home.'

'No. I can't leave you till I see you on to that ambulance. I wouldn't be satisfied with myself.'

'It's like being on a platform waiting for a train. I know why people say they hate to see anyone off. One runs out of conversation.'

'You shouldn't be talking anyhow. You had better lie down and get under the blankets. I'll go and see what I can find out.'

Left alone, Isobel gave way completely to panic. She hid herself under the blankets, clinging to the bed, feeling as if it was a raft on an unknown ocean.

Mrs Delaney came back, saying, 'They've rung North Shore from the office. Apparently they've picked up another stretcher case. It's holding them up.'

She came close to the bed and touched Isobel's shoulder.

Isobel muttered, 'I'm frightened. Plain bloody terrified. Sorry.'

Mrs Delaney put her arms around her and gathered her into an embrace.

'Darling, I know. This waiting is the last straw. You've been so good up to now, but enough is enough. Come on, have a cry if you want to. It's only to be expected. But everything is going to be all right. Doctor Stannard says so and he knows what he is about.'

Her voice was crooning, hypnotic.

Isobel was trembling violently. She tried to clench her chattering teeth to still them and uttered instead a little whimpering noise.

'Ashamed of this.'

'Well, don't be.'

Mrs Delaney stroked her shoulders, which was comforting.

Isobel thought, with surprise, that it was the first time anyone had ever touched her in kindness. It was a new sensation, remarkably steadying. Though perhaps it was the thought that was steadying.

'That's better,' she said.

'Don't talk. Just lie still and I'll sit with you and say nothing. They are going to ring from downstairs when...'

'The tumbrel comes.'

Isobel said this with a giggle.

'You don't stay down long, do you?'

'Don't stop holding me.'

'No. Wait till I get comfortable. Don't want to break my arm, do you?' She lifted Isobel's head onto her warm, plump lap and continued to stroke. 'Just relax.'

Later, she said, 'You actually dropped off. Best thing in the world for you.'

'Retreat from reality.' Isobel sat up. 'Sorry I was such an ass.'

'You expect too much of yourself altogether. They've taken your suitcase down.' Mrs Delaney was holding out her coat. 'Better put this on. They're bringing a wheelchair. It'll be here in a minute.'

Isobel shrugged into the coat.

'What on earth can I say to you? You say "Thanks" when somebody opens a door for you.'

'Just look after yourself and get well.'

There was a knock at the door. Eric was waiting with the wheelchair.

'Just thought I'd see you off. Bernie couldn't get here.'

He set her into the chair, handbag and duffle bag beside her, and wheeled her to the lift, Mrs Delaney following with the suitcase.

At the reception desk, a man in uniform was talking on the phone.

'I've got two cases in the back, I tell you.'

He listened.

'Well, I wasn't paid for this.'

He looked with disfavour at Isobel. He listened again, then said to Eric, 'Get her a face mask, will you? This her suitcase?'

He picked up the case and walked out.

'Charming,' said Eric. 'Maybe I'd better get him one too.'

He patted Isobel's arm, disappeared and returned with the face mask, put it on her and wheeled her out into the street where the ambulance was waiting.

'Look after yourself, kid. Nice knowing you.'

He lifted her into the front seat beside the driver.

'Say goodbye to Bernie for me.'

He handed in the duffle bag and the handbag. They held hands for a moment. He closed the door. The driver started the engine and they moved away.

I I

MORNINGTON B GRADE

Clearly the driver was not inclined to conversation. That was as well, for she was too exhausted to speak to him or to notice the scenery as they climbed into the mountains. She sat with her face turned away and saw the light fade and felt the air grow colder. The discomforts of her spell in the theatrette were returning: shudders ran down her body and her head was heavy.

It was completely dark when they stopped at the lighted entrance to the building that bulked against the sky.

The driver got down and was about to disappear.

She said, 'Will you help me down, please?'

He walked to her side of the vehicle and extended an arm, which served as a rigid support while she climbed down. Resentment of his reluctance gave her strength enough to walk through the doorway into a vestibule where a woman sat at a large reception desk.

The woman said sharply, 'Are you Isobel Callaghan? We'd quite given you up. You have no business to be up and dressed. You're supposed to be a stretcher case!'

Behind Isobel the ambulance men were carrying a stretcher through the room and into a further doorway.

'I'm sorry,' said Isobel, who had been given no choice and felt very much like a stretcher case.

'And all the wards have had their dinner now. You will have to go to the dining room.'

Isobel did not know whether she should apologise for this, also. She stood at the desk while the second stretcher case was carried past behind her and said with desperation, 'Please may I sit down?'

'I'll get a chair. It won't be long. Sit over there for the moment while I find out what to do with you.'

The ambulance driver carried in her suitcase and her duffle bag and set them down at the desk.

The woman talked on the phone.

'A Ward? Right. She'll have to go to the dining room for dinner…Well, they'll have to find her something…I don't know.' She covered the mouthpiece of the phone and said to Isobel, 'Where are your night things?'

'In the overnight bag.'

'She has them separate in an overnight bag…Right. You can take that with you and leave the rest. We'll see to it in the morning.'

A chair meant a wheelchair. It arrived pushed by a very tall, redheaded young man who was greeted as Max.

'You're an hour or so late, mate.'

'Take her round to the dining room and see what you can get for her, then down to A for the night. She'll need that overnight bag for the moment. I'll ring Sister Mackenzie to expect her.'

Something in Isobel's appearance had amused Max.

As he helped her into the chair he said, 'You can take that mask off now, kid. You're among friends.'

She clawed the mask off her face and dropped it into her lap, feeling foolish.

He set the small bag on her knee. They set off again, through the inner doorway into a corridor.

'How long have you known?' asked Max as he wheeled her along to an open double doorway and through it into a dining room with small tables flanked by chairs of bright orange plastic.

'About a week.'

'Longest week of your life?'

'So far, I suppose. Yes.'

'Gives you a turn, doesn't it?'

Max left her wondering if he too...He was arguing at the hatch which led from this room with tables and chairs to what must be a kitchen.

'He'll have to find her something. Come on, have a heart. She came up by the ambulance. Should have been on a stretcher, they had her sitting up in front with the driver. Got to get her fed and to bed.'

Isobel said, 'I don't want anything to eat. I want to go to bed.'

Her tone was fractious, infantile. It shamed her.

'That's dirty talk around here. They can give you soup and bread and butter. Okay?'

'Yes.'

He brought her a bowl of soup and a plate of bread with a pat of butter.

He perched on a plastic chair, long legs extended. He was a large-boned loose-jointed young man whose appearance, since it lacked sophistication, inspired confidence.

'Listen,' he said as he watched her spoon up soup. 'It's not half bad. Honestly. They are a decent bunch and the doctors know their job. I can vouch for that.'

'Were you a patient then?'

'A couple of years ago. Then I took a job in the wards. Kind of got used to the place. You'll find you do. Have some bread?'

She shook her head.

'Can't.'

'Okay. You tried and I won't peach. Off we go again.'

He wheeled her out of the deserted dining room into the corridor, through another set of double doors, along another corridor, and repeated the process.

'Can you stop at a bathroom?'

'I shouldn't, but okay. Don't be long. We're expected.'

He helped her up at a bathroom door. She used the lavatory, washed her hands and wiped them on the discarded face mask. He came to the door and supported her into the chair.

'Shouldn't have let you do that, I think. Better say nothing about it.'

Isobel was learning a new vocabulary.

101

'I shan't peach.'

'That's the style! And here we are.'

They had arrived in a lighted ward with eight beds. One of them was empty and beside it a small grey-haired woman was waiting.

She came forward, saying, 'It's Isobel, is it? We had given you up.'

'The ambulance was late.'

'Yes. We know that now. Thank you, Max. Are those her night things? Right. Now I'll fetch some water for a wash and you can change into your pyjamas.'

She said to the onlookers, 'You mustn't get her talking. She's had a long day and she's a sick girl, so leave her in peace.'

The woman had a soft Scottish accent, which was reassuring.

She left to fetch the hot water. Isobel sat on the bed. The patient in the next bed said, 'How long have you known?'

'A week and a bit.'

'Ah.'

It was a sympathetic sound, echoed from other beds.

There were no curtains here. Isobel fetched her pyjamas from the bag, slid out of her sweater and then her pants, thankful this time for knickers, and changed with all possible modesty and great effort into her nightwear.

Sister Mackenzie came back with a jug of water, a towel, a washer, a basin and a glass which she filled with water from the jug.

'You'll be wanting to clean your teeth. Do you want a pan?'

'No thank you.'

'Face and hands and then clean your teeth and we'll settle you for the night. Now don't stir.'

Having her face and hands cleaned with a wet wash-cloth made her feel decidedly juvenile.

'I shan't be doing this for you every day, I assure you.'

'I hope not.'

'For the moment you just keep as still as you can. You can clean your own teeth. There we are then. Settled for the night. Do you want a sleeping pill?'

'No thank you.'

'I'll say good night, then. Sleep well.'

She went off carrying the equipment and saying, 'Good night to you all. Pleasant dreams!'

'Fat chance,' someone said when she had gone.

Another voice said reproachfully, 'Never knock back a sleeping pill. Remember you've got friends!'

'Well, she has some manners, Sister Mackenzie. More than you can say for some.'

'I want a fag. Anyone got a lighter?'

'You'll get caught, Pat. Have to front up to Stannard. Brrr!'

'I'll hand it straight to you, dear, and just sit there looking innocent. Besides, he knows. Turns a blind eye.'

'How do you know?'

'Joe said he heard him say, "They'll only smoke under the bedclothes and set the place on fire if you try to stop it."'

'Then why don't they allow it?'

'They want to keep it down, I suppose. Hey, I want a lighter. Quick, before lights out. Thanks, Eily. And just in time. There they go.'

A cigarette shone in the dark. Isobel hoped it would not set the place on fire.

Someone said, 'Nine o'clock. Back to boarding school.'

'You get more holidays in boarding school.'

'You're telling me. More holidays? You get holidays.'

'I tell you what. At boarding school you don't meet men wandering down the corridor in their pyjamas. Some of those men are rough. Open all the way down the front. No trouble. Never heard of buttons.'

'Ah. It's cruel to sew buttons on flies!'

A voice said, 'You know what I'd like just now? I'd like a nice gin sling.'

'Ring the bell then, dear. That's what it's there for.'

'I don't think I'll bother. The service in this hotel is rotten.'

'Lois, where are you going tonight?'

'I haven't quite made up my mind.' Lois's voice was light, girlish and remote. 'I hear there's a new pianist at the Pink Tights, but I don't know...maybe the Rococo, or Spangles.'

'Better make up your mind, love. Time's getting on.'

'Time! I've got all the time in the world. If I go with Hooky, it had better be the Rococo. It's more like Hooky's style.'

'What are you going to wear?'

'Um. It had better not be my black lace with the cut-outs. Not with Hooky. But I don't know that I'll go with

Hooky. He hurt me this morning with his great big needle, and Bart said to him, "You hurt my girl," he said, "and I'll twist your bloody nose off." Hooky said, "Who's hurting her? And don't you go calling her your girl or you'll hear from me." "Don't fight over me, boys," I said. "I know I'm good, but no woman's that good." I just might go with Bart, for once.'

'Oh, how I would love a nice gin sling.'

'You know what I'd like? I'd like to go home.'

A voice floated. 'Think I'll go back home next summer…'

'Ssh! Ssh! Ssh!'

'Keep it till after her rounds.'

'You're quiet tonight, Eily.'

'Got me mind on that damned bronc.'

'Are you down for a bronchoscopy, Eily? I didn't know that.'

'Yeah. Thought that was it last time. But he said this morning, they'd better take another look. Reckoned he heard a wheeze. Another bronc. Great!'

'Rotten luck!'

'That's what you get for smoking, Eily.'

'Huh. Two fags a day if I'm lucky.'

'You could sell your body to science, Eily, and make a packet.'

'Wouldn't be much use to me without a body.'

'That's right. There's always a catch.'

'Who's that snoring?'

'Mrs P.'

'Well, nip over and wake her up. Go on!'

105

'Mrs Partridge, wake up! You were snoring, keeping everybody awake.'

'Come on, Lois. Tell us what you're going to wear.'

'I think...pale blue chiffon trimmed with white fox. A floaty cape with fur all round the bottom. So that it swings out when I turn round.'

'Not much good for dancing.'

'You take it off when you dance.'

'Hooky will take it off my shoulders and drop it on a chair, and there I'll be in my low-cut chiffon dress all ready for dancing. No jewellery. Perhaps one thin diamond bracelet.'

'I can tell you where you got all that. Out of that old film they put on last month. With what's her name. Rita Hayworth. Pretty old-fashioned.'

'The thirties are coming back. Look at the songs. Anyhow I don't care about fashion. I only care about what suits me.' She sighed. 'I hope we don't have trouble with that waiter again. There's this Italian waiter who's so crazy about me he can't control himself. He keeps hanging about making sheep's eyes and saying things in Italian and you can see that Hooky doesn't like it. He doesn't like to make scenes but he won't put up with much more of it. I hope he doesn't do his block, that's all.'

'I thought you were going with Bart.'

'No. Think I'll stick to my old love. Last time he was looking so nasty at that waiter that I thought we'd better not go there again, but really there's nothing like the Rococo. Such lovely suppers.'

Other voices joined in the fairy tale.

'Little meat pies.'

'Cocktail frankfurts with tomato sauce.'

'Oyster patties.'

'Caviar on white bread.'

'Yuk. You can have that.'

Another voice said sourly, 'Stewed mince and curried dishcloths.'

'Don't remind us! Me, I'd like a nice gin sling.'

'Is that Mrs P. snoring again? Some people have no consideration. Mrs P., wake up! You were snoring again.'

'I say, did you hear about Pam? She's going home.'

'Going home? Is she cured then?'

'No. Not cured. Doctor Hook told her they decided not to operate. I met her when I came out of X-ray and she was coming out of the office. She said Doctor Hook was very nice about it, said they thought she'd be more comfortable at home. A local doctor can give her her AP.'

'How was she taking it?'

'Looked more puzzled than anything.'

'The strep didn't take. They can't operate if the strep doesn't take. You get a spread.'

'Ssh! Little pitchers!'

This was said in a tone of warning.

'Oh, she's asleep. Hasn't stirred.'

'Poor little sod.'

Isobel, lying still and listening in fascination, and pity for Mrs Partridge, wondered who had inspired their sympathy.

A torch shone in the doorway and a voice taut with anger spoke from behind it.

'The noise in this ward is disgraceful. It's the same story every night, singing and carrying on till all hours, then in the morning it's the devil's own business getting you awake to take your temperatures. Well, this is just once too often. Doctor Hook will hear of this in the morning and I wouldn't be surprised if you all went back on B grade.' The light moved. A small large-eyed, fleshless face stared mildly like an insect caught in its beam. 'As for you, Lois, Doctor Stannard said he was going to have to put you on silence if you showed no improvement. Keep that in mind. No thought for anyone but yourselves, the lot of you.' The voice was receding and the torch was lowered.

There was a brief silence, then the talk began again in tones of indignation.

'Well, I must say! What a lady!'

'Rotten mean saying that to Lois.'

'Look what you've done with your snoring, Mrs Partridge.'

'Think she'll really tell Hooky?'

'Nah. Back on B grade and who'd be carrying the pans? She wouldn't risk it.'

'Well, she's gone for the night. What about a singsong?'

'What'll it be?'

'"Once in a While".'

'Why did I ask? Okay.'

The voices whined sweetly in the dark.

'Once in a while will you try...to give one little thought to me...Though someone else may be...nearer your heart?... In love's last dying ember...one spark may remain...If love love still can remember...that spark may burn again...'

Lulled by the sound, Isobel slept.

'If ever I was to write about this,' Isobel told herself sometime later, 'I should call it "Adventures in the Third Person".'

The singers of the night before had indeed woken sluggish and disgruntled, muttering protests as the thermometers were thrust in their mouths.

'What about her?'

'She isn't staying here. Doctor's coming to see her later.'

Isobel went back to sleep, or retired rather into her voluntary coma.

A nurse did say, 'Can you get up?'

She considered the question carefully.

'I think so.'

'Well, make up your mind. Can you get to the toilet?'

One of the voices from last night spoke.

'I'll give you a hand, kid, if you want to get to the toilet.'

'Thanks. Very much.'

'Well, just let me know when you're ready.'

'Right.'

That was a weight off her mind. She withdrew again.

Breakfast came and went without her participation.

'Listen, love. Do you want to go to the bathroom? Doctor'll be here soon. You ought to freshen up a bit, you know.'

This was Eily, who was threatened with another bronc but retained sympathy for others. She was a tall, strong-boned young woman with heavy black hair which fell to her shoulders. Though she was comely enough, something in her appearance suggested the prizefighter. The long, delicate nose flattened at the bridge, the upper lip full enough to appear swollen, hinted at misfortunes in the boxing ring. Her voice, low-pitched and husky, did not contradict the impression.

'Got to pretty yourself up for Bart. Where's your toilet stuff?'

She found it in the duffle bag, took the towel which hung at the end of the bed and led Isobel away to the bathroom.

Isobel used the lavatory, washed her face, and combed her hair.

'That's a bit more like it. Come on, I'll get you back to bed. You don't want to worry too much about Nurse Piper. Got a permanent case of them, she has.'

A case of what? Isobel did not ask. She clung gratefully to Eily and wondered why she needed another bronc. She appeared strong under Isobel's clinging arm.

Her bed had been made while she was away. Two young women in white coats and wearing face masks were making beds. Lois and the unfortunate Mrs Partridge sat in cane armchairs by their beds; other patients, like Eily, walked about in dressing gowns or went out to the bathroom.

All was in order before the doctor arrived with Sister Mackenzie.

'This is Doctor Bartholomew.'

Isobel looked with interest at this partner of Lois's dream life. He did not seem at all likely to twist anyone's nose. He was a small, neat man who radiated earnest good will.

He nodded to Isobel, then spoke to Sister Mackenzie.

'Doctor Stannard wants her to have a day to settle in before she goes to Medical, Sister. Unless there's something urgent to deal with. Anything to tell us?' He asked Isobel, who shook her head.

'Nurse said she slept well, but she didn't touch breakfast.'

I am an important parcel.

'She's to go up to C Ward, Room 5. We won't disturb her just now. If you'll send for a chair.'

'Yes, Doctor.'

'Sister Connor is expecting her. Right, then.'

He nodded to Isobel, intending reassurance, walked across to Lois's bed to ask after her health, nodded to Eily and departed with Sister Mackenzie, leaving behind him an awed silence.

'Well, what was that about?'

'I don't know.'

Eily said, 'You never do know why they do anything. They just tell you what's going to happen.'

Isobel said, 'The ambulance was late.'

'That's right. Stannard was hopping mad. I heard Sister Mackenzie tell Stinker that she sat up all the way in the front seat with the window open. Lovely.'

Isobel pondered the vision of Doctor Stannard, chieftain of the eagle tribe, hopping with rage. It turned into a kind of war dance in which that elegant gentleman was flourishing a tomahawk. She giggled.

'What on earth?' asked her neighbour.

She whispered, 'Hopping. Stannard,' and shook her head.

'Well, you haven't lost your sense of humour.'

'Leave her alone. She's not supposed to be talking.'

The wheelchair arrived, pushed by a nuggety small man and a tall dark young woman, both in white coats, the young woman carrying a blanket over her arm.

'I'm Diana,' the young woman said. 'I'm on C Ward and I'll be looking after you in the mornings. Room 5, Joe. Get her bag, will you?'

She sat Isobel in the chair, tucked the blanket over her knees, put her bag beside her and they set off, Isobel waving goodbye. There was another journey, along corridors, through two sets of double doors and into the long corridor they had travelled from the dining room the night before. There the journey ended in a small room with two unoccupied beds, each with a cabinet beside it, one close to a large window which looked out on a long verandah and in the background mountains that extended to the horizon.

Diana said, 'Thank you, Joe.'

She helped Isobel up and Joe departed with the chair. 'You're to take the inside bed.'

Isobel subsided on the inside bed. Her suitcase was standing at its foot.

Diana unpacked and stowed her belongings. Her outdoor clothes would remain in the suitcase and be taken to the luggage room.

At the prospect of being parted from her outdoor clothes, Isobel uttered a cry of protest which made Diana laugh.

'Kind of brings it home to you, doesn't it? Most people do react that way when you take away their clothes. I did myself. Thinking, now I'm really stuck with it. But you get them back as soon as you make D grade. It's a great day when you put your shoes back on, I can tell you.'

So Diana, like Max, was a graduate, one who had got used to the place and taken a job in the wards.

In a shallow cupboard that faced the foot of Isobel's bed, she hung Sara's rose-coloured dressing gown, then in front of it the dragon coat, over which she had raised her eyebrows without comment. The Turkish slippers were arranged on the cupboard floor, Mrs Delaney's emergency socks tucked into them. Beside them were the shabby scuffs from her attic room. Perhaps they would be less conspicuous than the slippers, over which Diana had paused a moment too long.

'Well, that's it. No Medical today. You're to take it easy. You didn't eat your breakfast. Can I get you a glass of milk?'

'Yes, please.'

Settling in. She was settling in. It was a daunting thought. Diana fetched the milk, set it on the cabinet, said, 'Anything else you want? If you want the pan, you ring the bell.'

'Thanks,' said Isobel, blessing Eily.

'Right. You're on your own till I bring your lunch. Doctor's orders. Sister Connor might be along later, I don't know.' It was clear that Diana was perturbed by the thought of Isobel's solitude. 'I suppose they know what they're doing. I'll be off, then.'

113

Solitude was no burden. Indeed, it was not absolute solitude for long. People began to pass by the window, some in dressing gowns, some in outdoor clothes. They did not come in, but most as they passed paused to smile and one or two to stand in the doorway and give a thumbs up sign which she found comforting.

The hour passed. The verandah was deserted.

Diana arrived with a lunch tray bearing an omelette, bread and butter, an orange and a glass of milk.

'Nice to be some people. Make the most of it. It won't happen every day.'

It became a matter of honour to eat the omelette. She needed no urging to eat the orange.

Diana came to take away the tray, approved of the empty plate and said, 'I'm off duty now. Sure there's nothing else you want?'

Isobel shook her head.

Enough for one day.

A trolley rattled in mid afternoon. Someone looked in. She played possum and the person went away.

The evening meal arrived, no longer a special order. She thought about curried dishcloths and stewed mince; this must be the dishcloths. She decided that she had done her duty by her stomach, pushed the plate away and closed her eyes.

A tall woman came in and looked regretfully at Isobel's plate.

'Now, darling. You must try to eat, you know. It's so upsetting for the cook if things go back to the kitchen. You must think about other people's feelings.'

Like Sister Mackenzie she wore the blue and white striped dress and the starched cap with floating strings which must be the uniform of a sister. She was large bosomed and broad hipped; her round head seemed rather too small for her ample body; her face wore an expression of sweetness which matched her coaxing tone.

'I had a big lunch. Honestly, I'm not hungry.'

'Well, eat your bread and butter. You must eat something.'

The tone was as unappetising as the stew, but Isobel did take a mouthful of the stew. It did not improve on acquaintance.

At least this indication of her good intention sent her visitor away.

An orderly arrived and cleared away her dinner without comment.

The same large woman arrived later accompanied by a young Chinese who said with formality, 'Good evening. I am Doctor Wang. I hope you have had a quiet day.'

'It took some coaxing to make her eat her dinner, Doctor.'

'Oh, indeed.'

This matter appeared to be of little interest.

'I shall be seeing you tomorrow after you have been to Medical. So until then, good evening and sleep well. You have already met Sister Knox, I see, since she persuaded you to eat your dinner.'

He nodded and they moved on.

His face had been quite expressionless, yet he left Isobel with the reassuring impression that he thought Sister Knox ridiculous. She wondered how he had conveyed that, but was too tired to wonder long.

A nurse came in and asked if she wanted the pan.

Yes, she did.

The nurse brought a basin for washing and a glass of water to help her clean her teeth.

That was the last ordeal. Lights out and sleep.

The day began with a thermometer thrust into her mouth and a hand clasping her wrist to count her pulse beats.

She opened her eyes and seeing Diana smiled at the sight of the familiar face.

'Hi.'

'Well, you're brighter this morning. Sleep well?'

This could be answered only with a nod, since Isobel was sucking a thermometer.

Diana released her wrist, made a note on a chart, withdrew the thermometer and removed herself to the doorway to read it in the morning light.

She shook down the thermometer with an expert flick Isobel could never master and set it in a glass of water cloudy with disinfectant which stood on a shelf above the wash basin.

'You're supposed to buy your own thermometer. Sister will tell you about that. You're to go up to Medical today. How do you feel?'

Isobel tested her extremities and decided that she was languid but mobile.

'*He* says the sooner you start treatment the better. So if you can make the effort...'

There was no need to ask who *he* was. The one who knew all and promised that she would get better.

'It'll be all right.'

'You'd better eat your breakfast. Morning tea will be along in a minute.' She took Isobel's handbag from the cabinet. 'You'd better put this in the pocket next to the wall.'

The pocket was one of the pair which hung like saddle bags on either side of the bed, and were formed by a fold at each end of a wide strip of material which passed under the mattress. Isobel thrust her handbag into the hidden pocket.

When Diana had left, Isobel pondered the ethics of a trip to the bathroom which she had noted on the journey by wheelchair. It was almost opposite.

If she was well enough to go to Medical, she must be well enough to go to the bathroom. The trick was to do things before anyone had thought to stop you.

She got up to fetch the rose-coloured dressing gown and the scuffs and was pleased to find herself much stronger, even with a reserve of strength which would take her to the bathroom and back without difficulty or at least without disaster.

The corridor was deserted and the lavatory was vacant, though the bathroom door was shut and she could hear running water.

She went back to bed triumphant, the lavatory problem solved for the present.

A trolley rolled to the door and Max looked in. 'Cup of tea?'

'Yes, please.'

'You're looking a bit brighter this morning. Had a good night?'

She nodded, still wishing to save breath whenever possible.

He poured her a mug of milkless, sugarless tea, her preference, grinned and moved on, saying, 'I'll be back with breakfast in an hour. Keep you busy round here.'

There were sounds, voices, doors opening and shutting. She drank her tea and drowsed.

People gathered in the corridor outside. There was some talk, some clatter of dishes. Max brought in a tray with cereal drowned in milk, a bowl of sugar, a boiled egg and bread and butter.

'Get around that lot. No excuses.'

She got around that lot, slowly, with perseverance. Max returned for the tray and grinned approval. 'That's a good girl. Nice clean plate.'

She found that she did not resent this return to childhood. In her present uneasy situation, any word of approval was welcome.

After breakfast, two young women in white coats and wearing face masks appeared. One was small, exquisitely modelled, with bright blond hair braided around her neat head. Above the mask grey eyes beamed at Isobel.

'I Tamara. She Elaine. We come to make bed. Out, please.'

She fetched Isobel's dressing gown from the chair where she had dropped it. Isobel got up, put it on and sat in the chair as seemed to be required of her.

'We no talk to you. Not allowed. Is too tiring.'

Behind her mask, her taller, less striking companion must be smiling apologetically.

'She means it's too tiring for you, you know. We were told not to ask you questions or get you talking. You can ask us, of course, if you want anything.'

Isobel nodded.

The two women did however talk to each other. 'That very nice fellow you with Saturday. Why no marry, eh?'

'I don't like him in that way.'

Elaine was coy, embarrassed. Her embarrassment did not deter Tamara.

'What way? What you mean. What way you no like?'

Her English was heavily accented, but ready and confident. It seemed that, having adapted the language to her purposes, she meant to give it no further consideration. Elaboration was for others; euphemism had no place.

'Oh, you know. I mean…not to go to bed with.'

'Huh.' Tamara shrugged her shoulders. 'Go to bed!' She tossed a sheet with contemptuous ease. 'Anyone can go to bed. Is easy.'

Elaine giggled shyly.

Isobel pondered the proposition.

Was that true? Funny. She had, she supposed, found it easy enough. That is what most people would say of her. An easy lay. Yet she sympathised with Elaine rather than with Tamara. She had never been an easy lay for anyone she liked. That was unthinkable.

She didn't suppose that Tamara, who even in a face mask was extremely beautiful, would have been an easy lay. Perhaps she thought going to bed was easy because it was to her an aspect of devotion.

Elaine's appearance suggested a rag doll that had been left out in the rain; bright, damp blue eyes below plucked eyebrows and a fuzz of brown curls added to the impression of softness which extended to her figure, slight as it was.

She helped Isobel back into her orderly bed with firm, economical movements at variance with her appearance, and the two departed, leaving her waiting for the next event.

This was the appearance of Diana, pushing a trolley, carrying on its upper tray a basin, a jug and towels, on the lower the hated china shoe.

Isobel eyed it with distaste.

'I went to the bathroom this morning.'

'Well, you shouldn't have. You're on B grade. If you want the pan you ring the bell there.' She reflected. 'Just make sure you don't get caught, that's all.'

Not getting caught proved to be a principal feature of life at Mornington.

Isobel decided to take the risk. She could go back so far to infancy but no further. Being sat on a potty was too much. Diana closed the verandah door and pulled down the window blind.

'Listen, kid. Don't crack hardy. You're here to get better. Okay, a trip to the bathroom, I suppose, but remember, the more you rest, the sooner you get better. Come on. Pyjamas. Down as far as possible, up as far as possible. You can look after "possible" yourself.'

'Well, that's a mercy.'

Isobel rolled over onto the towel Diana had spread on the bed.

What an extraordinary experience it was to be washed by somebody else. The surrender of responsibility was restful, but made one vulnerable. She was thankful for Diana's professional detachment as she soaped, rinsed and dried the body that Isobel had handed over to her care.

'You weren't washed at all yesterday. Don't bother to mention that to Sister Connor.'

Not being caught went both ways, it seemed.

'I wouldn't dream of it.'

'There you are, then. Clean pyjamas. I'll send these to the laundry. Best to wear pants under your pyjamas. It cuts down on the washing. You'll do your own washing on C grade.'

'When will that be?'

'When the gods decide.' She pulled up the blind and opened the door. 'There you are, all ready for Medical. You might as well sit up.'

She fetched Isobel's dressing gown, put it on her and paused over the slippers.

'Do you think they are peculiar?'

'Better than those scuffs, dear. No, really, I think they are cute. And I just love that dragon coat. Where did you get it?'

'It was a present from Hong Kong.'

Truth at one remove.

Ten minutes later, a small, trim woman of straightfor-ward gaze and reassuring aspect came in and introduced herself as Sister Connor.

'I'm sorry I couldn't get to see you yesterday. I had a busy day. How are you feeling? Are you up to going to Medical? The sooner the doctors have the information, the sooner the treatment can start.'

Isobel had been nodding assent.

'Right. Max is outside with the chair. Here she is, Max!'

Isobel took her seat, they took another journey, this time back to the block where she had come in by the front door, into a large laboratory where Doctor Bartholomew was waiting, in company with a burly, dark-haired individual whose face seemed to be set in a permanent sneer.

This was Doctor Hook, Lois's dream lover.

Isobel supposed at first that the sneer was an accident of the flesh, like Eily's boxing past, but she learnt in time that Doctor Hook despised all sufferers from tuberculosis. At worst, they were doing it on purpose; at best, they had only themselves to blame. It seemed that he had chosen to specialise in the illness as an outlet for his inborn misanthropy. His abrupt manners and his brusque commands earned him great respect as a doctor. It was generally agreed that Hook knew what he was doing. Otherwise why would such an unpleasant character ever be given employment?

Lois's choice of Hook as a lover paid tribute to the absurdity of dream as well as to its autonomy. Handsome Stannard wouldn't be a safe subject for dreaming, but it did make it easier to endure Hook's snappish commands to strip to the waist when one thought of him turning his bad temper on an amorous waiter. How frustrating that he would never know of it.

122

She stripped to the waist, had her chest measured, first relaxed and then expanded. The difference was noted by Doctor Hook, while Doctor Bartholomew, who appeared to be in a state of constant apology for his colleague's bad manners, said nervously that her lung expansion was very satisfactory. Isobel reflected that it had often got its owner into trouble.

Then came the X-ray and what she thought of as the new mantra: Strip to the waist, please. Chin, elbows, lean forward, breathe in, hold, breathe away. It did indeed become familiar as a mantra.

In the laboratory she struck trouble. A young man trying to draw blood from her fingertip grew irritable.

'Shake your hand about a bit, will you? This is like trying to get milk from an old dry cow.'

'Sorry!'

She shook and massaged, feeling shame at her incompetence, and at last the young man got his due of blood which he squirted from his hypodermic into a test tube.

'That's it, then. You can go back to the ward.'

Max was waiting outside with the wheelchair. The journey back to the ward was speedy, since it was lunch hour.

There was no special lunch today.

Meatballs and mash.

Food is muscle.

Couldn't have been better put, she thought, and for all her determination could manage only half a meatball. She pushed the plate away and decided to plead fatigue if she was questioned.

In mid afternoon, Sister Connor returned.

'You're to see Doctor Wang. Can you walk it? It's only a few doors along.'

'Sure.'

Sister Connor led her to the end of the corridor, knocked at a door, said, 'Here she is, Doctor,' and departed.

'Will you strip to the waist, please? And lie down on the couch.'

More tapping, listening, prodding and noting.

The young Chinese, who had seemed like a stripling beside Sister Knox, gained in stature as he practised his profession.

How much one learnt from the touch of hands: skill, confidence and a kind of courtesy—like freedom, thought Isobel. You can't define it, but you know when you don't have it. Doctor Wang passed the test of touch.

As she put on her pyjamas, he asked, with some amusement, as if he recognised the question as a password, 'How long have you known?'

'You too?'

'Oh, yes. I am a member of the world's least exclusive club.'

His question, she perceived, had been a kind of intelligence test. She appeared to have been given a pass mark.

'Shall I see you back to your room?'

'Thanks. I can find my way.'

She wondered, as she made her way down the corridor, how many of the staff had tuberculosis and whether there was any way of telling them apart.

Next morning, after Diana's visit, an orderly appeared and left the now recognisable manila envelope at the foot of her bed.

After it came Doctor Stannard, less daunting in a limp and sagging white coat, and with him Doctor Wang and Sister Connor.

'Feeling a bit better?' asked Stannard.

'Yes, thank you.'

'That ambulance trip did her no good, Doctor,' said Sister Connor. 'Sitting up all that way next to an open window. Clare was on Reception. She had it out with the driver but he said he had had no instructions, and the attendant had to travel in the back with the stretcher case. He hadn't been told she was a stretcher case.'

'They were not cooperative,' agreed Doctor Stannard.

Clearly it was us against the world at Mornington.

'Why was she not at North Shore in the first place?' asked Doctor Wang.

Isobel looked warily at Doctor Stannard.

He said vaguely, 'It was an emergency.'

He had taken the two X-rays from the envelope and was studying them.

'I'll have the fever chart, please, Sister.'

He reflected. He named a number of ccs of streptomycin.

The strep didn't take. Pam had been going home not cured because the strep didn't take. But that didn't happen often.

Doctor Stannard said to her, 'Now you're on your way. Starting tomorrow morning.'

125

He handed the fever chart back to Sister Connor, put the X-rays back in their envelope, nodded and departed with Wang.

Sister Connor stayed to say, 'Any questions?'

Isobel shook her head.

'I'll just wait and see.'

Sister Connor departed.

The orderly appeared to take away the X-rays and life resumed its pace.

Streptomycin was administered by injection into the buttock every morning by Sister Connor. Pulling down pyjama pants, even to the discreet distance the injection required, established forever one's social status, which was humble.

The side effects of streptomycin were controlled by a drug which the doctors called PAS and the patients, without affection, called Paz. It too had side effects, such as nausea. This was known to the patients as feeling pazzy. Later in their acquaintance, Doctor Wang made a small grimace and begged Isobel to refer to the drug as PAS. Isobel replied that she had always found it wise in Rome to do as the Romans did. He answered this with the silent laughter which was his usual response to a retort.

PAS presented its own difficulties. It came in enormous tablets with the circumference of a two-shilling piece and as thick as a stack of four of them. Diana, who distributed six tablets to Isobel every morning, instructed her in the technique of swallowing them. One dunked a tablet on a tablespoon into a glass of water, waited for the precise moment when the covering softened to the consistency of an oyster, then tipped it down the throat in one movement. If one delayed too long, the covering dissolved and the life-giving contents fell into the water. One then had to drink the water, a fate to be avoided, or, if one was not under observation, tip it quickly down the sink.

Though the administration of streptomycin was humiliating, its effect was startling. Isobel gained strength every day. She negotiated with Diana, refused the bedpan and asked to be allowed to go to the lavatory. This was condoned, so long as she escaped the attention of the authorities. The authority in this case was Sister Connor, whose movements could be easily monitored.

The bathroom itself was out of bounds, but she took the washcloth from willing Diana and washed herself, feeling catlike but more independent.

Periods of energy grew longer.

She took out her poets and read some familiar pieces, not yet ready to tax her brain with the new.

The doctors visited again and were pleased with her progress.

After ten days, she went back to Medical for an X-ray.

Now there were three in the large envelope which the orderly brought. The third one, it seemed, brought good news.

Doctor Stannard held it to the light, compared it with its predecessors, said, 'This looks to me like a sudden flare-up. No spread. Fundamentally pretty stable.'

He looked at Isobel. 'Too much high living? Too many parties?'

Isobel thought of her cold attic, the newspapers stuffed for extra warmth between the mattress and the sagging iron frame of the narrow bed, the gas ring, the sink, the latrine bucket in the corner.

She said sourly, 'You flatter me.'

Doctor Stannard retreated into abstraction.

'Certainly a very positive reaction,' said Doctor Wang.

'Think she can handle C grade, Sister?'

'I hear that she has promoted herself already,' said Sister Connor.

So she had not been unobserved.

'Right. Give it till the end of the week. She could go into Room 2.'

'What is C grade like?' Isobel asked her informant Diana, when she came to take her afternoon temperature and her pulse and ask whether her bowels were open.

'The same only more so. Have you gone up a grade?'

'Yes. Starting next week. I'm moving to Room 2.'

Something flickered in Diana's face.

'What's wrong?'

'Oh, nothing. Well, you've got nearly a week, so make the most of it.'

III
MORNINGTON C GRADE

Room 2 was, like Room 5, part of C Ward, a row of small rooms, each with two beds, opening to the west on the wide, open verandah, which, with its planking and its waist-high railing, suggested a ship's deck, though it overlooked not sea but an oceanic expanse of mountains. The inner door of the room opened on a corridor which separated it from a corresponding row of bathrooms, lavatories and store rooms.

It linked the administration block (reception, offices, Medical, laboratory, X-ray, upper wards, dining room and parts unknown to patients) with the lower block (surgery, recovery ward, main wards, kitchen and other parts unknown). At each end of the verandah there was a flight of three steps, leading beyond Room 1 to Doctor Wang's office, beyond Room 12 to a small room furnished with a couch, a table and chairs, known as the visitors' waiting room, though no visitor was ever seen to wait there.

Room 5, though situated in C Ward, was not of it. It was kept for emergencies, for patients needing special care. Now Isobel was to become one of the crowd, a genuine member of C Ward.

On Monday morning, Diana came immediately after breakfast with the bath trolley.

'Make the most of it. You'll be head of the bath queue tomorrow. Six o'clock and not a minute later. All baths have to be over by ten o'clock. I hope you don't mind cold baths.'

Isobel, plying her washcloth, took this to be a joke. She discovered next day that it was not.

'The girls will be wanting to strip your bed. As soon as you've finished there, you can start moving your stuff to Room 2. You might as well get into your dressing gown now and I'll take you along to meet Val.'

C grade was certainly a change of pace. Isobel, bathed and towelled, put on pyjamas, dressing gown and slippers, and packed books and toilet gear into her duffle bag with the required speed. Diana cleared the wardrobe and the cabinet of scuffs (which Isobel obligingly hid in the duffle bag), clean pyjamas and dragon coat, which she carried over her arm along the corridor to Room 2, Isobel following, glad of her promotion but apprehensive about the future.

'Well, here we are. Val, this is your new room mate. Her name is Isobel. You can tell her anything she wants to know.'

Diana hung Isobel's clothes in the new wardrobe and departed, saying, 'See you later.'

Val was a woman in the late thirties or early forties, Isobel thought—she was not good at estimating age. Val's red-gold hair was not yet touched with grey. It was drawn back severely from a rounded brow and a handsome face, somewhat marred by the smallness of her green eyes and the near invisibility of her eyebrows.

She greeted Isobel with an eagerness which was disconcertingly like a drowning clutch.

'I hope you speak English.'

'Well, yes. It is my native language.'

'Oh, what a relief! The last one hardly spoke a word of English. I told them I could never put up with such a thing again. "At least," I said, "give me someone who speaks English!"'

She had, it seemed, suffered terribly from the proximity of Olga, a *New Australian* who, besides speaking little English, wore earrings in bed and had visitors who spoke a foreign language without the slightest consideration for Val's feelings. Her resentment of this insult vibrated in her voice.

'Once, she had visitors who stayed for two hours and spoke a foreign language the whole time. At the end of it, I was so exhausted and I had such a terrible pain, here in my spine and in the nape of my neck, that Sister had to call Doctor Wang. He was very nice about it. He gave me a tranquilliser to calm me down and he talked to me about stress and explained why people talk about pains in the neck.'

Isobel, who had been listening to this outburst with dismay, and finding Val's English quite as exhausting as

131

any foreign language, said, 'To Doctor Wang, English is a foreign language.'

Silenced for a moment by astonishment, Val brought the full force of her intellect to bear on this extraordinary statement.

At last she said, slowly and firmly, 'English is not a foreign language.'

Isobel decided not to argue.

'I thought they would move her to another room when they found out how much she was upsetting me, but they didn't. Sister did apologise and said, if I was upset by Olga's visitors, I could go and sit in the visitors' room. Though I don't see why Olga couldn't have gone there instead of me. It didn't happen again, thank goodness.'

'What became of Olga then?'

'Oh, she was always complaining to the doctors about pains here and pains there, and eventually they took her up to X-ray and then they moved her straight away in an ambulance. Found more than they were expecting, apparently.'

Isobel wondered dismally if any of Olga's pains had been in the region of the neck.

Bed making had begun.

A reedy young voice from the next room cried, 'Haven't you got a kiss for me, beautiful? You don't know what you're missing!'

Tamara came in laughing, saying, 'Funny little ting!'

Elaine followed, saying, 'I don't think it's funny at all. At his age. You ought to report him.'

'Is not worth fuss. No harm done. If he lays finger I smack hard, no worries. Hullo, Isobel. You got move, eh?'

132

'Yes, I've made C grade.'

'Good. Out of bed now.'

Isobel wondered what Val thought of Tamara's demonstration of English as a foreign language. Herself, she was delighted to hear it again.

She mustn't take against Val. She mustn't go on first impressions.

It will settle down, we shall co-exist, she thought as she unpacked her duffle bag and thrust her handbag into the pocket between the bed and the wall.

Then she climbed into bed and waited for the next item on the day's programme.

That was the arrival of Sister Connor with the strep injection, and the added embarrassment of the presence of a room mate at this humiliating ceremony.

She averted her eyes from Val's naked posterior and trusted Val to show her the same consideration. One learnt the special courtesy required in institution life.

Morning tea or coffee came next. One was not left long alone at Mornington. Food and drink arrived with frequency: early morning tea, breakfast, morning tea, lunch, afternoon tea and dinner. Lunch was the main meal, dinner rather resembling supper.

After her cup of milky coffee—Isobel was conscientious in the ingestion of milk, and coffee essence was a good way of disguising its taste, which she disliked—the moment she had been looking forward to with eagerness arrived. Free hour.

On C grade, patients were allowed to get up for an hour before lunch. They could drag (but not carry) their cane armchairs to the verandah, they could walk about and visit other rooms, so long as they did not stray beyond C Ward.

As soon as the hooter sounded, Val got up, put on dressing gown and slippers and went out, leaving Isobel to make her own way.

Isobel followed, feeling shy and thinking that Val might well have waited for her and introduced her to other patients.

Fortunately, on the verandah she met Eily, who greeted her as a friend and was truly happy at her promotion.

'How did the bronc go, Eily?'

'Waste of bloody time. They didn't find a thing. Only got to put on a bit of weight and I'll make D grade. According to the old firm of Stannard and Wang, I'll be home in a month.'

'Oh, Eily! That's wonderful.'

'Well, yes and no.'

Eily stared gloomily at the mountains. Home, it seemed, had little to offer.

'Oh, Gawd. Here comes young Romeo.'

The remark was overheard, as no doubt she had intended, by the youth who was approaching. This must be the young sex offender of the morning, who would get hard smack if he laid finger on Tamara. He did not look like a sex offender. He had a keen, clever face in which dark eyes shifted uneasily like small animals seeking escape, and short dark hair on a fine head set on an emaciated body with stooped shoulders pitiably bowed.

'This is Lance, wolf cub from Room 1 and a right little nuisance. Just keep him in his place.'

'Oh, Eily!'

Lance belied the intelligence his face promised by assuming a ludicrous air of melancholy.

'Dying duck in a thunderstorm,' said Eily without sympathy.

'Eily, don't be so cruel. You know that, deep down, you truly love me.'

'Maybe so. I haven't got down as far as that yet. Get on your way, you silly little bugger. And pick up your feet.'

Isobel was to hear this admonition often. The dragging step with which Lance had approached was known as the TB shuffle, and was monitored by any patient who observed it. The cry 'Pick up your feet,' was often heard on the verandah and was obeyed without rancour by the offender.

Lance responded by exaggerating the dragging step as he moved away.

Eily stared after him, saying, 'Poor little bugger,' with an anger which was not directed at the boy.

'You've moved into Room 2, have you, with Val? She's buddies with my room mate Gladys. She'll be down there this minute giving her the news.'

'I hope the report is good.'

'Mmm.'

Eily glanced thoughtfully at Isobel but said nothing.

'It's a pity about Gladys. She was doing fine until she had that last baby. Shouldn't have had it. After all, she had three kids already. Now all the kids are in care and Glad is eating her heart out. Her husband does his best, takes them every weekend. The more she frets the longer it'll be, Sister Connor keeps telling her. Talk's easy. Poor old Glad.'

'Doesn't she ever see them?'

'You can't bring kids in here. Sometimes he brings them up on Sunday and they stand in the garden and wave to her. It's risky talking to Glad those Sunday nights.'

'How's Lois?'

'Huh. Still the same when I left. The others play up to her too much. She'll wake up to herself some day, maybe.'

Isobel had been enchanted by Lois's dream life with the amorous doctors. She was saddened to learn that Lois must pay for it.

'Do you have anything cheerful to tell me?'

'Well, you've done all right. Three weeks ago you were on your last legs.'

'Doctor Stannard says it was a sudden flare up. Accused me of riotous living.'

She was sorry at once that she had offered this opening to the past. She did not intend to arouse any interest that might lead to the discovery of her entry into Saint Ursula's, knickerless and raving.

Eily however showed no inclination to enquire further. This too was part of institution manners. If you wanted to tell your story—she was soon to discover that many people were eager to do so—then you found listeners, but nobody asked you how you came to be there.

This was the Foreign Legion. Your past was your own affair.

The hooter sounded. They nodded goodbye and returned to their beds for the midday meal.

136

Isobel, annoyed by Val's rudeness in leaving her unintroduced, ate her cottage pie in silence.

After lunch, Sister Connor came to see how she was faring.

'I feel a bit tired.'

'First day up. You're bound to feel it a bit. Just shut your eyes and rest up this afternoon.'

'Well, really,' said Val, when she had left, 'she might have asked how I was.'

Exposure to the company of Isobel was apparently an ordeal which might affect the health.

Isobel lay with her eyes closed as recommended by the authorities while Val turned with a flounce towards the window.

Can one flounce in bed? Apparently so.

It can't be as bad as this. She must improve on acquaintance.

The sound of a trolley trundled right to her bedside roused Isobel.

It was, she saw with delight, loaded with books.

'Hullo. So you've made C grade. Congratulations. Would you like something to read? Mystery, romance, travel, adventure, biography?'

The speaker was Mrs Kent, the librarian. Diana had identified her as she passed the window of Room 5: a small, brisk woman of the parrot persuasion, though not excessively so. A blunt, curved nose, high pink complexion and grey hair were enough to sketch in the likeness.

Isobel had forsworn reading for escape on her three-and-a-half flight attempt on Parnassus. She was pleased to think that now she was entitled to indulge herself.

'Mystery, thank you.'

She examined the offerings and chose a mystery by Margery Allingham.

'I know your style, dear. Detective with aristocratic connections, very sensitive, long difficult courtship of intellectual female.'

'I've read Lord Peter Wimsey right out.'

'Well, when you've finished with Allingham, what about Ngaio Marsh? There's a cultivated type for you, Detective Inspector Roderick Alleyn, very high-class background, in love with famous artist, very classy dialogue.'

'Can he detect good?' asked Isobel.

'Oh, quite the best. He'll keep you going.'

'I don't mean to be here so long.'

'Well, that's the spirit. And you've done very well so far. Val, how are you getting on with your library book? Don't you want to change it?'

Val looked startled. She fumbled in the pocket of her saddle bag and brought out a book which she handed to Mrs Kent.

'I'm afraid I haven't had time to open it.'

Mrs Kent bristled.

'Haven't had time! What a thing to say to me. When I do so much. May I ask what you do with your time?'

Val looked blank.

She's in Czechoslovakia with Mr Vorocic, thought Isobel. This was her own habitual refuge in moments of difficulty, and it gave her her first feeling of sympathy for Val.

Having expected no answer, Mrs Kent departed with private thoughts and raised eyebrows.

Isobel opened *Flowers for the Judge* and prepared to enjoy the afternoon.

The hooter sounded its imperative.

Three o'clock. Rest period.

Isobel closed her book.

They lay back, arms extended above their heads, and remained motionless.

At four o'clock the hooter sounded. They came to life and were served afternoon tea.

Isobel opened her book.

Val uttered a whimper of dismay.

'You're not one of those people who read all the time, are you?'

Isobel closed her book with a sigh. It was in any case time for Nurse Morris to appear, to check pulse and temperature and enquire into the state of their bowels.

One was not left long alone at Mornington.

Dinner.

Voices rose. They called from room to room, just out of earshot. Lance's voice took on the rattle of light artillery, though Isobel could not hear what he was saying. He got no response from his room mate and seemed to need none.

Sister Knox could be heard at the door of Room 1, saying, 'Now, you will settle down like a good boy, won't you, Lance?'

This produced silence until she was out of earshot.

139

At the door of Room 2, she said, 'You will be quiet, won't you, darlings? You know, it's little me who gets into trouble when the ward is noisy.'

In what dimension could statuesque Sister Knox count herself as 'little'? Certainly not physically.

She went from room to room, apparently repeating this plea. This was preparation for the doctor's final round.

She returned almost immediately with Doctor Wang, who looked weary but smiled at Isobel and asked how she was liking C grade.

'Very much, thank you.'

There were times when truth must give way to courtesy.

Lights out.

Lance's voice rattled on in the dark.

Shouts rose.

'Lance! Shut up! Shut up and go to sleep!'

Silence at last. The ward slept.

Tuesday began with Diana's familiar cold hand round her warm wrist and a thermometer thrust into her mouth.

'Wakey, wakey!'

Isobel watched as Diana counted seconds on her wrist watch and made a note on the chart, removed the thermometer, read, noted and flicked in the familiar routine.

After that, things were different.

'Bath time. Up you get. When you've had your bath, knock at Room 3 next door and call Pat. She's next. Don't take too long about it.'

Without giving her body time to protest, Isobel tumbled out of bed, put on dressing gown and slippers without waking up entirely, seized towel and toilet bag and crossed the chilly hall into the chillier bathroom.

Diana had not been joking. The water was cold.

It seemed odd that one must suffer from tuberculosis to have the experience of bathing in freezing water on a winter morning in the mountains, but after the first shuddering shock she found the cold water stimulating, though it did not tempt her to linger.

Back in her pyjamas, clean, virtuous and glowing, she knocked on the door of Room 3 to call Pat, a small, gypsy-faced girl who answered with a pardonable growl of discontent but appeared shortly at her door in dressing gown and slippers, saying briefly, 'Thanks for nothing.'

'Don't mention it. The water's fine.'

'I'll bet.'

Pat managed a grin. Common misfortune was a bond.

Isobel got back into her warm bed in a good frame of mind and settled down to sleep again.

Val had not stirred. Isobel drifted into sleep.

'Isobel!'

A voice was calling from the past, breaking into her dream.

'Isobel! Wake up!'

The voice was here, close at hand. Someone nearby was in trouble and calling for help.

She started awake.

'What's the matter? Is there something wrong?'

Val said, 'It's morning. It's time to wake up.'

'Uh.'

Isobel closed her eyes again.

Val persisted.

'You're not going to sleep all day, are you?'

Isobel mumbled, 'Too early to say.'

'Oh, why won't you wake up? You've been up and had your bath and now you want to go to sleep again.'

The distress in her voice was so compelling that Isobel resigned herself to staying awake. She looked at Val in astonishment, wanting an explanation of what she took to be very strange behaviour, and saw terror in her eyes.

I am stuck with another Mr Richard.

She said, 'Did you sleep well?'

'You certainly did,' said Val pettishly.

'Aren't we supposed to?'

Patients did usually sleep well. It was generally supposed that there was *something in the tea*.

'I don't snore, do I?' she asked uneasily, thinking of Mrs Partridge.

No, she had not snored. Her misdemeanour, it seemed, had been to sleep while Val was awake.

It became clear during the day that Val's existence required the active cooperation of another person. To read, write, meditate or even sleep in her presence was an act of cruelty which caused her genuine suffering. Solitude was terrifying to her, and so was silence.

She was therefore a compulsive talker, with the added disadvantage that she found talking a laborious affair, requiring the racking of brains. She talked, thought Isobel, as if she were drowning and only the sound of her own voice kept her head above water. Even when she had subject matter at her disposal, her delivery resembled a slow, laboured swimming stroke. This made it tiring to listen to her, for one had to resist the urge to come to her rescue.

Isobel could soon have told Mrs Kent what Val did with her time. She looked out the window, watched and wondered, giving Isobel what was rather a trudging than a running commentary on the sparse events she observed.

'I wonder what Ron is doing out of the laboratory at this hour.'

'There goes Janet's husband. Poor man. But I wonder why he doesn't cheer up a bit now that Janet and Brett are doing so well. Doctor says the lesions are clearing up wonderfully.'

Janet shared Room 4 with her five-year-old son Brett, both victims of the infection.

'Last week he came in the mornings. Now he's coming in the afternoons again. He came yesterday afternoon and now again today. I wonder...'

'What's his job, then?'

'He's a sales representative. The firm were very good, changing his territory to the mountains so that he could be near his family, but you'd think he'd want to come at the same time every day, so that Janet would know...'

'Perhaps he had to fit in with appointments or something.'

Having done her duty by the conversation, Isobel opened her book, refusing to be deterred by Val's sigh of dismay.

*

143

Wednesday differed from Tuesday only in bringing a visitor for Isobel.

After lunch, a short, broad-shouldered man, clothed and shod, appeared smiling in the doorway.

'Hullo. I am Boris. I am come to ask if you want anything from the store.'

'Oh, please! Do they sell writing paper and envelopes, and stamps?'

'All of that, and they post letters, local but not overseas. If you want to write overseas, Mrs Kent will take your letter and post it for you in the town. And Val, can I get something for you?'

Val shook her head.

'My name is Isobel.'

Isobel wondered if Val had heard of the custom of making introductions.

'Oh, I know that. You have been on B grade and very interesting. Now you are on C grade, not so interesting but I hope healthier.'

Isobel never did discover how information was disseminated at Mornington. It seemed to pervade the atmosphere, omnipresent as dust mites or the Deity. She had misjudged Val. Introductions were obviously unnecessary.

She smiled at his summing up of her situation.

'Much healthier, thank you.'

'I am glad of that. I shall not be long with your shopping.'

Boris's face, broad at the cheekbones, narrowing to a pointed chin and radiating kindness and humour, put her in

144

mind of the Cheshire Cat. His grin seemed to remain upon the air after his departure. She found it cheering.

He arrived shortly with her purchases and her change and settled in the doorway to tell his story. He was a Yugoslav who had been working as a commercial pilot in the Northern Territory until the dreaded dengue fever had struck him down and brought the breakdown with it.

He had migrated to Australia after World War II, in which he had been a fighter pilot, first for Yugoslavia, then for Britain.

'The trip was free, you understand, so I took the longest, and here I am.'

He shrugged, amused at fate. Isobel discovered that this was his usual stance, though sometimes one could detect a tremor in his laughter.

The hooter sounded for rest period and sent Boris away.

One hour, arms over head, lie motionless, *relax*. Just that little thing.

When the hooter sounded again and the ward stirred, the trolley came rolling with afternoon tea. She ate her biscuit, drank her milk coffee, then set about writing to Mrs Delaney.

She had to make it clear that this was an expression of gratitude and also of farewell. Such charity as Mrs Delaney dispensed could not be maintained for long.

That Mrs Delaney saw it as a brief adventure to be undertaken with enjoyment was its most endearing feature.

Isobel reflected and wrote:

145

Dear Mrs Delaney,

I am sorry to have been so long in thanking you for your great kindness to me in a time of need. I have thought of it often with gratitude and should have liked to write to you sooner, but have only this week been promoted to C grade and allowed to indulge in such activities as letter writing.

I have made good progress and the doctors are pleased with me, so the future looks good.

I hope the dead dinosaur is not too much in your way. I shall find a new home for it as soon as possible.

I remember what you said about handing on good deeds and hope that some day I shall be able to follow your example.

Yours most sincerely,
Isobel

She had given considerable thought to that conclusion. Signing had had to mean 'signing off', a clear indication that she expected no answer.

She folded the letter into its envelope, addressed and stamped the envelope, all with a quite extraordinary sense of achievement.

'What does one do with letters?' she asked Val.

Val looked startled.

'I don't really know.'

'But people must write letters. Somebody must take them to the post.'

Since this topic seemed to make Val uncomfortable, Isobel said no more. She would find out tomorrow on the verandah from other letter writers.

Thursday was the big day. Thursday was Rounds. On Thursday one had one's moment of fame as the doctors studied one's latest X-ray, compared it with the earlier ones, checked one's fever chart and answered the question one was bound to ask: 'Any change, doctor?'

Immediately after breakfast, bed making and strep injection, over which Sister Connor was brisker than usual, an orderly brought the great buff envelopes and propped each one at the end of the appropriate bed.

One tidied one's cabinet, was warned not to disarrange the bed, then one waited. One waited. Never was there such silence, such anticipatory tension in C Ward as in the ten minutes which preceded Rounds.

They are coming. The doctors are coming.

There they were in the doorway, Stannard and Wang coming in followed by Sister Connor with the fever charts fastened to a clipboard.

Isobel's moment of fame was brief. Doctor Stannard nodded, said, 'Settling in all right?' glanced at the fever chart and moved to Val's bed. Sister Connor slipped the chart to the back of the pile and followed.

It was then that the ordeal began. The impression Val gave of snatching at words to save herself from drowning was at its strongest when she spoke to the doctors. Her situation was made worse by her conviction that a greater degree of elegance was required when one spoke to a doctor.

The objective case of the personal pronoun she judged to be unfit for a doctor's ears. Her reasoning in this matter was clear. Since to say 'Geoff and I' was refined, while to say 'Geoff and me' was common, the pronoun *I* must always be preferred in refined speech to the pronoun *me*. This led to agonising pauses. 'The doctor said the climate was affecting…was affecting…' before refinement triumphed over usage and she plunged on: 'The climate was affecting I.'

Isobel wondered why she should agonise over Val's difficulties as she did.

Doctor Stannard did not agonise. Isobel watched him in wonder as Val with her mouth open waited for the next word to come down the chute. His gentle and attentive gaze showed not a flicker of any suppressed emotion.

Doctor Wang's inscrutability was of a different nature. Stannard's countenance was open, Wang's was closed. Inscrutability, Isobel decided, was a screen for private feelings. What his private feelings were she did not care to speculate.

At last it was over. Val had communicated the uncomfortable effect of PAS on her system and the interference with her breathing to be noted immediately after lights out.

'We'll have to keep an eye on that, Val,' said Doctor Stannard, moving away, leaving Isobel exhausted and Val dissatisfied.

'I do think he could have taken some action!'

As soon as the doctors were out of earshot three rooms away, Lance came in from next door tense with rage and sat himself on the end of Isobel's bed.

'She told him I'm always out of bed! How can she know that? She isn't always here!'

'Well,' said Isobel, 'where are you now?'

'That's not the point! She isn't here, is she? And what she doesn't see she can't say!'

He had the air of a brilliant barrister addressing a jury as he argued his case.

'She just wants you to stay in bed and get better, you know.'

'She ought to tell the truth, that's all!' He mimicked furiously. '"Doctor, he's always out of bed. I can't do anything with him."'

'What did he say?'

'Oh, he told me that I had to keep the rules if I wanted to get better and it was on my account that Sister was worrying. Like hell it's on my account. Bloody old mischief maker.'

Sister Connor was neither old nor a mischief maker.

'That's true, you know. You're the one she's thinking of. And the weight of probability is all on the side of Sister Connor.'

'Oh, shit. You would be on her side. You're just as bad.'

Though that concluded the argument, Lance did not seem inclined to move.

'What's this?'

He picked up *Flowers for the Judge* from Isobel's cabinet.

'It's a book. You don't read books?'

'Ain't got much time for them, kiddo. Too much like school. Didn't go much on school. Used to cut it a lot.'

149

Perceiving that she was being drawn into an illicit conversation, Isobel said, 'Better get back to bed.'

'Everybody'll be up as soon as rounds are over.'

'Well, that's not now, is it?' said Isobel, feeling sympathy for Sister Connor.

'Once,' said Lance, 'we was down in the park, a couple of fellows and me, and a prefect came down and told us we was caught and we was to come straight back and go to the head and we was going to get death when we got there. Didn't know what to do. One of the fellows said he was going home. His old woman would give him a note to say he was home sick all day.'

This was said with the unemotional rapid-fire delivery she had overheard from the next room the previous evening, but his expression was one of recollected dread.

'No use asking the old man. Well, he might have, but you'd never find him. Don't work regular, see. He's on the pension. Does a good thing of raffling ducks in pubs. Wouldn't have known where to find him, see.'

'What did you do, then?'

'Went back.' His eyes were stilled by remembered horror.

Isobel did not press for details.

'How about getting back to bed now?'

Her tone was softened by a sympathy which she soon found to be a serious error.

He could not be dislodged, but sat silent, hunched and gloomy, like a bedraggled raven, until patients began to appear on the verandah. Then he left without a word and went to join them.

Conversation was particularly brisk on Thursdays. There was news.

Pat was for surgery.

'I asked him, "Any change?" and he grinned at me and said, "The time has come, the walrus said." No laughing matter to me.'

'Well, it had to happen sometime, Pat, and the sooner the better.'

'Yes.' Pat sighed.

The remote future did not compensate for the immediate threat.

'When he smiles at you, watch out!'

Eily was for Medical next morning, as a preliminary to her promotion to D grade.

Others had news for their particular friends.

It was on the verandah that Isobel received her education.

We are wogs. We know that we are wogs. That is what we call ourselves. We speak with envy and anger of famous people who are just as much wogs as we, but have somehow managed to beat the rap. A famous film star, known to be a wog, starred in a film made in the US. How come they let her out? She's just the same as we are, really. Doctor Stannard has done a lot to educate people, to employ wogs, to get over their prejudice against us. He goes to international conferences, raises money for the fight against TB. They reckon they're going to wipe it out. With strep they'll wipe it off the earth. That'll be the day. 'I like Doctor Wang myself, as a doctor, I mean. After all he's one of us. Knows what it's like.'

Once D grade had been allowed to go into town once a week, until a few hoodlums came back drunk and Doctor Hook put a stop to it. Spoilt it for everyone. Of course that's Hook. He's tough. Well, that's his job.

Some of D grade were on their third time round. They would go home, break down, come back. Different now with the operations. People had lobectomies, got better for good. But I wouldn't care for a thoracoplasty. Rather have my bugs, I reckon, take my chance. What's a thoracoplasty? They saw through your ribs, collapse your lung for good. Dorothy had a thora. She says it's like carrying a bundle under your arm all the time. And she's one of the lucky ones. What's the difference then with an AP? Except that you have to go on having it? Give me my old AP. Kept me going this far, hasn't it? What's an AP? They feed air into your lung to collapse it. That's why pregnancy is good for wogs. The pressure compresses the lung...But what you gain in pregnancy you lose having the baby.

Voices are hushed then. Poor Gladys. Poor old Glad. Never should have risked it.

Sunday was the day for general visiting. Relatives and friends arrived from the city. Lunch was early, cleared away by half past twelve, so that the visitors had more time before the hooter went at three o'clock. Isobel thought when she heard that hooter on Sundays that the message was *visitors ashore!*

On that first Sunday she met Val's regular visitors, her husband Geoff and a young woman named Pauline, the daughter of their next-door neighbours. Pauline was a tall young woman of magnificent bearing, sleek, dark brown hair worn short and close to her shapely head and pale skin pitted with acne scars. Geoff was shorter, thickset and somewhat Celtic in appearance, black-haired, blue-eyed and blue chinned. They came with clean washing, bags of fruit, cakes home-made by Pauline's mother, and anxious enquiries about Val's health.

Pauline was also well-mannered. She circumvented Val's reluctance to perform introductions by smiling at Isobel and saying to Val, 'You have a new room mate,' and to Isobel, 'This is Val's husband Geoff and I'm Pauline.'

'Isobel Callaghan.'

Isobel nodded in appreciation of the social effort.

Pauline unloaded and stowed the offerings and asked Isobel's permission to borrow her armchair.

Permission given and an apology offered, Pauline settled with her back to Isobel, who lay admiring the straightness of her spine and the graceful set of her head on her shoulders.

The conversation was about constipation. This was a matter of some importance in a regime which excluded exercises and offered a diet high on milk and low on fruit and salads. A nurse came round in the evening dispensing doses of cascara to defaulters.

Val disapproved of aperients. One became dependent. Isobel had grown accustomed to the daily report on Val's bowel movements: failure, causes of failure, success, cause of success, degree of success, degree of difficulty, time involved, quantity and quality of output. When the last was minimal, Val was faced with a serious intellectual or ethical problem: Could she honestly say that her bowels were open? This problem occupied her, and therefore Isobel, at some length.

Isobel had been tempted to suggest, 'Ajar?' but perceived in time that the suggestion, apart from its unseemly levity, was capable of misinterpretation.

The conversation today was more general. It was not precisely a conversation, since Val talked while the others listened.

Pauline's father had been a martyr to the condition and had cured himself by an effort of will, going every day at exactly the same time and *sitting and sitting*.

'Like me at the typewriter,' thought Isobel, who should not have been listening. And that after sometimes going five days without. The number of days one could safely go without...the folk remedies...Val had heard from someone that an infallible cure was to eat a very ripe banana, very slowly, first thing in the morning.

'Of course your state of mind has a lot to do with it. You have to keep very calm while you eat it.'

Isobel, who had been devising a mantra that would assist the calm ingestion of the curative banana, and had decided on a hushed murmur: *Slither thither*, was overtaken by a mannerless guffaw which she tried to disguise as a racking cough.

The manoeuvre was painful, which served her right, and was not instantly effective, since she saw Pauline's body stiffen and understood that she was not deceived.

Isobel stared at her book and felt her face redden. Pauline's manners were a reproach to her own.

Of all the dirty, mean, commonplace little tricks... none of her business what Val and her visitors talked about, and listening in to conversations while indulging a private snicker was...plain damned vulgar.

Isobel had many sins, now filed firmly away under the heading 'Illness'. This one was new.

I am in danger of going stir-crazy, in a small, mean way. Have to watch it.

She tried to fix her attention on the adventures of Albert Campion, resolved in future to respect the privacy of others. First lesson of life in confined spaces.

On Monday there was a special visit from members of the Red Cross.

The Red Cross supported Mornington. From time to time members of a branch of that association came on an excursion, to see the results of their fund raising, their fetes, their theatre parties and their afternoon teas.

These visits were not welcomed by the patients.

'Not my idea of fun,' said Eily, 'rubbernecking at people in bed. It takes all sorts.' When the special early lunch had been cleared away, Sister Connor came along the ward, looking in each doorway to order away any causes of embarrassment such as panties draped over armchairs, unwashed glasses or any other signs of disorder, and to remind the occupants that these ladies worked very hard in their interest and were entitled to courtesy at the very least.

'We shall be good little orphans,' said Isobel, who was beginning to feel some confidence in Sister Connor.

'Well, yes. I hope so.'

She nodded and went on her way.

The visitors had been entertained in Medical by Doctor Wang. Now they began to drift along the verandah, looking into the rooms with tentative smiles, to which Val responded with much eagerness.

'We weren't exactly asked to wag our tails,' thought Isobel sourly.

However, Val was an excellent buffer, always ready to answer that she was indeed lucky to have such a beautiful view, that the doctors were wonderful, that everyone was very grateful for the wonderful work of the Red Cross. To the credit of the visiting ladies, this last remark usually sent them hurrying on.

One stout lady, encouraged by the friendly reception, paused in the doorway, saying, 'Would it be all right, dear, if I came in and sat down for a bit? So much walking!'

'Oh, do!'

She came in and took the armchair beside Val's bed.

'Lovely to get the weight off your feet and have a bit of a chat. Wonderful work, of course, and so polite, that nice young Chinese doctor showing us the X-ray machines and the laboratory and all. A wonderful place, but I thought I might just miss the grounds and have a rest. Though I shouldn't be saying that to you, should I? Being one of the lucky ones myself. I went to one of those buses they have at the railway stations, you know, with the signs up: BETTER SAFE THAN SORRY and IT COULD BE YOU. Dorothy, my sister-in-law Dorothy, said it was a duty. She is a very serious-minded girl. Oh dear. She won't be too pleased if she notices that I'm missing. I'm hoping she won't notice.' The visitor sighed.

'Well, I went into the bus and had the X-ray and believe me I was relieved. They say the unlikeliest people. Is that how you found out, dear? What a shock it must have been, you poor girl.'

'Everything went black,' said Val. As soon as I saw where the letter was from. Fortunately my next-door neighbour came in. We're very close, she drops in most mornings for a cup of coffee, and she found me, just blacked out. She opened the letter and read it, and she rang my husband up at work. Geoff has been marvellous. Of course it was detected very early, before much harm was done to my lung. That's the point of all these mass X-rays. As Geoff said, better to find out early than late. I was in bed at home for a month, then the doctor thought I would be better off here. And Geoff comes to see me every Sunday. He never fails. Some unfortunate people never have a visitor. You'd think everyone had forgotten them.'

Isobel hoped that this was tactlessness rather than malice, but she felt uneasy.

So did the fat lady.

'It's a long way to come from the city, isn't it?' She looked towards Isobel and added, 'What about you, dear? How did you find out?'

'It just crept up on me.'

Val asked, 'What part of Sydney do you come from?'

They were on their way to discovering common acquaintances when the visitor looked at her watch.

'I'll have to be going. It's your rest period soon, isn't it? During your rest period we have to go and look at Surgery, the operating tables and all, to which I don't look forward.

Only through the glass door, thank goodness, we can't go in. A doctor's going to tell us all about the wonderful operations. I only hope I don't pass out. Well, it's been lovely talking to you. So nice to meet you.'

She got up refreshed, smiled to Isobel, squeezed Val's hand in appreciation and walked out.

In two minutes she was back, looking scared and puzzled.

'I think there's something wrong with the boy next door. The one in the bed by the window.'

Val looked at Isobel, who had somehow assumed responsibility for Lance.

'I'll go and see what he's doing.'

She put on her dressing gown and slippers and went to investigate.

Lance was sitting up in bed looking malevolently cheerful.

'What did you do?'

He responded by raising each fist to scratch an armpit in an ape-like gesture, turning to climb the bars of the bedhead, leaning outwards with one hand to snatch imaginary peanuts. It was a lively performance, but most unlikely to impress Matron.

Isobel giggled.

'Well, you shouldn't have. Now I have to go back and tell the nice lady what a rude little beast you are.'

He scratched at his armpits, snarled and said, 'Suit yourself.'

Isobel returned.

'He was playing at being a monkey in the zoo. Catching peanuts. Sorry,' she said.

The visitor was thoughtful.

'That's just what I said to Dorothy. I said, "I wouldn't thank anyone to come looking at me in bed as if I was an exhibit in a zoo." But Dorothy said we had to support the Society and I supposed she was right. All the kinder of you to make me welcome. The little boy was really very clever. I'm sorry I was too dumb to see the joke.'

'You could have thrown him a peanut,' said Isobel as she climbed back into bed.

The visitor said, uncertainly, 'Would he have liked that?'

'No, but it would have served him right.'

'I think it's wonderful of him to show so much spirit. Well, it was so nice to meet you. I really have to go. I'll just call in on the little boy and tell him I appreciate his humour.'

That'll fix him, thought Isobel with satisfaction and felt positively affectionate towards the visitor.

'That was a very nice woman,' said Val.

'Very nice indeed,' agreed Isobel.

'Dear me. I thought she'd be too normal to suit you.'

The hooter went then to mark the beginning of rest period, which spared Isobel the need to reply.

Janet's husband was observed to have changed the time of his visits to the morning.

'It is very strange,' said Val. 'If he comes tomorrow morning…there has to be a reason.'

159

In the afternoon Miss Landers, who was in charge of occupational therapy, came to visit Isobel. She was also of the bird persuasion, but more ibis than parrot or raven—a long-legged bird, recently startled. Her kind, open countenance went well with her job. She offered Isobel the choice of basketry, soft toys or knitting. Isobel chose knitting. Miss Landers departed and returned with a bundle of heavy, iron grey wool and a carton containing knitting leaflets and needles of various sizes. She looked depressed as she counted out skeins of wool, as if she wished she had better to offer.

Isobel took two leaflets, one with directions for a classic pullover, the other with directions for a blouse knitted with fine wool in a complicated pattern of narrow vertical leaves outlined and veined with lace. She took a pair of No 8 needles for the body of the pullover and finer needles for the basque.

'If you can get somebody on D grade to help with the winding, dear. Don't overdo it.'

Arm movements were still restricted on C grade.

That somebody was already at the door, smiling his Cheshire Cat smile.

'I can do this for you,' said Boris. 'So often I have held the wool for my mother while she rolled the wool into a ball. I know to wind over my fingers in the proper way. You may hold the wool and keep your arms still, while I roll the ball.'

'Yes. That would be the best thing,' said Miss Landers with relief. 'So good of you, Boris.'

She left. Boris took the armchair and separated a skein from the bundle. He looped it over her hands and set to work.

This was restful, for he did not seem inclined to conversation.

Val said, 'I'd like to see the pattern.'

Boris handed over the leaflets and continued to roll the wool.

'What do you want this one for?'

Val held up the leaflet with the directions for the lace pullover.

'I thought I'd like to try the stitch.'

'But it's for 2-ply. You don't have any 2-ply, do you?'

'I'll reduce the number of repeats, that's all.'

'But isn't that wool 8-ply?'

Val pursued the topic with the tenacity she devoted to the observation of the movements of Janet's husband.

'But it will work out all right if I reduce the number of repeats.'

'You don't mean that you're going to knit a lacy pattern in 8-ply. You can't do that!'

'Why not?'

'Well, you can't. Everybody knows you can't. Nobody ever knits lacy patterns in 8-ply.'

'Always a first time.'

Boris finished the ball and went to retrieve the leaflets. Val appeared to be in such distress that she was capable of confiscating the offending pattern. He set them on Isobel's cabinet, gave her a private, sympathetic grin and separated another skein from the bundle on the floor beside him.

Isobel found herself forced to placate Val.

'I'll just try it and if it doesn't work, I'll pull it undone and try something else.'

Talk about measuring out your life with coffee spoons! Salt spoons would be more like it.

'Of course it won't work. I don't know why you waste your time trying it.'

They rolled a second ball.

'Enough for today,' said Boris. 'I shall put your wool in your wardrobe and I shall come back tomorrow morning. Put your arms down and rest now.'

Isobel had no intention of resting. She cast on, counted her stitches and began on the basque, frustrated when the hooter went. The hooter was the law. She put down her knitting without finishing the row and took the rest-period position.

Her mind however was not in the rest-period mode. She was angry.

What the hell does it have to do with her? Bloody odious woman.

Her rage was affecting her breathing. That wouldn't do. She controlled the breathing and with it her rage.

Keep calm. Keep calm. Don't let her get to you. I'm going to do it my way, I'll finish it my way even if it's a disaster. But that's letting her get to me, too.

Breath control again.

I'm not here. I'm in Czechoslovakia with Mr Vorocic.

If that didn't work, she would proceed to the next resource, silently reciting a favourite poem.

Oh, do not die, for I shall hate
All women so, when thou art gone...

The metre was soothing. She finished the hour in the proper state of remedial torpor.

With thick wool and coarse needles, and Isobel's pleasure in the movement of her liberated fingers, the work went quickly.

Next day, she was ready to start on the disputed pattern.

'You're not really going to knit that ridiculous stitch, are you?'

Isobel nodded, reading aloud from the leaflet, 'Purl 2, wool round needle, knit 3, wool forward, slip 1, knit 2 together, pass slip stitch over, wool forward, knit 3.'

Against this argument, Val had no defence. She sighed in exasperation and was silent.

Lance wandered in.

'Wotcher doing, Izzy?'

'Knitting. And go back to bed.'

He settled instead on the end of her bed preparing to watch her at work.

To continue to knit would be to condone his presence—his too frequent presence. She put down her knitting, repeating, 'Go back to bed, Lance.'

How many times already had she said those words?

'Yeah, in a minute.'

'Lance, don't you have anything to do? Don't you have correspondence lessons or something?'

163

'Finished with all that stuff, kiddo. Turned sixteen. Never made much of school. Knocked a bit of fun out of it sometimes, me and Buzz and Trigger. Buzz used to get some great stuff from the joke shop. Got a smoke bomb once, set it off in the science lab and got the school cleared out for the whole afternoon. That was great. Lucky for Buzz they never found out who planted it.'

His face expressed no pleasure in the memory. It retained its air of absent-minded melancholy.

'And once he got a farting cushion and put it on old Mary Lawson's chair. That wasn't too bad. Gave us a real buzz when she plumped down on it and oh! Boy! The class hit the roof.'

'Charming. What did she do?'

Lance showed genuine emotion.

'Oh, that bitch! You could never reach her whatever you did. Always chasing you for homework and keeping you in…She picked up the cushion and put it on the desk and gave it a great bang like you could hear the fart next door. "And that expresses my opinion of the perpetrator of this vulgar trick." And then she did it again. You'd have thought she was enjoying it. Pretty crude, for a teacher.

'The boys thought they'd got to her at Christmas. Trigger found an old kettle on a dump, and they put it in a box and wrapped it up in fancy paper, like a real Christmas present, ribbon and all. We was all waiting to see her open it. Bitch! She never blinked, just took it out and held it up and said it was lovely of us to give her something that would always remind her of us. A dirty old kettle. And then she turned it up, it had a rusty bottom with three holes in it,

164

and she put on a goofy look and said, "Whenever I look at it, I shall see your dear faces." She should talk about faces, the old bag. She'd never see thirty again, I bet.'

Who was it said that teaching was a contest with Marquis of Queensberry rules on one side and all-in wrestling on the other?

'Did you think she was going to love you for it?'

'That's not the point. She's a teacher, isn't she? Teachers aren't supposed to get personal. They ought to know better than talk about people's looks.'

'I don't believe she was thinking about your looks. She might have been looking into your nasty little minds.'

Perhaps she had not been so badly off after all, with Mr Richard as her only burden.

'You're just as bad. Should have been one yourself.'

'Well, you don't have to put up with me. *Go back to bed*.'

'Tea'll be along in a minute. I'll go back then.'

'And stay there.'

Lance assumed his dying duck expression.

'Don't you love me, Izzy? Sending me away, it isn't nice.'

'I love you enough to want you to get better. Now be off.'

He sighed, shrugged and shuffled away, leaving Isobel to reflect that he had shown one genuine emotion, hurt over the teacher's sarcasm. The antics with the wares from the joke shop had seemed to be a wretched substitute for anything called fun. His juvenile attempts at sexual insolence were just as much a wretched substitute for love.

'You play up to him,' said Val.

'I don't want to. I try not to get drawn in. I really want him to stay in bed. How about telling him yourself? He might listen to you.'

'Why should I? It's none of my business. He doesn't come to talk to me.'

Isobel might have known that flattery would get her nowhere.

She mastered Embossed Leaf Stitch in spite of interruptions and managed to complete two repeats. She liked the effect of heavy iron grey lace. It put her in mind of balconies in Paddington.

'You're wasting your time, you know. You're going to have to pull it out in the long run.'

'Well, I think it's all right, myself.'

'It is simply ridiculous.'

Being involved in the tricky business of knitting two together through the back of the loop, Isobel let the comment pass.

On Thursday morning, Doctor Stannard paused and frowned over Isobel's fever chart.

'Time that fever settled down.'

If you had to spend your time keeping Val's head above water and keeping Lance in bed, she thought, you might have a fever too.

The news on the balcony was that Eily had failed D grade.

'Have to put on more weight. He said to give it another couple of weeks. But I never do put on weight. It isn't my nature. I'll be here for ever if that's what they want.'

'Try drinking water, Eily. Fill yourself up before you go up there. That'll do it.'

'I'm near enough to wetting myself when I'm up there anyhow. Wouldn't want to risk it.'

Pat was to move down to surgery next Monday.

Gladys was called to witness that Isobel's knitting was ridiculous.

Cautiously, she agreed that maybe it looked a bit funny.

'Who's going to wear it?' asked Eily, with meaning.

'Isobel, I suppose,' said Val. 'I can't imagine that anyone else would.'

'May I have it back, please? Or would you like to put it back where you found it?'

This missed its mark entirely, since Val could see no wrong in taking Isobel's knitting from her cabinet and putting it on display without her permission.

On Friday, Val watched Janet's husband walk along the verandah.

She said, 'I have a terrible thought about this. I think Janet's husband is having an affair with Nurse Baker.'

Isobel was startled.

'What makes you think that?'

'I think that is why he changes the time of his visits. He comes when she is on duty.'

'But they never have a word to say to each other.'

'And that's another thing. It's not natural. It's not just that they don't speak. They pretend not to see each other. I saw them pass each other on the verandah yesterday and they didn't exchange a look. That isn't how people behave, unless they have a reason. What other reason could there be? And they both look so wretched. He ought to be happier now that Janet and Brett are doing so well, but he's looking more and more worried. And she was looking wretched too when she walked past him.'

'Well, I hope you are wrong.'

She hoped also that, if Val were right, Janet's husband would have the sense to vary the time of his visits. Hadn't the unfortunate lovers heard of the telephone?

On Sunday Geoff and Pauline came to visit Val. Isobel, remembering her breach of manners the week before, opened her book and tried to withdraw from the scene. She was distracted from Ngaio Marsh by the mention of her own name.

Val said, shrill with exasperation, 'I cannot get Isobel to wake up in the morning. I have to keep at her and keep at her!'

Since Geoff and Pauline in response stared at her in shame and consternation, she said, 'She would lie there all day if I didn't wake her.'

Isobel said dryly, 'I don't have a train to catch.'

She regretted her sarcasm at once, for it increased the embarrassment of the visitors.

How odd this human connection was. Isobel felt for Pauline, who felt for Geoff, who must feel for, or at least because of, Val, who felt for no-one.

How odd, too, that Val, who could hunt down unhappy lovers with whom she had no connection, did not seem to notice the harmony of feeling which prevailed between Geoff and Pauline.

Perhaps they were not guilty lovers, but most observers would see them as lovers. Sex was not the whole of it, after all.

'Look at it this way,' said Isobel to herself. She was lying motionless, arms above her head in the prescribed position, while she surveyed her situation. That was probably against the rules, but fortunately undetectable. 'You are a public patient. You are getting every morning a life-saving shot of streptomycin with six large dollops of paz, free for nothing. The state is even going to keep you.' This thought brought a quite perceptible wince, which was certainly against the rules. She had, under the eye of Mrs Blair the almoner, filled in an application for the invalid pension. No help for it. As she had written her name in the space allotted to the signature of the applicant, she had promised herself that one day she would write that name in a more honourable place, but the vow had brought little comfort. 'So, in these circumstances, enjoyment is not to be looked for. Tough it out. Survival techniques are required.' But what techniques? Retiring to Czechoslovakia with Mr Vorocic was for the moment only. Besides, it was not practical here, where she was, face it, trapped and exposed. Her usual invocation of Saint Thomas More: 'Both must ye die, both be ye in the cart carrying forward', would not do here. One did not invoke the rumble of the cart when the cart was standing at the gate. 'My problem is that people are making claims I resent. Well, sort it out. There are false claims and true claims. Val wakes me up in the mornings because she's afraid to be alone. That's a true claim. I can just about carry on a conversation with her without actually waking up. That's the best I can do. But I don't have to squirm when she makes a fool of herself on rounds. She's not asking me for anything. I must detach. That's not true pity that makes me squirm, it's some sort of false vanity, identifying. She's doing it. I'm not. Detach. This is like family life—enforced intimacy. But this doesn't last so long.

'Lance, now. That's different. All his claims are true, poor little devil, but somehow they aren't direct. Well, no-one can really meet them. Make me well, make me happy, give me love. And all the time, making himself the most unlovable little bastard out. Well, that figures. I'll just have to do my best from minute to minute with that one.

'I wish I could set Val and Lance on to each other. No such luck. Val has a son, nineteen years old. Why doesn't she ever ask about him? Why doesn't Geoff ever mention him? Not my business. Survival is my problem.'

Mental discipline was required. 'I shall learn a poem by heart, every day.' That had worked before, a survival technique she had forgotten till now. 'I shall start with Hopkins, because he is the toughest. And maybe the most supportive. I can sneak a line or two at odd moments, something to hold on to.'

Pat went to surgery and was replaced by Donna, who took Isobel's place at the head of the bath queue.

She came as instructed to call Isobel for her bath—a plump, pink and gold young woman who said in a tone plaintive and puzzled, 'The water's cold.'

'That's right. The heating starts at half past six, but the baths have to begin at six, because they have to be finished by ten. That's when the bathroom is cleaned, you see, and we can't use it after that. You get used to it.'

One more move and Isobel would be in hot bath territory. She thought it would be heartless to gloat over the prospect.

'Well, it seems odd to me.'

Isobel discovered later on the verandah that many things seemed odd to Donna and were met with the same plaintive bewilderment. Her children, like Gladys's children, were in care for the time being.

'They haven't written to me once since they were at the home. Not once. I wrote and asked the Matron why I wasn't getting letters from the children and she just wrote back and said that the children hadn't heard from me.'

She looked at Isobel as if she were waiting for an explanation of this extraordinary attitude.

Isobel could only shake her head in sympathy.

I have desired to go
    Where springs not fail,
To fields where flies no sharp and...

Hopkins was proving to be a support.

After lunch Miss Landers paid a visit.

Val told her to look at Isobel's ridiculous knitting. 'She's just wasting time. It'll have to be pulled out.' Miss

171

Landers came and looked and was dubious about the grey lace.

'But if Isobel likes it...You knit beautifully, Isobel. I wouldn't have expected that, somehow.'

'Life is full of surprises,' said Isobel, smiling at Miss Landers, who was receiving little encouragement in her progress along the rooms.

Garry would have no part of occupational therapy. He met Miss Landers's timid suggestions with a look of sullen contempt which made persuasion futile. Lance had added half an inch to the basket he was weaving. Eily had not begun to put together the pieces of white lambswool she had been given to make a toy koala for Gladys's baby.

'I did spread it all out and looked at it, Miss Landers. Then all at once I thought, "Bugger it!" and put it away again.'

This Miss Landers had met with a nervous laugh.

Gladys was using the same grey wool to make a cable sweater for her elder son. This was an added reproach to Isobel.

'I thought knitting was supposed to keep you warm,' said Val. 'It won't be much use with those great holes in it.'

'You're wrong there, Val,' said Miss Landers. 'Weight for weight, lace fabric is warmer than solid. It does seem strange but it's true. It traps air pockets, I think. That's why cellular underwear is so warm.'

Val met this with silent disbelief.

Miss Landers braced herself.

'How are you getting on with your own cardigan, Val?'

Reluctantly, Val rummaged in her saddle bag pocket and brought out a sleeve in progress.

'Dear me. Isn't that the same sleeve you were doing last week?'

Her small store of courage being now exhausted, she did not demand an answer.

Isobel continued to knit.

When Miss Landers had left, she said, 'Val, why do you care so much about it?'

'But it's wrong and you won't be told.'

'Right and wrong don't apply to knitting patterns. You drop stitches or you don't, that's all.'

To fields where flies no sharp and sided hail
        And a few lilies blow.

At evening rounds, Doctor Wang came across to pick up the book of poems from Isobel's cabinet.

'I can't read this Hopkins,' he said. 'I find him too difficult. Such odd word order and strange words. It all seems to me unnecessarily complicated.'

'Not unnecessarily,' said Isobel. 'I know he's difficult, but that's part of his...what he calls his inscape. The struggle for expression is part of his subject matter, always.'

'Well, it seems to me uncivil for a poet to betray his difficulties to his reader. Shouldn't he conceal them?'

'It's a very individual style, more like forging poems out of metal than simply writing them.'

'You like poetry, then?'

'Very much indeed.'

173

'Do you know of our great poets Li Po and Tu Fu?'

'I've heard of Li Po. Didn't he fall out of a boat and drown while saluting the moon?'

'It's a sad thing that our great poet should be known only for the folly of his death.'

'Well, it's nothing against his poetry, I suppose.'

'Would you care to read some? I can bring you some of his work in translation.'

'Yes, please.'

'And you may help me to understand Hopkins. I should like to know more about English poetry. My education is lacking in the subject.'

The conversation had demanded too much of Sister Knox's loving-kindness. She began to move restlessly from foot to foot. The hint was not to be ignored. Doctor Wang nodded and moved on.

On Thursday Sister Connor followed Doctor Stannard into Room 2, still protesting at Lance's misconduct.

'He's oftener in this room than he is in his own bed.'

'Well, it isn't my fault,' said Isobel. 'I keep telling him to go back to bed and he takes no notice. The only way I could keep him in bed is to move in with him and that is just too much to ask.'

'Oh, quite beyond the call of duty,' Doctor Stannard agreed, retreating into vagueness and picking up Isobel's chart, over which he looked thoughtful. He put it back without speaking and went to ask about the wheeze in Val's chest.

The caravan moved on.

Val said, 'You shouldn't speak to Doctor like that. You could see that Sister was annoyed with you.'

'She was annoyed with me because I let Doctor Stannard off the hook. He doesn't want to think about Lance. The boys are a problem he can't solve and he doesn't want to be reminded. I gave him the chance to get off the subject, that's all.'

She was sorry she had spoken: she was forming the opinion that Mornington functioned on the brilliance and the charm of Doctor Stannard and hard work and worry from others, such as Sister Connor.

Val, who read people as others read books, had to agree with this.

'You shouldn't have been so free with him, just the same.'

'Next time I'll remember to tug my forelock.'

'What nonsense you do talk.'

After lunch Doctor Wang arrived with the promised book.

'These are not the best translations. The best are made by Ezra Pound. His translation of "The River Merchant's Wife" is very true, very good indeed. I must find it for you. The notes in this book are good. They will help you to understand the text. Much in the poems is traditional. And now,' he said, taking the armchair, 'would you read me a poem of Hopkins?'

She had been in line for a stroke of luck and here it came. She turned to 'Spring and Fall' and began to read aloud, with annotations.

He asked, she explained. They talked.

They struck out like swimmers who had been trapped in the wading pool, energetic and joyful.

Doctor Wang was very young, it seemed, not long exiled from the Quadrangle, the Buttery, the café, the noisy river of talk which one took for granted until fate silenced it. He was as lost among the medical staff of the hospital as Isobel was lost among the patients.

'I have kept you talking too long,' he said. 'I shall come back and find out what you think of Li Po. And I want to know more of Hopkins. Perhaps tomorrow.'

'Great,' said Isobel.

'You mean he came right in and sat down and talked to Isobel?'

Val said, thinly, 'He didn't get much chance to talk to me.'

He didn't want to talk to you.

'We were talking about poetry. That's all.'

Fortunately there was another subject for conversation. Nurse Baker had left, without notice and without explanation.

'They said in Room 10 she just walked in and said she was leaving. She was in a fury but she wouldn't say why.'

'Didn't Diana say anything?'

'According to Diana, Matron sent for Baker yesterday morning and she came away looking like a ghost. White as a sheet and shaking. Diana had to do the afternoon round by herself.'

'I thought she looked a bit off when she was taking our temperatures.'

'And Sister Knox wasn't herself when she did evening rounds with Wang. And come to think of it, Wang was pretty quiet, too. He usually has a nice word for everyone.'

'Something must be up.'

'Well, she's gone.'

'Not much loss, I reckon. I always thought she was standoffish, myself.'

'Funny, just the same.'

Val said nothing. She must have been right in her suspicions of Nurse Baker, but she did not even look as if she could have spoken to the point if she had cared to.

This was much to her credit. It was the first time Isobel could record anything to Val's credit but it was, considering her eagerness for notice, a very good mark indeed.

Reading was now an activity sanctioned and even encouraged by a doctor.

Isobel began to study the poems of Li Po and read Hopkins, looking for the next offering.

She tried to ignore Val's distress. She had once been on the point of asking, 'Why don't you try it yourself, Val?' but she was checked by the growing suspicion that Val was illiterate.

Was this possible? Could it be that a woman who, if not quite of the bourgeoisie, was far above the submerged masses, could not read nor write? There was that very odd answer she had given to Mrs Kent about the library book. And she had not in all this time read anything, not even a caption under a photograph in the *Women's Weekly* which was passed every week from room to room. Illiteracy showed up in odd places. They had discovered during the war that very many recruits were illiterate. Perhaps she could manage a word at a time, with visible effort, sounding out, moving her lips...if this was so, being thrust by misfortune into a literate world, burdened with a companion who read books, talked about books and, finally, diverted doctors from their proper duties in order to talk about books, would explain her constant terror and her need to dominate, even in the matter of knitting patterns. She must be compensating for that hidden helplessness and suffering the fear of exposure as well.

See her as a frail, domestic shrub uprooted by a storm and drifting in a flood where she was exposed to monsters, foreign languages, books, strange talk...

Isobel was feeling much kindlier towards her because of her silence in the matter of Nurse Baker and Janet's husband. What could she do to show goodwill?

She didn't intend to give up reading. She could not sacrifice conversation with Doctor Wang. She did not even intend to unpull her knitting, which had progressed so well that she was about to shape the shoulders and cast off the back section.

The most I can do, thought Isobel, is protect her from discovery. She won't know about it, but it will make me feel better.

She went back to her book and looked for a poem which would help Doctor Wang to the insight he looked for into the Western mind.

*

The trouble with reading, memorising and discussing poetry was that it prompted the urge to write, which would certainly have to be suppressed.

Reflecting that Hopkins seemed much more difficult when one planned to explain his poems to somebody else, she settled on 'Pied Beauty' and began to read it with care.

Val stared through her window at emptiness.

The hooter sounded. They reclined, hands above head, eyes closed, breathing quiet and regular.

At four o'clock the hooter released them. Isobel sat up and opened her book. Val sat up, sighed and stared through the window.

At evening rounds, Sister Knox said, 'Isobel. About your admission form...'

'Yes.'

'What is your religion, dear?'

Isobel temporised.

'Isn't it on the form?'

'OD. That isn't a religion, is it? Now, dear, what does OD stand for?'

Might as well be hung for a sheep as a lamb.

'Orthodox Devil-worship.'

Sister Knox met this with a brief angry titter. Beside her, Doctor Wang glimmered quietly.

'Now you mustn't be silly, you know. There isn't any such religion.'

'But indeed there is, Sister. And with some very interesting ceremonies. Isobel must tell us more about them,' said Doctor Wang.

179

I'll murder you, you smooth bastard, thought Isobel, eyeing him with meaning and feeling suddenly cheerful.

'It means Other Denominations, that's all.'

Sister Knox was gently reproving.

'I don't really think that it's a thing to joke about.' Doctor Wang must be experiencing a rush of blood to the head.

'It's a paradox, Sister. The people who make jokes about religion are often the ones who take it seriously,' he said.

Sensing communication from which she was excluded, Sister Knox responded with a prim little smile of annoyance and said no more.

Later, in the dark, Isobel asked herself why it was impossible for her to make a false statement on the subject of religion. She had not intended any sort of heroic stand. Given that one must not leave a vacant space on an official form, she had supposed that OD would be an adequate offering. She could not offer more.

Why not? It's no use pretending that you never tell a lie. You tell plenty when it suits you. Then why not say she was Church of England? Why not that particular lie? She could find no explanation for this obstinacy, yet she knew she could not escape it.

But then, why did they care so much? She hadn't noticed anyone praying. Maybe people did, of course. Maybe there were silent prayers rising in the night, but those prayers wouldn't be coming from conformists, she was sure of that. They want too much. Whoever they were. Placating these

180

unknowable authorities seemed to require eternal vigilance, like liberty.

All too difficult. She closed her eyes and slept.

Next day Doctor Wang arrived after lunch. She read 'Pied Beauty' aloud, first with annotations, then without.

'To Hopkins, then, the beauty of the world is an affirmation of God's existence?'

On the edge of Isobel's field of vision, Val sat upright in her bed, mouth open, gasping for speech, body straining, quivering like a puppy waiting to be taken for a walk.

Isobel narrowed her field of vision and spoke with haste.

'Yes. It's an intensely religious poem, that's true.'

'Are you a believer, then?'

'Um.' Isobel reflected. 'You know that Voltaire said, if God had not existed, it would have been necessary to invent him. Well, He doesn't exist, and we do invent Him. Sometimes for good and sometimes for evil. With Hopkins, it's for good, that's all.'

Wang nodded.

'And sometimes very much for evil. That's an interesting thought. Is it man's responsibility to invent the true God?'

'We haven't made much of a job of it yet.'

Wang grinned at her.

'About that OD?'

'Oh, dear. At the other hospital they said I had to have a religion, so I thought I'd be a Buddhist. I've always liked the idea of it. Oh, am I being offensive? Are you a Buddhist?'

181

'Of all religions, it is the one I respect most. But I agree with you, I think. There is no religion men will not use as a source of power and an excuse for doing evil. Buddhism is as vulnerable as any other faith.'

'We should read "God's Grandeur". I'm not sure how well I can manage it, but I'll try.'

Wang stood up.

'We shall travel hopefully.'

He nodded cheerfully to Val as he departed.

'It would be very nice,' said Val in fury, 'if I could be allowed to get a word in.'

Deliberately obtuse, Isobel answered, 'I didn't know you were interested in poetry, Val.'

Val did not answer. In silence, she breathed banked-down fire.

Doctor Wang continued his visits. They moved from Hopkins to Auden. He read Li Po and Tu Fu aloud, and even, at Isobel's request, in Mandarin.

This provocation was not deliberate. She had forgotten Val's sensitivity to foreign languages. It could only make the situation worse for Val, who was suffering the torments of Tantalus. To be in the glamorous, life-enhancing company of a doctor while being denied his attention brought her to the limit of her endurance.

'Am I ever going to be allowed to talk to Doctor Wang?'

'Of course you can talk to him, Val. But not about your symptoms.'

'He's a doctor, I suppose.'

182

'Well, yes, but he's off duty. He can take half an hour off, can't he?'

'If he can listen to the rubbish you talk, he can listen to me.'

'If there's something worrying you, you can keep it till evening rounds. That isn't very long to wait.'

'It's not the same. It's not like having a doctor sit with you and listen. There are a lot of little things I could ask him about, if you didn't talk all the time.'

Val had as much chance of joining their conversation as an obese cripple of jumping on a moving bus. The bus must stop, wait, she must be helped aboard. This did not occur.

Doctor Wang's unorthodox visits also kept Lance most unwillingly in bed.

'Shouldn't be hanging about patients' rooms,' he grumbled, as he came shuffling in a minute or two after the doctor's departure.

'Better tell him so yourself,' said Isobel, who maintained obstinate calm in the face of all attacks.

I'm having this. You won't take this from me.

Doctor Wang remained unaware of the disturbance he was creating in the lives of the patients, and of the bitter glances that were directed towards Isobel.

Isobel had reached the armholes of the front section of the disputed grey sweater. She was measuring the one against the other when Mrs Kent arrived with her trolley.

Mrs Kent took the completed section and held it up for display.

'What a clever little puss you are, Isobel. I didn't think anything could be done with that awful grey wool and look

183

at it! It's absolutely charming. For all the world like cast iron lace. Don't you think so, Val?'

Val answered with a deep sob and a spurt of angry tears.

Mrs Kent, with raised eyes, sought reaction from Heaven, then stared at Isobel.

'Val doesn't think the pattern was right for the wool.'

'But...'

Mrs Kent despaired, shrugged and pushed her trolley away, shaking her head as she went.

Isobel put her knitting aside, but only to look into the new library book.

Is it possible to cause so much misery to another human being, simply by being oneself? she wondered, feeling a reflection of that misery. No help for it; she must continue to be herself.

Isobel had an unexpected visitor.

When she saw the tall figure in the doorway, she held out both hands, crying out in amazement, 'Olive!'

Olive came across the room to her bed, kissed her on the cheek, set down a paper carrier bag and her handbag on the floor and took the armchair beside Isobel's bed.

'How did you get here? How did you find out where I was?'

'You took some finding,' said Olive with a severe note in her voice. 'But Frank refused to give up. I don't think he has thought about anything else for months. First of all, we thought you were coming back. We all thought you'd turn up on pay day. After all, they owed you three days' pay. Why should you let them get away with that?' She shook her head in disapproval. 'But the week passed, and then the fortnight, and there wasn't a sign of you, so we got really worried. Frank went right into Mr Walter's office... I've never seen Frank so angry. He really shook him up. He told him that if he couldn't find anything better for his boob of a brother to do than torment decent hardworking members of staff, he'd better keep him out of the office. You know that's the first time anyone ever said right out that Mr Richard wasn't...'

'Not the full quid?'

'Frank's very words. Not to Mr Walter, of course.' Olive relaxed into an unladylike giggle. 'I think he was frightened that Frank would leave. They could never do without Frank. Anyhow, Frank got the full fortnight's pay for you. He said you'd been driven beyond endurance and it was constructive dismissal and you should have pay in lieu of notice. Then he went after holiday pay and got an extra week. He said, while he had them running, he was going to do his best for you. I've got the money here. And how could you, walk out and let them get away with it?'

'I was too embarrassed.'

'You didn't have to be nice to them, did you? You only had to turn up and collect what they owed you. Well, we saw that you had cleared out your desk and we realised that you weren't coming back, so Frank went to your room to give you the money. That's when we got really worried. They said you'd left and hadn't left a forwarding address.'

'I didn't think of it. I wasn't expecting any mail.'

'So we didn't know what to do. We didn't know any of your friends and we knew you had no family. Then Sandra remembered that you had a story in a magazine called *Seminal*. She went out at lunch time and found a copy in a bookshop. We thought they might know your address. Frank got me to write to the editor and ask him if he knew where you were living. He wrote back to say he couldn't give out addresses but he could send on a letter. So I wrote again to tell you we were worried and wanted to hear from you, and then we waited. Weeks. At last Frank took the morning off and went to the office of the magazine and saw the editor. A very nice man.' Olive made no attempt to disguise the length and the severity of this odyssey. 'He said he was worried too, because he'd written to you and had expected an answer, so he gave Frank the address.' Olive paused in remembered horror. 'Isobel! *That place!*'

Isobel whispered, 'The rent was cheap. I kept myself to myself.'

'I should hope so. But if you had seen Frank's face when he came back from there. Didn't you ever think?'

'No, she does not,' cried Val, who had been listening with avid interest to Olive's story. 'That's what I keep telling her. She's just too self-centred.'

Olive turned in astonishment and said gently, 'I thought you would understand that this is a private conversation.'

After one gasp of outrage, Val slid down under the covers, turned and presented her back to the undeserving world.

A brief silent dialogue of raised eyebrows and shrugged shoulders—Olive could not know that telling Val to

186

mind her own business was like telling a carnivore not to eat meat.

'Well, you'd gone from there, too. My letter was there in the rack, and the letter from the editor. I have them here. Mine doesn't matter. The other one...'

She fetched from the carrier bag a bulky envelope addressed to Isobel herself in her own handwriting.

A returned manuscript. Isobel accepted it and put it aside, deferring dismay and disappointment.

'I did miss you all,' said Isobel, who had been listening with increasing pain and mortification. 'I was just too embarrassed. After what I had said to Mr Richard.'

'It was a little strong. But Frank always said you bottled up too much and one day you'd boil over.'

'I boiled over all right.'

'You weren't yourself. We all thought you were ill, you know. You never seemed to shake off that cold... you should have had more time off. That's another thing Frank threw at him, that he was too lousy to give you a bit of sick leave...oh, words flew, I can tell you. But you were always sucking cough drops, and you were so quiet. We all missed your funny little sayings. It was building up.'

'But you found me.'

'Frank got another idea. He wanted to know if you'd cleaned out that room yourself. He had it fixed in his mind that you were sick. If you'd cleaned it out yourself, then he'd know at least you were on your feet.' At Isobel's whimper of shame, she said without mercy, 'I hope you do feel badly. So you should. Well, he went back to that place and asked the woman in the office—not a very nice woman, she couldn't

187

have cared less—but she did admit that somebody else had come to pack up for you and she had kept the letter in case of trouble. I think that's the only reason that woman would ever do anything. And there was a note from you, folded up in the back of the rent book, and it had the address of a hospital. Well, at least we knew.' Olive sighed.

'Not very cheery, of course. But at least we knew a bit more. So Frank was off again this time to that hospital. They weren't very helpful either. At first they didn't want to know.'

'It was a classy private hospital. They didn't like having me there.'

'How did you get there?'

'It's a long story. Go on.'

'There wasn't any date on the letter and they weren't going through the Admissions Register unless he could give them a date. He waved your letter at them and asked to see this Mrs Delaney who had packed your things. Then they got moving. They got her on the phone and she talked to Frank. She said she had your things at her house and was minding them for you, and told him that she'd had a letter from you. Which,' said Olive with emphasis, 'is a lot more than we had had. But she said you were making good progress.'

'I only wrote once, to thank her. She was so good to me.'

'Yes. Well. It was a bit of daylight, for poor Frank. The first bit of good news he had had. By that time…well, I was about to go on leave, so we decided to wait until I could come up myself, and here I am.'

'I'm sorry I gave you so much trouble.'

That was an understatement. She was conscious that she had done a grievous wrong. Committed a grievous sin, though she could not name it. Examination of conscience must wait. 'Tell Frank...tell him I miss him. Who's checking his invoices for him now?'

She was wistful. Checking the invoices for Frank had been her favourite task. She saw Frank lifting a monstrosity out of its packing while she translated from the abbreviated German: 'Bowl, footed, green, frosted, fluted, gold rim.'

'And a very nice present for your favourite ma-in-law.'

She, considering the object, amending, 'Wedding present for the bride who's marrying the man you love.'

They had laughed together over the worst excesses of Lingard glassware. She had not imagined that this shared laughter was creating a durable bond.

'Oh, that's young Jenny. She took your place. She can't handle German, of course. She just checks the numbers.'

'Who does handle the German?'

'Oh! Oh!' Olive hid her face in her hands for a moment. 'That is old Mr Oskar. If you call it handling the German! He's a friend of old Mr Stephen. They got him in to help. After all, he is German. Nobody was expecting any trouble. They didn't realise that his English wasn't up to it, and they can't get rid of him. Since he's a friend of their father, he just orders them about. And he won't type, of course.'

Isobel nodded. It was understood that no man was ever asked to shackle himself to a typewriter.

'So Sandra has to take dictation and it's driving her mad. He's so slow. What you would do in a morning takes him a day and a half, and once when Sandra asked him if he couldn't hurry it up a bit—after all, she has her own job to do—he went round and told Mr Walter that he wanted Sandra dismissed for impertinence. They won't need to worry about sacking Sandra if this goes on. She's looking around for another job now.' Olive shook her head. 'When I think what you used to do, and for a junior's wage. Frank even had to bully you to go ask for a rise.'

Isobel reflected that she had been trapped in Mr Richard's fiction, having accepted his assessment of her skills.

'Mr Richard is not popular, my dear. He has not been seen around the office since the day you walked out.'

'Well, I suppose that's something gained.'

'That old man can't even read the invoices. If a label comes off and Frank wants a description there's all the trouble in the world.'

'It's difficult at first, because they abbreviate the words. But the thing is there in front of you, so you can learn fast enough if you want to.'

'Jenny is trying to learn. She's picking out the colours. She's a good little thing.' Olive burned suddenly with a clear flame. 'Do you know, they came looking for your dictionary! Your little paperback dictionary. They thought you might have left it behind.'

Isobel too was indignant. That dictionary, packed away now in the dead dinosaur, was a love object, the careless gift of a bookseller on her first day at work. It had conferred a blessing and she cherished it accordingly.

'Sandra said, "If you are looking for the German dictionary, Mr Walter, it was Isobel's personal property

190

and I am glad to say that she took it away with her." Once, nobody would have cheeked Mr Walter. He has come down a peg or two. He went quite red and walked out without saying anything. I tell you, Mr Walter rues the day.'

'I did not die in vain,' said Isobel.

'Don't talk like that!'

'Only to Lingard Brothers. Truly, I'm doing very well. Oh, Olive, it's wonderful of you all. And I am so sorry. Poor Frank. All that trouble and misery, and all through my thoughtlessness. I'll never forget it.'

'Mmm.'

Olive's tone said, See to it that you don't.

The reproach was unnecessary. Isobel would never in her life forget that wretched odyssey and her responsibility for it.

'Are you going away for your holidays?'

Isobel wondered if she had caused more human expense by delaying the holiday excursion.

'I'm getting married on Saturday. Terry has put his mother into a home at last.'

'Oh, Olive!' Isobel grasped her hands in delight. 'You've kept the best news to the last!'

'Yes. I'm sorry it isn't happy all round. His mother is very bitter against him. But he couldn't give her proper care and when I offered to give up work to look after her, she went wild and said she wouldn't have another woman in her house. So unreasonable. I was relieved, really, when she said no. Then the doctor talked straight to her and said if she wasn't prepared to cooperate, he would simply have to get her committed and she'd have no choice. She was a danger

191

to herself, as things stood. So Terry has got her into a very nice place, though she won't see him. That is, he goes to see her and she won't speak to him. It upsets him, but he had no choice, and we can't help being glad about getting married. We just hope she'll come round and accept the situation.'

'Not much loss if she doesn't.'

'That's what people always say, isn't it, when they're not in the situation. But she's his mother and he remembers her when she was different. I'm not sure that she was very different, myself, but he likes to think so. It's a bit of a cloud, but we're getting married at last, and it's fun fixing the house. It's a big place. And that's something I wanted to talk about with you. We'll have a spare room, and if you have nowhere to go when you leave here, we can let you have it while you are looking about. Terry's happy with the idea. You won't have any excuse.'

'You're very kind.'

'Well, don't forget it. Don't ever do that to us again.'

Isobel nodded acceptance.

'Did Lingards give you a present?'

Olive grinned.

'Six sherry glasses out of stock.'

'Lucky they weren't liqueur glasses.'

'But Frank and the girls gave me a lovely silver sandwich tray, and they're coming to the wedding. It's going to be very quiet, of course.'

'I wish I could be there.'

'Yes. We all wish that.'

'What time of day? I'll be thinking of you.'

'Three o'clock in the afternoon.'

'Oh, good. That's rest period. I'll be able to concentrate.'

'They warned me about rest period. I'll have to be off. There's a bus back to town, too. About this money? Do you want it in cash, or shall I write you a cheque? I didn't know what would be best.'

'A cheque, thanks. How marvellous of Frank. There's a sort of bank–post office at the store and Boris will bank it for me. Boris is a friend, on D grade. They're the walking wounded. Very useful.'

Olive had begun to empty the carrier bag.

'This is from Frank and the girls. We didn't know what to bring you. Sandra was for talc and scent and stuff to cheer you up, but we thought food would be better.'

She unpacked cracker biscuits, a circular box containing a wheel of foil-wrapped wedges of cheese, a bag of oranges, a block of chocolate ('Special from Frank'), and a jar of jam over which Olive smiled.

'That's from Jenny. It's a jar of her mother's marmalade. I know it seems a bit odd, but she hears so much about you from Frank…'

'It's lovely of her.'

'We remembered what you used to eat for lunch. I hope it's all right.'

'Couldn't be better. I'm dribbling. I'm going to make a pig of myself.'

'And don't forget, you have to write. I'll give you my new address.' Olive took a notebook from her handbag and wrote.

'And your new name? Or is it bad luck to anticipate?'

Olive shook her head.

'Winterton. Mrs Terry Winterton.'

In her voice and in her face there was so much joy and gentleness that she was for the moment transfigured.

There it was again, that unknown, unexplored territory.

The hooter sounded. Isobel kissed Olive on the cheek, they clasped hands and she departed.

Isobel spent the rest hour in painful reflection.

The sympathy she had left behind her at Lingards caused an astonishment which reached deeper than the mind. She had taken for granted always that when she closed a door behind her, she disappeared entirely from the minds of those behind it. That this was not so was disconcerting; it created a responsibility she did not wish to bear.

I can't. I can't. I don't know how.

There was no escaping it. She could never deny responsibility for Frank's ordeal or cease to suffer from the thought of it.

This was what the Church called a sin of omission, but what sin? If there was a sin, you could be sure the Church had a word for it.

She was not indifferent to other people. She had cared about Olive and her problems with Terry's mother. She cared for Frank. But could not write a letter, never expected that anyone would care for her. So Frank had trudged, worried, persisted.

As a sin, it partook of the nature of suicide. Dismissal of others.

Why, she thought, finding relief in amusement, I'm doing what I used to do when I was a kid, trying to name my sin. That was for my deathbed repentance, to save me from the fires of Hell. This one is for here and now and the aim is...amendment.

I have to live as if...I have to assume that I have some importance to other people. I have to live accordingly. I have to step out into space.

I can't do it. I don't know how.

I begin to sympathise with Val. What illiteracy is really like. I have my own illiteracy. I get impatient, think, 'Why doesn't she ever try?' Then, why don't I?

I say, 'I can't do it!' Can't do what?

See myself as a person acceptable in the eyes of others. I might have to live up to their expectations, can't guarantee satisfaction. Easier and safer to be nothing.

And so Frank trudges and worries.

It won't do.

The responsibility is there. I can ignore it, but I can't abolish it.

And Robbie. Not for the first time, I reject a man because I can't accept myself.

I have to write a poem about that. Could I send him a poem? Explain? I'll write it even if I don't dare to send it. The first thing I'll write when I start again.

If I had looked into your eyes instead
of my beleaguered mind where monsters...

Oh, what a dodge, diving into poetry. Coping with everyday is what we're after.

> the inward gaze made monsters of
> the cherished shadows

Now, cut that out.

Stepping into space, is what I call it. That's what the fear is.

But the fear is irrational, because the ground is there. This is like agoraphobia or any other phobia. I have to accept that the ground is there.

Dear old Frank. He won't have taken that journey for nothing, if it is just to persuade me that the ground is there.

What am I afraid of? Making a fool of myself, earning a snub or two?

Toughen up, will you?

There's a margin for error. I did behave badly and Olive let me know it, but she came and brought gifts.

Her animal joy in the prospect of appetising food was in the circumstances a strong support. It helped her to endure a considerable degree of moral suffering.

She wished she could write all this down. She needed a new mantra.

No man is an island. John Donne had it right. Not even Isobel Callaghan.

And that is the kind of talk you abstain from, or Frank will have trudged in vain.

*

These painful and laborious reflections had occupied the whole of rest hour. The liberating hooter took her by surprise.

She was faced now with the problem of Val, who continued to lie silent and motionless as if she had not heard it.

'Val!'

No response.

'Val. Look, I'm sorry I didn't introduce you to Olive. I was so astonished to see her that I didn't think of it.'

'I'm sure I'd be the last to interfere where I'm not wanted.'

Except, of course, in the matter of Doctor Wang's visits. But how could one ever convince Val that she was not wanted?

'It would have been all right if I had introduced you to her and I didn't think of it at the time. I'm sorry.'

Oh, Lord. Here I am straight back into difficulty. What's wanted here? What do I owe?

Damn it, it was a private conversation.

Val expressed her own grievance unprompted.

'Why don't you ever tell anyone anything? I didn't even know that you worked in an office. You never say anything about yourself. You are really a very strange person, Isobel.'

Was this owed, then? Was this what she must do?

She could hear Frank saying, 'Tell the nosy old bag to mind her own business.'

One didn't have to offer everything.

Meanwhile there was money for the bank account and, more important, the food. Her pleasure in that prospect

197

gave her the strength to open the disappointing envelope and face Fenwick's rejection slip.

What accompanied the rejected manuscript was not a rejection slip but quite a long letter.

Dear Miss Callaghan,
This is an interesting and original story. I am returning it because I feel strongly that you should rework it as a novel. There is really too much incident for a short story, and relationships you hint at—as with Paul and Sophie—seem to rouse the reader's curiosity without satisfying it.

If you are prepared to rework it as a novel I should be happy to read it, and if it comes up to the standard of your short stories, recommend it to a publisher.

Do think this over. I am sure it would make a good novel.

Sincerely,
Tom Fenwick

PS There isn't any law against describing scenery, you know.

Isobel forgot her shortcomings. She lay holding the bundle, letter, manuscript and envelope against her chest, like a small girl cuddling a doll.

Then she roused herself to look at the date on the letter. Nearly three months ago. Was it too late? Had he taken offence? Had he changed his mind?

Down with paranoia!

She found pen and paper and wrote,

C Ward
Mornington Sanatorium
2nd September

Dear Mr Fenwick,

Thank you for your letter, which has just now come into my hands. I am grateful for your advice and your confidence in my writing. I am not at present in a position to write a novel, but I shall think about your advice and hope in the future to be able to follow it.

I am well placed at the moment to study scenery, especially mountains.

Sincerely,
Isobel Callaghan

She folded the letter into the envelope, addressed it and stamped it, and laid it on her cabinet. The first D grade visitor who dropped in would put it in the box for her.

Val was watching. She was however still so daunted by the ferocious snub Olive had dealt her that she did not venture to ask a question.

Overflowing with love for all, Isobel would have liked to make a peace offering of information. 'An editor who published two of my stories wants me to write a novel.' No, it wouldn't do.

She said instead, 'Would you like a biscuit and cheese?'

Val accepted the offering.

She did show the letter to Doctor Wang next day when he called in to return her copy of Donne.

He shared her excitement to a gratifying extent.

'It could be managed, you know. When you make D grade. We could find you a place to work.'

'Yes,' said Isobel. 'When I make D grade.'

There was no question in her voice. She would not condescend to question him on the matter when he came to visit.

Val said, 'Doctor Wang!'

'Yes?'

He was all polite attention.

'I get this funny jerking feeling in my legs at night. It makes it difficult to get to sleep.'

'Indeed. That must be most uncomfortable.'

'Speaking of Donne,' he said to Isobel, 'there seems to be the same intimacy with his God as you spoke of with Hopkins. I do think this strange.'

Did he know how cruel he was being? For that matter, did Val know it? Isobel remembered her resolution, to avoid the arrogance of thinking and feeling for others. Otherwise she might never make D grade.

When the doctor had departed, Val said, 'He was really nice about it, you see,' but her tone was defiant and her expression uncertain.

'Yes,' lied Isobel.

*

It was Lance who put a stop to the unofficial visits of Doctor Wang. Lance had acquired a set of joke teeth, which fitted over his front teeth and projected like Dracula fangs over his lower lip. With fangs projecting and a thumb dragging at the outer corner of each eye to convert it to a sinister slit, he put his head in at the doorway shrilling, 'Me Wun Bung Lung.'

Doctor Wang got up from his seat at Isobel's bedside and walked out through the inner door into the corridor.

Isobel spoke in fury.

'You disgusting little beast. You ever work a trick like that one again and you will not step into this room ever again. I shall never have another word to say to you.'

'I didn't know he was there.'

Lance didn't tell lies as a rule. He did not see the need. That he was prepared to lie on this occasion was a hopeful sign.

'That makes no difference. It was disgusting behaviour and it would be disgusting whether he saw it or not. You've no right to come here disgusting us.'

Lance wrenched the joke teeth out of his mouth and said sulkily, 'It was a joke.'

'Then keep your jokes for those who share your sense of humour.'

Val sprang a surprise.

'How do you like it when people make jokes about Jews?'

Lance stood transfixed.

201

'You never told me you were Jewish!' Astonishment had replaced anger in Isobel's voice. 'But then why would you? That's got nothing to do with the price of fish, I suppose.'

Lance said bitterly, 'Some people know without being told.'

'The way they know that Doctor Wang is Chinese? Don't start feeling sorry for yourself. There weren't any prejudices around here until you started it. You should be proud of being Jewish, anyhow. I often wondered where you got your brains from. Not that you make much use of them. Get back to bed. Just go hide your face. We've had enough of you.'

Lance shuffled away, resentful but shaken.

Isobel said to Val, 'Who told you he was Jewish?'

'Nobody told me. You just have to look at him. You don't notice much, do you?'

Val was smug, Isobel reflective.

Doctor Wang did not visit in Room 2 again.

Next morning he joined Isobel on the verandah, pulling up a vacant chair to sit beside her.

'Lance seems to think I am physically repulsive.'

His voice was tremulous with hurt and offence.

'Lance is repulsive. He got such a roasting that he actually stayed in bed all day. I think he figured that it was the only safe place for him.'

Doctor Wang refused to smile.

How vulnerable he was and how young! Hardly older than herself.

'He's only a pathetic little larrikin, you know. And you don't have to take notice of him. And believe me, if Chinese people are slit-eyed and fang-toothed, then you must be a notable exception to the rule. You are a very good-looking young man. That is, according to Western standards. I don't know how you rate in Hong Kong.'

Indeed, the only details of his appearance that might offend the Western eye could also be considered beauties: a sprite-like cast of countenance which would prevent his ever looking mature and a redness of lip which combined with the honey colour of his skin gave a disagreeable hint of the epicene quite alien to his character.

Fearing that sympathy had led her into impropriety, she added in haste, 'Is your wife a beauty?'

'I think so.' His face lightened. 'And my son is particularly handsome. For his age.'

Little Wang was six months old. The doctor's joy in him transformed his face.

'Look,' she said urgently, 'I know Lance is a blight. But look at his situation. He doesn't seem to have anyone to care about him or think about his future. He honestly is very bright and responsive if you can get to him. I've tried to get him reading. I gave him *The Old Man and the Sea*. And he loved it.'

Lance had brought the book back woebegone.

'Ah, kid, dem bloody sharks! I was with him all the way! Poor old bugger!'

Just the sort of response that Hemingway would have liked.

Doctor Wang had ceased to listen.

'I should like you to read this poem aloud if you don't mind. I cannot really appreciate the metre until I hear it.'

The literary talk was transferred to the verandah, where it drew others to listen.

Boris came first, ready to be of service.

Surprisingly, Eily drifted close, said, 'Any charge for admission?', drew up a chair and attended in silence.

Isobel looked up once to find an audience of six listening while she read aloud Byron's 'When we two parted / In silence and tears…' It was quite like the ideal of life in a sanatorium, inviting the soul.

Quickly, it became a settled arrangement. If Doctor Wang was busy, he came to apologise, briefly, before he went about his duties.

The weather was good that spring. Mornington lay below a ridge, sheltered from the wind. There were few rainy days; on those rare occasions, Wang did not appear. Isobel missed the poetry hour intensely.

She wanted to write. The urge to write was beginning to torment her. She thought she might take advantage of the rainy mornings, when Val went down to talk to Gladys, but solitude never lasted long.

Rain or shine, Isobel had her own visitors.

There was Madeleine, a small, neatly made woman who told the serial story of her strange, episodic marriage to the handsomest taxi driver in Haberfield.

'That's what he used to say, love. Look at himself in the glass when he was shaving and say, "Who's the handsomest taxi driver in Haberfield, Maddy?"'

'Not a wide field.'

'No, there wasn't that much competition. But you see, love, he is always looking for a woman who sees what he sees in the glass.'

'And it never lasts?'

Maddy shook her head sadly.

'Never. I wish to heaven it did, so he could settle. Last time he left, he told me he'd only come back out of pity. I said to him, "Keep your pity for yourself, mate. You're the one who needs it."'

'Would you really take him back again?'

The taxi driver had written her an affectionate letter, asking after her health. Madeleine shrugged. The gesture seemed to say, without enthusiasm, 'What else is there?'

The taxi driver had been the study of Madeleine's life, the only story she had to tell.

There was Peter, who worked in the laboratory with Ron, lived in one of the chalets, which were Isobel's dream, did tapestry and longed for love.

He would set out for Sydney at the weekend, expecting that the skies would open and send him a lover, coming back on Sunday night dejected and needing comfort.

This was mysterious, since Peter was a personable young man, somewhat slight in figure and slightly feminine, though not effeminate, in face.

He blamed the sanatorium for his lack of success in courtship.

'As soon as I say where I work, they start running.'

It was a dilemma.

He would not take up with a *wog*. Never. Yet he could not summon up courage to leave his job, his chalet, his security.

Isobel never had the courage, or the brutality, to ask him if he were *one of us*.

She could not use the word 'wog'. Doctor Wang had in a rare assumption of authority banned it.

'You will not use that word again, please. It is not necessary to out-Roman the Romans.'

Isobel grinned, guiltily, and complied.

There was Tamara, who did not visit formally, but lingered after she had made the beds to relive her spectacular life story of forced labour and bombings in Berlin, and of her passion for her son, Georgy, not her husband's child, the fruit of an earlier marriage or encounter.

Her great drama had been the struggle with the baby-sitter who had tried to rob her of Georgy.

'She say, "You young. You young! You have more children!" And my Georgy, he grow up, think mother is bish go leave him.' Tamara shook her head in fury, facing the kidnapper again. 'I pull, she pull, she pull my hair, I kick her shins, grab my Georgy and run. Left his good coat.' She frowned at this memory.

Tamara was the one narrator whose story Isobel truly enjoyed.

Tragic, comic, tough or tedious, she relived it with a gusto which raised the spirits of the listener.

Privacy was hard to find. Sometimes she felt that she was being eaten alive in very small mouthfuls.

*

'Sometimes,' said Val to Geoff and Pauline, 'I think Isobel is out of her head. The muttering and the mumbling she goes on with!' Her monotonous, mosquito voice rose to a high whine. 'It's enough to drive me crazy. You would think she might have a little consideration for other people.'

Geoff and Pauline, as usual the unwilling medium of Val's resentment, were sealed in a moment of embarrassment, unable to speak.

Isobel could not speak either.

What Val said was true.

It was the unwritten poem to Robbie that was escaping from her control like a live animal.

She had decided that her best approach to that moment with Robbie was in a monologue in the style of Browning's 'Men and Women'.

That token of love which you offered me—it
    was, I recall, a meat pie
offered with such words as might have turned it
    to larks' tongues
but for the poison I brought...

'Larks' tongues' and 'poison', that was all right.

The difficulty was with the look of love, the light of love in his eyes, which she had killed and must now give life to...it had to be an insect which stung and died.

Oh, do not take offence if I say 'insect'
I know that the word has unfortunate
    connotations—
but think of the dragonfly, think of...

The trouble was that the only insects durable enough to destroy monsters were more in the nature of dung beetles or white ants, which did not in any case sting and die.

She had been so happily engrossed in her thoughts that she had no idea she was murmuring them aloud until Val had said sharply, 'What on earth are you talking about? Dung beetles! I don't believe you know what you are talking about yourself half the time.'

Isobel too had been shocked.

It had seemed so clear cut, if not easy. Keep to the rules, do what they tell you and you'll get better. But what was the point of a healthy body if the mind couldn't keep up with it?

Poor Val. First a foreigner and now a madwoman and no use complaining about a madwoman who consorted with doctors.

Isobel had said, 'I'm sorry.'

It was no use resolving to renounce poetry. It would not go away.

She must somehow find the opportunity to write. Not a novel, of course, but a poem. One poem wouldn't wreck her health; it might save her reason.

The only available sanctuary was the bathroom. It was in use from six o'clock till ten, closed for cleaning until eleven and out of bounds, therefore empty and unvisited, for the rest of the day. Once when she was waiting for the lavatory to be vacated, she had stepped in there and enjoyed a moment of peace and silence. She had not done that again, finding the contrast with her living conditions too painful, but now she thought of it as escape.

She would have to take care. Discovery would be too humiliating; she could not expect Val to cover for her.

She would have to vary the times of her escape and limit the period of absence, say to ten minutes. If Sister Connor or anyone else came looking for her, she could always explain away an absence of ten minutes. Nobody would enquire too closely into what might still be a prolonged trip to the lavatory. They wouldn't have a clock on her after all.

The next time Val was out of the room, she hid her notebook and her pencil in the deep pocket of her dragon coat.

She was behaving like a school child planning a prank, but after all that was her exact situation at the moment.

So she became a rule breaker, one of the naughty ones, the smokers, the jokers, the truants.

To be caught would be calamitous, humiliating to her and also embarrassing to Wang. The risk made her nervous as well as cautious, but she could not give up those interludes of quiet, when she sat on the stool beside the bathtub and wrote, creating her mythical insect, the small bright-winged David which slew the monster madness as it died.

She had to ponder, too, a link between the meat pie and the love-light she embodied in the dragon-slaying insect.

Breath and light, both died...

She was so absorbed that she forgot to watch the time. On her third excursion, she looked at her watch and saw, with real fear, that she had been away from her bed for twenty-five minutes.

She put her notebook and her pencil in her pocket and made haste back to the room, trying not to look furtive. 'Where have you been?' asked Val.

'Oh, just about the place.' She added, trying in vain to seem casual, 'Has anyone been looking for me?'

No. She had got away with it.

'You're getting to be as bad as Lance.'

Isobel had an answer from Tom Fenwick: a parcel with two back issues of *Seminal* and two copies of the *New Yorker* and a note that read: 'What rotten luck. Shall keep up the reading matter. Please keep in touch and report progress. If I can help in any way, let me know. I mean PLEASE. T. F.'

It would be no trouble to respond to that one. She felt she was entitled to the services of people like Tom Fenwick. She had only to deserve them, an obligation she could not in any case avoid.

On the verandah a stranger appeared and approached the poetry-reading circle. A tall woman of imposing figure, silver hair plaited and coiled in a coronet around her well-poised head, approached them with small, slow steps.

Doctor Wang got quickly to his feet, crying, 'Mrs Soames! Elsa! You should not be walking, surely.'

He pushed his chair forward. The lady sat, with dignity, settling the skirts of her splendid gown of royal blue velvet in graceful folds.

'I took it slowly, doctor. I have come to no harm.'

Her voice was threadlike, but clear. Her serenity withstood reproach.

'You must not walk back again.' He looked to Boris, who nodded cheerfully.

'I shall fetch a chair. I am becoming a very good driver.'

'Thank you.'

Mrs Soames nodded to Boris.

'We are having a poetry session,' said Doctor Wang.

'So I heard. That is why I have come to hear for myself.'

'You must not come again, I am afraid. It simply won't do. Mrs Soames is recovering after a thoracoplasty,' he explained.

All those present looked with awe at Mrs Soames.

'But may I stay now that I am here?'

Doctor Wang sighed and yielded.

'Isobel and I are having an argument which perhaps you can settle. She had read a love poem of John Donne which I refuse to call a love poem. Isobel?'

Isobel read:

Oh, do not die, for I shall hate
All women so, when thou art gone,
That thee I shall not celebrate
When I remember thou wast one.

Mrs Soames nodded to interrupt her.

'I know the poem.'

'My objection to the term "love poem" is that one believes more in the poet's pleasure in the brilliance of his paradoxes than in the sincerity of his passion.'

'Say "joy", not "pleasure",' said Isobel, 'and I'll concede the point. But why should his joy in his power of expression detract from his love?'

'Love is self-forgetfulness, not self-expression,' said Wang.

Mrs Soames recited in her whispering voice:

How did the party go in Portman Square?
I cannot tell you; Juliet was not there.
And how did Lady Gaster's party go?
Juliet was next to me and I do not know.

'Now that,' said Wang, 'I consider a truly Oriental love poem. Who is the poet?'

'Hilaire Belloc.'

'Hey,' said Eily. 'That's neat. I like that.'

Doctor Wang was amused.

'Are you taking to poetry, Eily?

'Beats some of the stuff you hear around here.'

'Well,' said Isobel, 'it's just as clever as Donne. Only sneakier.'

'We are back to our old argument. The art is to conceal art. Though I admit you have converted me to Hopkins. There is a difficulty there worth the struggle. Love is a simpler subject.'

'In art but not in life,' said Mrs Soames.

'That is the last word, I think. And now you must go back. And you must not do this again. We shall wait for your promotion, to join us.'

Boris had left them, unobtrusively, and was now returning, pushing a wheelchair. He and the doctor together raised Mrs Soames from her chair and settled her in the wheelchair. Boris propelled her away, through Room 2 to the inner corridor. Isobel had always found trips by wheelchair humiliating; Mrs Soames managed to give this one the appearance of a royal progress.

She looked to Wang for further information about the visitor. He, however, was leaving them as well. He had been gazing with a troubled face after Mrs Soames.

On the verandah, Lance walked past the poetry group, unseeing, wrapped in grievance. The mental gymnastics by which he had transformed himself into an innocent victim were beyond imagination—but, as Isobel had to remind herself, he was in all things the victim of fate.

She was relieved when after two days he resumed his illegal visits to Room 2, though they restricted her own freedom, making it more difficult to escape to the bathroom.

There was a change in him. Though he perched as usual on the end of her bed and resisted as usual her attempts to get him to go back to bed, he was silent, apparently sunk in thought, but observing her with an attention which made her uneasy.

'Izzy?'

'Yes?'

She looked up from her book.

'Your face. It gets me. Something about it just gets me.'

213

Isobel knew her own face well and could envisage it with all the intimacy of dislike: the small, full-lipped mouth—some people might call it a rosebud mouth but in moments of self-hatred she had an uglier name for it—round chin, heavy straight eyebrows set in a permanent frown. Illness had reduced the full cheeks she had likened to a baby's bum. She hoped they never came back.

She said sourly, 'I wish it got you back to bed.'

(And that, she thought later, was her first error. The proper answer would have been, 'Don't talk such bloody rot,' or something just as decisive.)

'Izzy, I mean it.'

He slid from his perch and came to kneel beside her bed, advancing his face to subject hers to a closer scrutiny.

She wanted to dodge. She had to control the disgust she felt at the closeness of his sick body. Poor little devil, she had to spare him that.

She said gently, 'Don't be a little ass, Lance. Go back to bed now.'

He got up and went, still thoughtful.

Who am I, she thought, to feel disgust? If he is diseased, so am I.

She hoped he would not come so close again, for all that.

The next day, he came closer. He came in and knelt beside her bed, brought his face close to hers while he peered with intensity at her features one by one, and she forced herself to control her dislike of the proximity, then with a purring sound he pressed his lips to her cheek.

214

She was paralysed by a conflict of emotion; the disgust she felt as his thin lips climbed her cheek like a small rodent was inhibited by the pity she felt for the fever smouldering in his flesh.

She withdrew to Czechoslovakia.

You would go to bed with any Tom, Dick or Harry who asked you, and you make a carry-on when a sick, unhappy kid kisses you on the cheek?

Yet what she wanted most to do was thrust him away, with violence.

It could be the final rejection, the blow that would finish him.

The look on his face as he withdrew was strange, remote, with an almost religious serenity.

Was that good?

Why was it so difficult to tell the difference? Why could one not have some sort of litmus test for right and wrong?

She could not take the responsibility of rejecting that physical contact. After all, there wasn't much to it, was there? Nothing you'd really call disgusting, nothing sexual about it.

So she endured, trying to talk herself out of the disgust she felt at his touch.

Enlightenment came one day in the corridor. An arm went round her shoulders and pulled her into a cheerful and careless hug.

'Love that dragon of yours!'

'It comes from Hong Kong, just like you.'

215

The arm released her and Wang went on his way laughing, leaving her with an important fact about body talk.

It was good or bad, like eggs, oranges or voice tones. There was no need to rationalise it. In Wang, good. In Lance, bad.

Bad above all because it did not communicate. Wang's hug spoke directly to her; Lance's body talked to itself.

Val would not have been fooled for a moment. Nor would Tamara. 'If he lays finger I smack hard, no worries.'

The next time Lance, on his knees beside her, closed his eyes and advanced his face to hers, she dodged and said firmly, 'Don't do that! I don't like it!'

He went at once into comic mode, whining, 'Izzy, don't you love me?'

She had given much thought to this and had her answer ready.

'The point is that you don't love me. This isn't what kissing is about. Some day you'll want to kiss somebody for the right reason, so keep it till then. Okay?'

The change in his expression was slight but startling, that trance-like serenity dissolving, his lips tightening and his eyelids opening to reveal rage.

He was baulked of revenge. She had aligned herself with authority, she was bitch Lawson, helpless and available for insult. This was the tin kettle in the Christmas gift wrap and she had been forced to accept it—but now, like bitch Lawson, she was escaping.

She looked at him in dismay while he got control of his rage, seeming literally to swallow it.

With his instinct for saving himself at the edge of the pit, he said thoughtfully, 'I think I'll go look for dumber company.'

He got up from his knees and walked away, for once without shuffling.

He won't find much dumber than I am, thought Isobel morosely.

'I don't know why you let that go on so long,' said Val.

Out of sheer damned stupidity.

She wouldn't give Val the satisfaction of telling her so.

The search for dumber company did not keep him away for long from Isobel's bedside. He returned next day, but with a significantly changed demeanour. He perched silent and thoughtful on the end of the bed and seemed to be looking for words in which to speak new thoughts.

Perhaps he had got new insight into his behaviour. Perhaps this was the time to tell him...tell him what? What prospect could one offer?

Better to have left him alone than to set him considering questions to which she had no answer.

She felt guilty and inadequate, but relieved not to have that insect mouth hovering round her face.

Oh, but she was tired of contemplating problems she could not solve.

Doctor Stannard lost patience with Isobel's fever chart.

After staring irritably at it, he picked up her latest X-ray, frowned at it, put it down and picked up the chart again.

217

'I can't understand this fever, Sister. Why isn't it settling down? There has to be some reason for it.'

Sister Connor could not offer a reason. Nor could Isobel.

Val spoke.

'She gets out of bed! She says she's going...' About to commit the impropriety of mentioning the lavatory to a doctor, she halted. 'She stays away sometimes more than half an hour and she won't say where she's been. She just says, "Oh, about the place." She does it every day.'

She inhaled a breath of righteous indignation, expelled it and sat proud and defiant, having done her duty in spite of all obstacles.

'Oh, indeed.'

Doctor Stannard turned his eagle gaze on Isobel. She met it with all the aplomb of a school prefect caught smoking in the lavatory block.

'Mmm. That will be B grade and bread and water, Sister, until further notice.'

The mischievous grin had been fleeting, almost subliminal, but it registered with Isobel, and also with Sister Connor, whose exasperation was far from subliminal. She suppressed it quickly out of respect for the white coat, but her expression boded ill to Isobel.

Doctor Stannard moved on, looked at Val's X-ray, asked after her health and departed. Doctor Wang followed him, avoiding Isobel's eye, avoiding everyone's eye.

Isobel hid her face on the arms she had crossed and supported on her propped knees. She did not stir or speak.

Val remained defiant, though she had done the unthinkable. Wog does not eat wog. Patients do not peach. One protects the smoker and the truant, since one does not know when one's own hour of need may come.

As soon as the doctors were out of range, Lance came running to Isobel and put his arms round her shoulders, grievances forgotten, the embrace expressing only sympathy.

He said to Val, 'You beast. You beast. Putting Izzy in. Getting her back on B grade.'

Isobel could not raise her head. She could not show her face. What she was hiding was not misery, but the shining of her eyes. A small, discontented animal which had long been prowling her mind had lain down, curled up and gone to sleep.

Picturing that grin again, she told herself, I'd do anything for him. I'd follow him anywhere.

She had not known that helplessness could be so exquisite a sensation.

Time to sober up, to bury this—in the heart, wasn't that the traditional burial place for such things? She must sober up and face the world.

She raised her head.

'It's all right, Lance. I'm not really on B grade. He was joking. Just B grade would have meant something. B grade and bread and water doesn't mean a thing.'

'Oh. No thanks to you, though,' he said to Val. 'It was a rotten thing to do, that's all.'

'It was for her own good,' said Val.

Her tone was sulky, her expression puzzled. Her attack on Isobel had not had quite the result she had anticipated.

Lance too looked puzzled.

'Why would he be joking? He doesn't joke when she goes on moaning to him about me. Just says not to do it again.'

'He doesn't put you on B grade either. Maybe he knows it wouldn't be any use.'

'S'pose you're right. No call for Val to go peaching, just the same.'

On the verandah after rounds, there was high drama.

'Isobel's back on B grade. Is that right?'

'Val put her in for getting out of bed.'

Val could not escape criticism for this breach of the unbreachable code.

'Somebody had to tell him. It was my duty.'

'Could have given her a warning. Back on B grade. That's tough.'

Val was a large, innocent bear chained to the stake of righteousness and baited by yapping dogs.

'I had to do my duty.'

She did not try to correct the notion that Isobel had been sent back to B grade.

That was left to Isobel.

'I'm not on B grade. He was joking.'

'Joking? Stannard doesn't joke.'

The tide of opinion began to turn against Isobel. Friendship with Doctor Wang was almost acceptable, since he was one of us and Chinese, after all—but joking, being teased by Stannard...

'No joke when the rest of us get caught getting out of bed.'

'One law for the rich!'

She was forced to smile.

'Nobody ever called me rich before. Listen, it was sort of like a joke, but he meant it just the same. I mean, I know I mustn't do it again.'

She was tired. She was really extremely tired. No doubt it had been wrong of her to get out of bed to write poetry, and Sister Connor was angry with her.

'Well, he never jokes with anyone else, that's all I can say.'

'Oh, but Isobel isn't like other people. Isobel is different.'

'Oh, yes. Isobel is different!'

There came that eleventh commandment again: Thou shall not be different.

Was it going to pursue her all her life?

This time she had tried to conform, a wog among wogs.

She had called herself a wog until Wang had banned the word—but there it was. He didn't ban it with other patients. But what other patient would be using it to a doctor? And he had known very well that she was playing a game—out-Romaning the Romans, as he had put it.

It was all too difficult. One couldn't after all avoid being oneself, with all faults. They were right to resent her. Let them get on with it. She was too tired to try, too tired to care.

She roused herself, however, to defend Doctor Stannard.

'Oh, give it away, will you? Doctor Stannard is nice to everybody. And you mustn't say that he cares more for one patient than another. He cares about us all. He just knew I'd get the message.'

'And how do you know that? You on a wavelength with him?'

She had sometimes thought that this was so, that Doctor Stannard's moments of withdrawal were in truth moments of communication. She could not forget that comment he'd made at their first meeting, delivered without looking at her: 'Such things do occur.' She was sure that he had told no-one of her forced entry into the wrong hospital, had never spoken of the intervention of the police. But perhaps he had forgotten or thought it too trivial to mention. It did not do to be fanciful.

Sister Connor arrived after lunch on her disciplinary errand. She said to Isobel, 'There is no special dispensation for you, you know. You can keep the rules like everyone else.' To Val she said, 'And if you have any worries about another patient, you can bring them to me before you talk to a doctor.'

Val said, 'It was for her own good.'

Isobel said, in desperation, 'I'm not away long. I just have to be by myself sometimes, for a little while.' She added bitterly, 'To remember what peace was like.'

Val said, 'Well!' in outrage.

Sister Connor took pause.

'This room is like a railway station. There's always someone in here gossiping.'

'I don't ask them to come. I can't tell them to go away.'

Sister Connor seemed to be giving this matter more thought than it warranted.

'No, I don't suppose you can. Still, there's too much of it. Val, couldn't you do something about it? Limit the visitors? You can tell them that Isobel has had enough for one day.'

Isobel dared not look at Val. Her reaction to this impious suggestion must be quite astonishing. She saw its reflection in Sister Connor's startled expression.

'Well, perhaps not. No.'

Positively, Sister Connor was stammering, apologetic.

Isobel had been nursing her anger against Val since the morning.

'Right. I'll keep to my bed. And if you really are concerned about my health, you can stop bullying and pestering me to wake up in the morning. There's something very wrong with you if you can't put up with your own company for an hour or two. I'll stay in bed but I'm going to sleep as long as I please, and I'm not going to say an unnecessary word to anyone before ten o'clock. Not you, or Lance, or anyone else!'

'Do you mean that Val wakes you deliberately?'

'Yes. That is what I mean.'

Sister Connor turned on Val, who stared at her whispering, 'Morning. Morning.'

Sister Connor drew a deep breath and spoke.

'You do not take it upon yourself to wake anyone out of sleep. This is a rest cure and sleep is the best possible rest. You will not disturb Isobel's sleep again. Doctor Stannard is very worried...' She halted, alarmed, closing her lips on an indiscretion. 'You are not the only patient in this hospital. It's time you learnt to respect other people's rights.'

On this she departed, without taking notice of Val's reaction.

It was Isobel's turn to be defiant and self-righteous.

Val drew in a long breath and expelled it in a sob, which was the start of a bout of weeping. She slid under the covers, turned to the wall and gave herself over to her grief.

Isobel lay still, trying to absorb an unwelcome piece of information. He had said, 'Don't be frightened, we'll cure you. You're going to get better.'

She hadn't doubted that statement till now. Now she assembled evidence to the contrary: his frown at her X-ray, his complaints about the continuing fever, his general shortness of temper. Would he have joked, if things were so bad? But it wasn't actually a joke. He knew she'd take it seriously. And they hid things. You had to work it out for yourself.

Meanwhile, Val's crying had increased in intensity. It became frightening. It was no longer like a human sound, but the noise of an ocean in which a body was drifting helpless, awash, abandoned.

It can't go on like that, thought Isobel.

She wasn't doing it for effect, either. She wasn't doing it at all. It was something dreadful that was happening to her.

There was nothing Isobel could do. Her voice would not be calming. She was the cause of the trouble.

Maybe she's having a breakdown. Maybe she'll have a haemorrhage if it goes on.

It can't go on like this for long. She's like a baby. She'll cry herself to sleep.

Her crying slackened at last, but it did not stop, taking instead the steady, laboured pace of her customary speech. At that pace, it could go on forever.

Eventually Isobel got up and went looking for Sister Connor. She found her talking to Sister Knox at the end of the verandah.

'Sister, Val just won't stop crying. Do you think you ought to look at her?'

Sister Connor groaned and said, 'I'll fetch Doctor Wang. You'd better go into the visitors' room, Isobel. You can lie down on the couch there for rest period. Sister, get her a blanket out of store, will you? And just remember, Isobel, that none of this would have happened if you had stayed in bed as you should have.'

Isobel thought there were other elements in the situation, but she was not in a position to argue.

When Sister Connor had gone, Sister Knox put her arm around Isobel's shoulders and said, 'Isobel, you're such a sweet girl, with a kind word for everyone. Couldn't you just be a bit kinder to poor little Val?'

A finger of white bone had touched Isobel's chest in the fourth intercostal area and had left her chilled with dread.

She said, carefully, 'She's as big as I am, she's twice my age, she has a family and a home to go back to, she has a husband who comes to see her every Sunday. Now what would you like me to do for her?'

Sister Knox took her arm away. She went to fetch the blanket, brought it back and departed in dignified silence.

Isobel lay under the blanket, fuelling her indignation.

225

That would look well on a tombstone. Here lies Isobel Callaghan. She was a sweet girl. More fool she.

Asperity gave way to terror. That tombstone was real. It reared above her, threatening to topple and blot her out from this world she wasn't finished with yet. No. Not by a long chalk. *No.*

I won't. I won't go.

She lay cowering under her blanket, afraid to move, afraid to breathe. This was fear as she had never known it.

But Stannard wouldn't have grinned if it was too late.

And Wang. She would have known, she would have seen it in Wang's face.

They were worried, but not frightened.

She must just remember that death was a possible outcome.

She thought of the future, considering alternative outcomes. C Ward was a good place for considering alternatives. It displayed them all, except for those who had had successful surgery and were waiting in the upper wards to go home.

There was Billy, who was dying quietly and patiently in Room 12. He would not die there; some day he would be moved discreetly into unknown regions. People did not die on C Ward. There was Wilf, who shared the room with Billy and would one day share his fate. Isobel thought this hard for Wilf, but he was buoyant, humorous, given to teasing Tamara, saying, 'Don't come here with your naughty temper. Rum Zwoelf, no!' opening and shortening the vowel to a wicked mimicry of her accent. Wilf had sent Tamara scudding along the verandah and skidding across the linoleum to Isobel's bed blazing with rage to say, 'Thin-skinned what mean?' Nevertheless it was accepted that Wilf had turned that corner and was on the way downhill.

There were what Isobel thought of as the professionals, Eily and Gladys and others who had been in one hospital after another, who sometimes hopefully went home only to break down and return, recidivists. There were those waiting for a lobectomy like the two young nurses in Room 9. Those were the lucky ones; they would be as good as new. There were those whose future was not yet known: Lance, perhaps, and perhaps Isobel.

I'm going to get better. It's up to me. I'm not going to die being sweet little Isobel, no.

I'm a self-appointed bastard, she said to herself and felt a little cheered.

When she got back to Room 2 at four o'clock, Val was resting quietly. Doctor Wang must have given her a sedative.

Oh, dear, what must he be thinking of me?

She caught herself up. She must not care what others thought of her, not even Wang.

Next morning Isobel stayed in bed, while Val, still silent and unforgiving, went to visit Gladys.

Doctor Wang came in from the verandah to sit by her bed.

'Where do you go on your secret excursions?'

She studied him warily.

'You won't tell?'

He placed both hands upon his heart in a gesture worthy of Lance.

227

'Honour of a schoolboy.'

'You mean Scout's honour.'

'I beg your pardon. I never was a Scout.'

'I didn't suppose that you were. I hide in the bathroom and write poetry.'

'Ah. May I read it?'

'No. No one can read it yet.'

If he wanted her secrets, he must trade.

'Is my X-ray getting worse?'

Now less affable, he paused.

'Let us say that you are not progressing as quickly as we had hoped. But progress is not always steady. There are plateaux.'

'And reversals?'

He said obliquely, 'You must trust us. Meanwhile, I think you must give up the poetic excursions.'

Then with a professional nod and a smile, he departed.

That, thought Isobel sourly, was called evasive action.

Eily, who had been lingering by the door, came in a moment later and took the chair by Isobel's bed.

'Listen, kid. I've been thinking. Val is buddies with Glad. She's down there this minute moaning about her miseries. You and I get on all right. What about asking Sister Connor if we can switch? You'd keep nit for me if I wanted a fag and I'd cover for you if you went walkabout. Who wouldn't, in this place?'

'I'd like that very much.'

'I'll go down and talk to them while they're in a huddle. I can't see what's against it if we all agree. The only thing is, I wouldn't stand for that little bugger being in here all the time.'

'You'd be doing me a favour if you could keep him out.'

'Trust me. You let them all get on your back too much.'

Isobel had come to the same conclusion.

She waited hopefully while Eily went to consult with Val and Gladys and was disappointed when on Eily's return she saw at once from her expression that the suggestion had been rejected.

'Val squealed at once, "Oh, I must have the bed by the window!" and Gladys said straight away that she couldn't stand having the bed by the wall, never could.' Eily sighed. 'What do they think this is, the bloody Ritz? Fact is, dear, Glad listens to her moaning and encourages her, but she doesn't want to be stuck with it all day. So there you are.'

Eily too was disappointed. That was comforting.

Eily studied her with an admiring grin.

'Some day you'll have to tell me how it's done. Wang I can understand, but Stannard? Care to have a try for Hook? Bet you two bob to a pound you won't get him.'

Was this Isobel the siren, the charmer of doctors? What next?

'Don't be an ass, Eily. He was just being kind. He's kind to everyone.'

'Yeah. But not in the same way. Maybe he thought Val was being a bit of a bitch.' Eily shook her head. 'Hasn't got those green eyes for nothing.'

The hooter sounded; Eily got up and left.

229

Val came back, still wan from her emotional ordeal and the after-effects of sedatives. She got into bed ignoring Isobel.

That suited Isobel very well.

Lunch arrived. Val did not eat. Sister Connor came, observed Val's untouched curry and said without much sympathy, 'Pull yourself together please, Val. You'll do yourself no good like this.' Val pushed her plate away and turned her face to the wall. Sister Connor sighed and went away.

Boris was the next arrival.

He said to Isobel, 'I do not come to chat. I think too much is asked of you. Too many people come to talk, I come to guard. You must rest more. I shall guard your rest, as much as I can. So do not speak, but close your eyes and lie quietly, whenever possible, and I shall help where I can.'

So somehow the news was out that Isobel was in trouble. As usual, it had drifted in the air, through walls and under closed doors. No point in asking how.

'Boris, you are a dear.'

'You begin now. I keep the boy away, and any others.'

This was how to do it: lie doggo, breathe easy. She closed her eyes and rested while Boris kept guard in the doorway.

When Lance approached the door, Boris grinned and performed an athletic feat of some distinction, swinging up his legs and sitting in mid-air, with back and boot soles braced against either side of the doorframe, his legs thus forming a barrier in the doorway.

'Many beatings I received for this back home, since my boots marked the door. I can climb right to the ceiling. Do you want to see me do that?'

Something about Boris, the ease of movement or of manner, conjured the ghost of another man, one of power and authority, his humour made for the braving of danger and the command of men. It was a bleak discovery which filled her with sadness and anger.

'I want to talk to Izzy.'

'I am sorry. Isobel is resting. Doctor thinks she must have more rest.'

'Who said so? Which doctor?'

'I said so. I am doctor here.'

Boris beamed, imperturbable and immovable.

Val said, with exaggerated concern, 'Isobel is a special person. She has to have special attention.'

Defeated, Lance went away.

Isobel protested to Boris, 'I can't cut him out completely, you know. I'm the only person he has to depend on. I have to give him some attention.'

'You give him attention when I am not here. Okay? I give up my time so you lie still, rest and get better. You show appreciation of my sacrifice.'

He smiled to show that the sacrifice was not grudged. She smiled in return and closed her eyes.

Next morning Isobel kept to her resolution. When she got back from the bathroom, she drank her tea in silence and lay then with her eyes closed, shutting out the world.

Lance on his early morning visit stood by her bed repeating, 'You're not asleep. You're not asleep. You're only pretending.'

Bastards get better. That was the new mantra: Bastards get better.

Val said, 'You mustn't disturb Isobel. Isobel is resting,' with a nakedly malicious stress on the name. Other people, one must understand, did not demand special privileges.

Bastards get better.

Val was almost ready to make common cause with Lance. Her intervention however served only to send him shuffling away discontented.

Bastard or not, she had to come to an understanding with Lance. For the moment, she had a debt to pay to Boris, and to Frank and perhaps to others. The idea that her welfare was a debt she owed to others was still a novelty and a subject for contemplation. Frank's journey had acquired mythic status, sharing somehow the nobility of the descent into Hades of Orpheus, though she was no Eurydice.

Tamara and Elaine were subdued. They made the beds in silence, warned perhaps by Sister Connor or made uneasy by the atmosphere in the room.

Boris arrived to do guard duty. Lance approached the door, Boris grinned and swung his legs across the doorway and Lance retreated in anger.

The situation was ridiculous. Isobel realised now that she had reacted too strongly to a hint of danger—that was what being stir-crazy did to you, made you sweat on every detail, tone of voice, slip of the tongue, anything that affected the precious self. No need to overdo it, collapsing in terror over a bit of a setback. Also, Boris was making her conspicuous and quite ridiculous, standing sentry in the doorway shooing people away. 'Isobel is resting.'

Bastards get better. Silly bastards get better. And death was a possible outcome. No special dispensation for Isobel.

The news that Stannard had threatened her with B grade, joke or not, impressed the usual visitors and sent them away, though it could not discourage Lance.

As soon as Boris left, he arrived to take his usual place on the foot of Isobel's bed.

'That old Kraut is nuts about you.'

'Do you have to be such an ass? He isn't a Kraut, he isn't old, and he isn't nuts about me. He's a friend, that's all.'

'What's going on, anyhow? Lying there pretending to be asleep, nobody can get a word out of you. Have you got the shits because Stannard said he'd put you on B grade? You said yourself he was joking. Anyone'd think you were dying.'

The noise which came from Val could only be called an audible sneer.

'Oh, shit you,' said Lance.

Val got up and walked out by the corridor door to the lavatory, Lance saluting her back with an evil grimace, lifting the corners of his mouth with his thumbs and dragging down the corners of his eyes with his forefingers.

It was comic. She laughed and then was ashamed.

'You mustn't do that, Lance. She's very upset. And I shouldn't have been getting out of bed, you know. And neither should you.'

'No business of hers to go peaching,' said Lance virtuously.

Isobel made haste to take advantage of Val's absence.

'I got a scare. It wasn't Stannard. It was Sister Connor let something slip. I tried Wang but you know what they are. He just clammed up. I think my ray is worse. I'm just playing safe for a while, that's all. Be a pal, will you?'

'Bugger,' said Lance.

He came and knelt beside her, putting his head down beside her pillow.

'Oh, shit it, Izzy. Shit it all.'

'Yes,' she answered. 'Shit it all.'

He put out his arms and she gathered him in, this time without distaste.

His head was on her shoulder. She stroked his hair, dry and sharp as grass in drought country, she felt the fever burning in him.

Shit it all.

She had gained the right to sleep in the mornings, but at some cost.

Maintaining bastardy was a difficult business.

Fortunately, the next day was Saturday. On Saturday the voice of the race commentator thundered through Mornington, and Ron, who left his laboratory to run a book on the races, literally ran from ward to ward, taking bets and distributing winnings. Val came to life sufficiently to listen to the races, place her bets and even make a small return on her investment. Isobel, who usually found the

234

noise a trial, now found it preferable to the silence which prevailed otherwise.

Bastards get better. But being a bastard takes some getting used to.

On Sunday, Val told Geoff and Pauline that Isobel had a very sullen disposition.

The Sunday visits had been passing peacefully, with instructions from Val about the garden, messages from neighbours and news about their doings collected and relayed by Pauline.

Val had never complained to them about Isobel's monopoly of Doctor Wang. Perhaps she hadn't quite known how to put it without admitting that Isobel was a favourite.

Today she was ready to attack.

Since Isobel had seen Val's terrible reaction to disapproval, she no longer wondered why Geoff and Pauline sat silent and wretched, embarrassed by her comments, yet offering no opposition, two doomed souls caught in Val's drowning clutch.

At the news that Isobel had a very sullen disposition, they bent their heads in silent dismay.

'I had to do my duty,' said Val. 'Nobody else ever tries to check her. She's been getting out of bed whenever she pleased. Now I'm the worst in the world for doing my duty, getting nothing but abuse for it. I've been so upset by the whole affair that Doctor Wang had to give me a sedative. I don't think I can go on like this.'

'You were upset,' said Isobel, 'because Sister Connor told you not to wake me up in the mornings.'

'And why can't you wake up? Everybody else wakes up. Why can't you behave like a normal person?'

'Because I'm not a normal person. I have tuberculosis. Sister Connor explained to you that sleep is part of the cure.'

In some circles, thought Isobel, normal people read books. It's the people who don't who aren't normal. This however could not be said. It would be beyond the bounds of bastardy to draw attention to Val's wooden leg.

'Everybody here has tuberculosis. There's nothing special about you.'

Geoff and Pauline were in Czechoslovakia with Mr Vorocic.

'Eily offered to change with you so that you could share with Gladys. Why didn't you take her up on that?'

'Why should I give up the bed by the window?'

This was delivered in a tone thin and vibrant with fury.

Geoff and Pauline wilted together, their heads drooping like dying lilies.

I can remember this. The tormentors can always surprise you. You think you've heard the worst, then worse comes.

She sensed in them a longing for physical contact. They wanted to hold hands. That would be the physical expression of their love, not sex, but the comforting gesture, the physical expression of support and sympathy.

Pauline said, 'I don't think you should wake Isobel up, Val, if the sister says it's wrong.'

Val said patiently, 'But I shouldn't have to wake her up. She should just wake up like a normal person.' She said

236

in a burst of resentment, 'Of course, it's Isobel, Isobel all the way. Everything she does is right and everything I do is wrong. I don't know why these things happen to me.'

She sagged against her pillows, looking wan.

Unfortunately, she was indeed wan, strained, it seemed, beyond endurance.

'Well, I shan't be getting out of bed again,' said Isobel. 'So you got your way there. And I'm going to sleep in whether you like it or not. Apart from that, what am I doing wrong?' Being more or less under the protection of Geoff and Pauline, she ventured, 'We have to share the room and I'd like to get on better with you if I could.'

'Oh.' Val shook her head. 'It's no use talking to you. You'd never really listen to me.'

Isobel returned to the book she had left in order to defend her character.

This was getting more like family life every minute.

She perceived with astonishment that this time she was the favoured child.

That situation had unexpected disadvantages.

When Sister Connor, still somewhat terse in manner, arrived with the day's issue of streptomycin, she said to Val, 'Doctor Stannard is coming to talk to you this afternoon.'

At Val's frightened expression, she said more gently, 'It's nothing to worry about. He just wants to have a talk with you. Just make sure that the room is presentable and you're both in bed as you ought to be.'

With a side glance at unforgiven Isobel, she left them.

'Well,' said Val. 'As if I was ever out of bed.'

237

Isobel had put out her tongue at Sister Connor's retreating back, a vulgar gesture of which she was immediately ashamed. That was what having to pull your pants down and being treated like a naughty child did to you. The death of dignity.

'Oh, don't worry. That one was meant for me.'

She spoke to Val without malice. This development cancelled all past grievances and disagreements. It was a departure from routine.

Doctor Stannard himself was coming.

Isobel was glad there was nobody to count her pulse beats. This wouldn't do. He was coming to see Val. The other day's encounter had been an act of kindness only.

Get yourself together, she said to herself firmly. She could not allow herself to entertain what was understood as a crush on a doctor.

'I wonder what he wants,' said Val.

On the verandah there was speculation.

'It can't be surgery. If it was surgery, he'd have said so on rounds.'

'Stannard coming? That's odd. Must be something special. Maybe a transfer.'

'You're not going home, are you? No, it couldn't be that.'

Going home was good news or bad news.

Val was not in line for bad news.

'Funny, though, for Stannard to be coming himself.'

'Ah, but that's Room 2, dear. Try Room 2 for a doctor.'

This Isobel pretended not to hear.

*

238

After lunch Diana came to inspect the room for signs of human activity such as the washing of knickers and bras. She plumped up pillows and straightened bed covers, wiped the hand basin and put away toothbrushes and soap dishes.

Lance had been warned and was reminded that if Doctor Stannard himself caught him out of bed the consequences would be serious.

Then they waited.

This reminded Isobel of her first meeting with Stannard at Saint Ursula's, and set the disobedient pulse jumping again. It wouldn't do. Wake up to yourself.

He came in and with minimal recognition of Isobel's existence—that settled the pulse all right—he sat down beside Val and began to talk about her case.

There had been doubt for a while about the necessity of operation. However, in the light of the advantages... a lobectomy was the only complete cure yet known. The rest of the lung expanded to compensate for the absent lobe and very soon after surgery the patient was as good as new.

On the other hand, the lesion was minimal. (At Mornington, minimal lesion was a cause of shame. Val winced at the mention of it.)

Let us say that an operation was not absolutely necessary. If she took care of herself, the prognosis was good, but the operation promised a future free of tuberculosis. What did Val think?

'I'd like to take your advice, doctor.'

'Would you like to talk to your husband about it?'

'He would say the same. We both trust the doctors and we are very grateful for what has been done for us.'

Val was at peace, comforted by this attention.

Isobel, who would have been very frightened, was going to be very frightened when, if, her turn came, was impressed by Val's courage.

'Well, I think the operation is the better option. It is a very safe procedure, and otherwise, you might always have it hanging over your head…' he paused and decided not to threaten Val with the sword of Damocles.

The point was—the reason he had come to talk to her was—that there was an unexpected gap in the programme and they could take Val immediately. She could phone her husband from the office. There would be the special medical examination when Mr Prior arrived at the weekend.

Val listened and nodded.

There was the bronchoscopy, a procedure in which the doctors inserted a tube with a light down the patient's throat in order to inspect the bronchi. This was not to be feared. They had never lost a patient yet.

He was using a gentle, hypnotic tone intended to lull. It did lull Val.

It wouldn't have lulled me, thought Isobel. How could Val, who woke every morning with terror in her eyes and called for help, for company, to save her from a moment's solitude, be so composed when she contemplated a bronchoscopy and a lobectomy? Sixty stitches, they said.

At least for a lobectomy they put you out, you got a general. With the thora, you had locals, saw your own blood spurting…brrr.

Still, a lobectomy, and Val taking the news so calmly.

'Right, then. We'll have the special medical on Friday. Mr Prior will want to examine you himself, you understand. And the bronc next week. A month or so and you'll be home and as good as new.'

He got up to go, paused, meditating a final gesture, a squeeze of her hand, perhaps...decided against it in favour of a smile.

A man for all occasions, Stannard. As with Isobel. The atmosphere in Room 2 had now changed. Val's importance was restored and with it her equanimity.

As soon as rest period was over, discipline broke down and visitors gathered.

Eily, survivor of two broncs, was called on to report.

'You just have to go with it, and remember that they know what they're doing. It's not too bad, you know. They give you a shot of happy drug. Maybe they gave me a bit too much last time. I got the giggles and he got quite snotty with me. "Stop that nonsense at once, Eily." He sounded just like Hook. Shut me up all right.'

Gladys said broncs here were a whole lot better than in other places. The morphia made all the difference.

There were nods, encouragement.

'Pat's doing fine. Says it's the best thing that ever happened, knowing that it's gone. Gone for good.'

Val nodded.

'He said it was the only complete cure.'

'Yeah. Look at it all ways, we're lucky. Would have been different once.'

241

They nodded, remembering the often repeated story of Tamara's husband's young brother.

'Whole family move out and leave him. Only Alexey go back, take him food. He sitting on pan, say, "I think I like an apple," then he say, "Help me, help me," and Alexey put his arms round him to lift him and he die.'

The bad old days which it was sometimes salutary to remember.

Isobel kept to her resolution and lay before breakfast with her eyes closed, playing possum, though Lance stood protesting with great bitterness, 'You're not asleep, Izzy. I know you're not. You're just pretending. You're mean, mean, mean.'

That's right. I'm a mean bastard. Bastards get better.

Boris arrived on guard duty, but he was hardly needed, since Val was the centre of attention. He kept watch for all that, barring the way to Lance in the doorway.

Mrs Kent stopped on her round to talk to Val about the bronc.

'They say there's just one moment when you think you're going to choke. You think something has gone wrong and you panic. If you just remember that it's normal and it happens every time, you won't panic.'

Just about as easy as remembering a deathbed confession, thought Isobel. That list of sins she had memorised in her childhood for the deathbed repentance that was going to save her from hellfire—how worried she had been that death might be too distracting, might make her forget something in the list.

242

In Val's position she would be very frightened—not so much of suffering as of losing control and behaving badly. There was one woman who confessed to having attacked a doctor and ripped his shirt…'Somebody's shirt got torn,' she had said with a self-conscious giggle.

Suppose that was me? How could I ever face Wang again?

Bastards don't care what people think of them.

Besides, it isn't me. It is Val, whose calm, I admit, fills me with admiration.

Val had her bronchoscopy and came back in a wheelchair, croaking but triumphant, to report at length on all that had been said and done.

Isobel said, 'You should be resting your throat.'

In vain. The saga continued until Val had no voice left.

Isobel thought she must really be in pain. Could silence be so terrible that she must suffer to prevent it?

She did complain to Sister Connor that her throat ached terribly.

'Isobel says I am talking too much,' she said with injured dignity.

Sister Connor avoided Isobel's eyes.

'It's a factor,' she said. 'Your throat won't get better if you keep forcing your voice.'

This connection between cause and effect fretted Val considerably.

'Can't you give me something for it?'

'Silence is the best cure,' said Sister Connor.

Val maintained the healing silence for almost ten minutes.

Three days later she went to surgery.

Sister Connor reported that Val had had her operation and was making a good recovery.

And Isobel's fever was subsiding.

Sister Connor had prevailed. The boys were to be moved to a ward.

'Doctor Stannard thought at first that it would be better for them in a room. He didn't want them among the men, learning bad language and listening to rough talk.'

Isobel grinned.

'I think Lance could teach the men a few new words. He taught me some.'

'Well, you'll survive. It's just impossible for me to keep him in bed. There'll be more supervision in the ward and really, the men are quite decent. They'll look after him.'

'What about Garry?'

Isobel often asked herself that.

'Garry is all right. He just keeps to himself and concentrates on getting better. He is getting better.'

She looked despondent.

Isobel guessed.

'But Lance isn't?'

'I can't talk about other patients, you know.'

'No, of course not. Sorry.'

But she knew that Sister Connor would have shared the news if it had been good.

Lance followed and took his place on the end of Isobel's bed.

'We're moving. Going down to the wards.'

He looked depressed.

'Will you come and see me, Izzy?'

'Of course I will. As soon as I make D grade. And Lance...do try, love. Stay in bed and do what they tell you!'

'Won't have much choice. Real bitches, those nurses down there on the wards.'

'They'll be all right if you behave yourself. Lance, you just have to.'

'Nobody down there to talk to.'

'What about Boris? He'll come and talk to you.'

'Huh!'

He wandered away, disconsolate.

They'll be kind to him, Isobel told herself firmly. He would never have got any better if he'd stayed here.

And she had herself to think of.

The boys in Room 1 were replaced by two quiet young women happy in each other's company.

Katie took Val's place in Room 2.

Isobel moved further down the bath queue, into the hot water zone.

Katie talked, but mostly to her reflection in the glass. It seemed though that what she saw in the glass was not a woman in her thirties, somewhat run to tooth and bone, but a lovable little girl of six or seven.

245

Katie was on D grade. After strep, she was allowed to dress.

'I shall wear a big floppy bow,' she said fondly to her reflection as she dressed, 'I don't care who calls me Pussycat.'

This was very sad, for no-one seemed inclined to call Katie Pussycat or any other endearing names.

Isobel discovered Katie's problem from Sister Connor.

When Isobel rolled over and pulled down her pyjama pants to receive the injection of strep, Katie was still.

'Your course is finished, Katie,' said Sister Connor. 'You don't need any more strep. And your temperature has been normal for weeks. You know what the doctor says. You need more activity.'

At this Katie dug under the blankets, refusing to answer. Isobel thought of her own moment of terror, when she had cowered like a beast in hiding thinking of the predator outside. For Katie the predator was the whole world outside.

When she had gone, Katie said to Isobel, 'They should know I'm running a fever. My body temperature is much lower than the normal, so when it goes up to normal, I'm really running a temperature. I tell them that and they won't believe me.'

On Rounds, Doctor Stannard passed her by after saying, 'More activity, Katie.'

He was gentle and sympathetic, but one day soon he would call her in and tell her that her bed was needed and that she must go, into the outside world which she seemed to fear more than illness.

After his visit, Katie would be silent and depressed. Then she would rally, get up and put on a frilly blouse and talk affectionately to the little girl in the mirror. Then she would be off on a round of visits and Isobel would see her no more till rest period.

That was well, for her situation filled Isobel with fear.

I have to get out of here while I'm still able to face the world. You can get to be like those prisoners who don't want to leave gaol. If there's nothing in the outer world to call you...

She had Tom Fenwick's letter, his parcels of magazines, Olive's offer of a room. And she had her typewriter.

She finished the grey lace pullover and by it achieved some local fame. Miss Landers took it and showed it about in the wards. She came back to say, with new animation, that a woman in A Ward wanted to copy it.

'But she doesn't want to tackle that stitch. She wants an eight-row pattern with a purl back and, she says,' Miss Landers quoted shyly, 'no nonsense about knitting three together through the back of the loop.'

'I could knit you some samples, if you bring me the leaflets.'

Her pleasure in this small achievement was, she knew, immoderate. It was gratifying to see Miss Landers enlivened by it, but it wasn't the Nobel Prize for Literature. Nevertheless she took great pride in knitting the samples and sending them down by Miss Landers to the interested party in A Ward.

Boris was discharged and came to say goodbye.

247

'I'll miss you very much,' she said. 'And I owe you a lot. You'll write and let me know how you're getting on, won't you?'

She saw at once that this had dealt him a blow.

Through lips he could scarcely keep from quivering, he said, 'I shall get on well enough. I shall not write to you, Isobel, because I am forty-three and you are twenty-one, and for other reasons. I ask of you one thing only.'

'Say the word.'

'Please be well. Happiness one can't arrange for, but let me think that somewhere in this world you are alive and well.'

'If you'll make me the same promise. I'll keep to it if you will.'

That at least was better. He managed to smile.

'I promise. Goodbye then.'

'Goodbye.'

So there was love and there was sex. Did they ever come together?

It would take you over. You wouldn't have time for anything else.

'Miss Landers wants to take you round to the stockroom,' said Sister Connor, 'to have a look at the wool. You might get some bright ideas about it. Doctor has given permission.'

Since she was still looking askance at Isobel over her forbidden excursions, she found her mission embarrassing and had no difficulty in reading the message of Isobel's raised eyebrows.

'All right. Say it.'

Isobel however wished to please Miss Landers, who was waiting in the doorway smiling hopefully. Besides, a trip to the stockroom or into any unknown region had all the attractions of a weekend abroad.

'No disloyal thought has crossed my mind,' she said in virtuous indignation.

'And I'm Marie of Rumania,' said Sister Connor. 'All right, Miss Landers. Don't keep her too long, will you?'

'It's so kind of you, dear,' said Miss Landers, as Isobel in dressing gown and slippers followed her along the inner corridor into the upper block towards Reception. 'You were so clever about the grey wool. I do have a problem with the wool. One has to face it. It isn't very attractive.'

'Cheap at the price, though,' said Isobel.

She was proud of her ability to charm Miss Landers into a real smile, not the nervous apologetic twitch with which she responded to the comments of the patients.

'Yes. You have to admit that.'

Beyond the dining room and before reception there was a side corridor which led past Doctor Stannard's office and closed unidentified doors to Miss Landers's store room. It was a large room, shelved like a shop, with stacks of basket shapes ready for the hanks of raffia stacked above them, boxes labelled 'Koala' and, filling two whole shelves of the short wall opposite Miss Landers's table and chair and her filing cabinet, a stack of neatly twisted skeins of khaki wool.

'Oh, my God,' said Isobel.

'Yes,' said Miss Landers.

'How long has it been here?'

'I don't know, dear. It was here when I came.'

249

'It must have been a pleasant surprise. It looks as if it was left over from the war.'

'It must have been. The patients won't take it even for children's clothes. They like something a bit brighter, and you can't blame them.' She allowed herself a moment of resentment. 'I don't know why they suppose that TB sends you colour blind.'

'No.' Isobel had been contemplating the stack of wool, reflectively. 'They think it improves the character. Somebody had a vision of rows of good little wogs sitting up in bed, knitting socks for soldiers, proud to be part of the war effort. It doesn't work like that.'

'No,' said Miss Landers. 'Indeed it doesn't.' She sighed. 'Isobel, dear, I mustn't keep you standing.' She moved the chair from behind her table and Isobel sat. 'I was just hoping, you know, that you might think of something.'

It was astonishing, even disturbing, that Isobel cared so much to succeed in this small enterprise. Of course she wanted to help poor Miss Landers, but there was more to it than that, and worse. It's no big deal, she said to herself, knowing that it was a far bigger deal than it should have been.

'It's not such a bad colour, if you forget about socks for soldiers. Do you have any white?'

'Only baby wool. Or 2-ply.'

'I could double the 2-ply. Suppose I knitted a plain sweater with the Basques and the cuffs and neck band in white, and then sewed a flower onto the shoulder. In white, I mean. It might work. You could keep it for a sample and see if you get any takers.'

Miss Landers brightened.

'There might be other colours that would go. We could look through the bins.'

'Good idea.'

The bins were filled with odd quantities of left-over wool donated by the Red Cross. Two ounces would do, they agreed, for the contrast colour.

They spent a companionable hour rummaging in the bins, each holding a skein of the khaki wool against possible contrasts.

They agreed that turquoise was perfect, accepted baby blue, shuddered at lemon, considered and rejected pale green, had an unexpected success with pale beige, of which there were eight whole ounces, a bonanza.

'Oh, Isobel!' Miss Landers spoke impulsively. 'It's wonderful to have somebody to take an interest. It's so discouraging always. I'm just sure this is going to work. Just giving people something that they'll like...it isn't easy.'

Positively, Isobel blushed.

'I'll need patterns for the flowers. Do you have any books on Irish crochet?'

Miss Landers laughed.

'You truly are a surprise. Irish crochet! I never would have thought it.'

'My grandmother was Irish. She taught me. I'll never be as good as she was, but I can manage most of the motifs.'

'I'll look through the leaflets.'

'If we don't have anything, Mrs Kent can find us something in town. We'll make up kits. I'll keep the Koala boxes. This is fun.'

251

She looked at her watch and said in alarm, 'Oh, Isobel! It's nearly lunch time. You should have been back half an hour ago.'

Isobel was counting out skeins of khaki and white.

'This is important, too. We're not just walking lungs.'

'I'll get you a chair. You must be tired out.'

Indeed, Isobel could not face the prospect of walking back to C Ward.

She nodded.

Miss Landers hurried out to Reception to put in a call for a chair.

Maybe, if this works, thought Isobel, I'll have enough credit to get some help for the boys. English lessons for Garry, for a start.

There ought to be more to occupational therapy than knitting and weaving.

'Somebody must be leaving,' said Miss Landers, when she returned with the information that the chair would be there in five minutes. 'There are two suitcases in Reception. "I wonder who's going?" I asked Clare, but she said Max had just put the suitcases there and said nothing.'

'Maybe Max knows. You could ask him. He must have got the suitcases out of the luggage room.'

'I don't think it's quite the thing to ask Max.'

'Well, we'll know soon enough.'

There was no need for apprehension though Isobel had been so long away. Everyone was preoccupied. Sister Connor was flushed and agitated. She did not notice the time of Isobel's return.

Katie had left. Her wardrobe was empty, her toothbrush and soap dish were gone from the basin, her cabinet too was bare.

Now Isobel understood that Katie had been moved from C Ward so that execution could be carried out in reasonable privacy.

She was glad to have work on hand to divert her from the thought of Katie's terror, Sister Connor's distress—it would certainly be Sister Connor who had faced the unpleasant job of evicting Katie, who must now be having lunch in the dining room and, after that, waiting unwillingly for the bus that would take her to the station, where she must take the train to the bleak, unwelcoming city.

'So you're back. And about time,' Sister Connor did snap at her.

Isobel forgave the irritable tone.

'Mrs Soames will be moving in with you.'

'Oh, great!' Isobel's delight was tempered by astonishment. 'But isn't she post-operative?'

Post-operative moved either out or to the upper ward.

'Talk about something you know something about,' said Sister Connor.

'Sorry, I'm sure.'

Isobel, still forgiving, thought that the scene with Katie must have been very unpleasant indeed.

Sister Connor said, 'Oh, don't mind me. It's been a bit of a day. And I have to get the girls back to make the bed up again. Sometimes people just don't think.'

'I wasn't worried.'

'I don't know why I have to be picking on you, when I want you to do me a favour.'

Clearly, it was a difficult favour to ask. She looked at Isobel in honest remorse.

'Come on. Out with it.'

'Will you give up your place in the bath queue to Mrs Soames? The doctors don't want her to be disturbed early in the morning.'

'You mean back to square one, cold-water country?'

'I'm afraid so. I don't say, "Would you mind?" because of course you mind. But there it is. This,' she added, 'is what comes of making yourself popular with doctors.'

'Well,' said Isobel, with sincerity, 'I think it's a very healthy sign when they start neglecting your health and comfort. I'll bear up.'

Sister Connor smiled at her in relief.

'There are worse around here than you.'

When Diana arrived with the lunch tray, she said, 'Lost your room mate.'

'I don't think she wanted to go.'

Diana set down a plate of stew in front of Isobel and waited for information.

'How did she take it?'

'I don't know. I wasn't here. I was round in the stock room with Miss Landers sorting wool.'

'Do you think they got you out of the way on purpose? Gee, did they think they'd have to use force?'

Diana's eyes shone.

'No. I think it was just coincidence.'

She was very glad of the coincidence, for she would have had to describe the painful scene to Diana, who showed her disappointment.

'Who's moving in, do you know?'

'Elsa Soames.'

'But isn't she post-op? She had a thora.'

Isobel had a nugget to offer.

'There's something up. I have to give up my place in the bath queue for her. Go back to the top of the queue. Cold-water country.'

'That's a bit rough. Was that Sister Connor's idea?'

'No. I think that came from higher up.'

'Oh, ho!' Diana was amused. 'It doesn't do to get too pally with the high brass, dear. They take advantage.'

Isobel picked up her knife and fork, prepared to end the conversation.

'I'd a damn sight rather they were fussing about her than fussing about me.'

'You're right there.'

Diana departed to carry lunch trays and the news along the ward.

After lunch Tamara arrived, alone and in a bad temper, carrying clean linen for the bed by the window.

'Made this bed once this morning and my shift over, Elaine gone already. Some people no consideration.'

She punished pillows and wrenched at sheets.

'Why you no take this bed? Should have when Val left.'

'I never move fast enough.'

Tamara laughed aloud, anger forgotten.

'Me neither. Never move fast enough. That's good. Like Elaine gets bus and I get caught. Some people, they always move fast, get there first. You know this lady come in?'

'I met her once on the verandah. She's had a thora.'

Elaine must have caught the same bus to town as Katie. Poor Katie, the only one who could see the little girl in the mirror, the little girl with the fever which never got better.

'And wash down cabinet, pooh,' said Tamara. 'Is orderly's work. They think they are God, I suppose?'

She straightened the bedcover and departed.

After such portents, Isobel waited in awe for the arrival of Mrs Soames.

She came by wheelchair, Max driving, Diana following with a handcase, Doctor Wang walking beside the chair.

'You will be happy here, I am sure. You will find Isobel a serious and agreeable companion.'

His eyes turned towards Isobel were, however, unseeing.

I'll pump you tomorrow, thought Isobel. I'm not going back to cold baths for nothing.

'Thank you, doctor.'

She did not recognise Isobel's existence, but that gave no offence. It was clear that she was absorbing bad news.

Diana helped her out of the chair, out of her royal blue velvet dressing gown and into bed.

She hung the dressing gown in the wardrobe and unpacked the hand case. On the cabinet top she set out an interesting array of accompaniments to the hospital diet: black peppercorns in a small grinder, salt crystals in another, a jar of mustard and small jars of sauces which Isobel did not recognise.

One kept one's sputum mug out of sight and used it with discretion and concern for others. Diana put Mrs Soames's sputum mug in the cabinet, incongruous next to a silver-backed hand mirror and a matching brush and comb.

When Mrs Soames moved in, she took possession.

Isobel wound white 2-ply and wondered what was required of her.

At the moment, it seemed, nothing.

Mrs Soames lay back and closed her eyes.

Diana, with a speaking look at Isobel, departed.

Mrs Soames remained silent and quiescent through rest period, afternoon tea and the hour before dinner.

Sister Knox brought in a special meal of omelette and bread and butter.

'You must eat, you know.'

'Of course. Really, this is most kind.'

'And you've met our Isobel. You'll love her. She's quite a favourite.'

Bloody liar, thought Isobel. What are they trying to sell to the poor woman?

'We had met.'

Mrs Soames nodded and smiled.

'You introduced me to Belloc.'

'Oh,' said Sister Knox, somewhat confused. 'That's all right, then.'

Doctor Wang came in with Sister Knox on evening rounds and asked if Mrs Soames was comfortable.

'She ate a nice omelette for dinner, Doctor,' said Sister Knox, managing to give the impression that she had fed her the omelette spoonful by affectionate spoonful.

Isobel was delighted to see on Mrs Soames's face the glimmer of a smile.

When Mrs Soames got up to go to the bathroom before Lights Out, Isobel got up to fetch her dressing gown. That was a mistake.

'I must not be a burden to you, my dear. I am truly quite capable of looking after myself. I am sorry not to have been communicative. I had some disappointing news, and the move was tiring.'

Isobel retired, relieved. After all, the woman was on C grade, like herself. But not, like herself, on the way up.

Next morning on the verandah, Isobel took advantage of a moment of privacy to ask Wang, 'What gives with Mrs Soames?'

Wang was silent. To discuss one patient with another was against the law.

'Just tell me what face I must wear.'

'A sober one, my dear.'

'What about the thora?'

He shook his head.

'Let us say, and for your ears only, that the operation did not have the desired effect.' He added, with irritation, 'It has never happened before.'

'What must I do?'

'Nothing, truly. Just respond if she speaks, give help where you can, I mean, physical help if she needs it. Most

258

of all she needs quiet, and so, by the way, do you. She will I think remain reserved. It is a disappointment.'

And that was an understatement.

'Isobel.'

'Yes?'

'This does not have any relevance to your case. It is asking a lot of you, the situation, but we thought, you have resources. You must not allow it to depress you.'

'Oh. Thanks.'

'I am telling you more than I should. We don't know the future, except that she cannot leave, may not progress beyond C grade. You can be trusted to be considerate. I hope you can be trusted to...maintain your own good spirits. Where else can we put her, my dear? But I don't want this to depress you.'

I'm to share a room with a dying woman and he's telling me far more than he should because...well, to prepare me.

'She is a very fine woman, with wonderful manners. And remember that you are a writer.'

Yes, she thought sadly. But whatever became of youth?

'Too much is asked of you, in my opinion,' said Sister Connor, when Mrs Soames had been wheeled up to Medical. 'And I told him so, straight. It's not right for anyone your age to have the responsibility. All he said was, "Oh, she'll cope." Never can tell him anything he doesn't want to know. Oh, God, forget I said that.'

'It's forgotten. And I'm not a baby. I'm twenty-one. Doctor Wang says I only have to remember that she needs

259

quiet. And he said that would do me good, too. Rather pointed, I thought.'

'Well, you haven't exactly distinguished yourself. But that isn't the point.'

On this she did not care to elaborate. Instead, she sighed and said, 'We'll just have to keep our eyes open.'

Elsa Soames in her gentle, whispering voice said, 'I'm not a very suitable companion for a young girl, I'm afraid.'

Though she had for a moment entertained the same thought, Isobel answered, 'What's so hot about being young? It's the same old world for young and old.'

'Yes, so it is.'

Elsa nodded, smiled and closed her eyes.

The atmosphere in Room 2 was now as quiet as she might ever have wished.

Elsa joined them sometimes on the verandah, to listen in silence.

When she stayed in bed, no-one commented on her absence.

Eily had made D grade and came dressed in a red and white striped shirt and a narrow black skirt, her thin waist cinched with a black patent belt, her feet in high-heeled black sandals. She had done up her hair in a smooth chignon; the only recognisable thing about her was the grin with which she greeted Isobel's startled look.

'Clothes make the woman, eh?'

'You look fabulous.'

Outdoor clothes evoked the outer world, disturbingly. Isobel wondered about Eily's life out there. Her clothes appeared plain but were reminiscent of Mrs Delaney.

Eily grinned again.

'You should see me when I'm really trying.'

And that was true. The swollen mouth and the flattened nose did not detract from Eily's glamour. They made it intriguing. She looked like a fine classical piece which had met with an interesting misfortune.

Meanwhile, Lilian had joined the group on the verandah. She was young, sandy-haired, grey-eyed, with a spatter of faint freckles across her cheekbones. She had delicate features, the most conspicuous a small but pugnacious chin. Her eyebrows and her eyelashes were discreetly darkened with cosmetics, a detail which added to the sophistication of her conversation. She was a teacher of English, articulate, argumentative and extremely well read. Wang's knowledge matched hers; they talked and argued about writers and philosophies new to Isobel: Sartre, Camus, existentialism…This widened Isobel's horizon and put her nose quite out of joint. She was ashamed of this; her policy must always be to listen and to learn, and so she did, but without any friendly feelings towards Lilian.

She had never heard of Kafka, found it difficult to believe that a literary masterpiece could deal with a man who woke up one morning and found himself turned into an insect.

'Truly? An insect?'

But Lilian and Wang both seemed to take this seriously.

'There's one thing I understood. When they told me I had TB, I thought, "That's it! K's crime! I've got it!" I had always identified with K, without knowing why. The secret unfitness, the crime that sets you apart, that's it!'

'Oh, no.' Wang was emphatic. 'It was being Jewish, clearly. The alien in society, the outcast. It is clear throughout.'

He paused because Lilian was grinning at him and began to smile, himself.

'To each his own crime.'

'I am lost,' said Isobel.

She was also extremely, shamefully, jealous of the understanding between the two.

'I shall bring you *The Trial*,' said Doctor Wang, 'and you can tell us what K's crime was. Then we shall know more about you.'

'I'm not sure I care for that, but I'll read the book.'

She acquired prestige with Lilian by reading the *New Yorker*.

'Where did you get hold of that? Do you have a subscription?'

'A friend sends it on to me. Well, he's not a friend, exactly. I haven't met him. He edits a magazine and he's published a couple of my stories, that's all. It's very good of him.'

'You write stories and get them published? Oh, lucky, lucky, lucky you!'

She spoke fiercely, with heart-felt envy.

'It's always lucky to be published.'

262

'It's lucky to be able to write at all. If only I could!'

'But if you want to, why don't you? All it takes is pen and paper. I mean, you know much more than I do about books. And you can say clever things, why can't you write them down?'

'I've tried and it doesn't work. Forget it. Can I have the *New Yorker* after you?'

'Yes. You'd better have it first. Then hand it on to Wang.'

'Can I read your stories?'

'There are only two of them. They're packed away with my other things. Somebody's minding them for me.'

'What's the magazine then?'

'*Seminal.*'

'You must be pretty good then. We had better shut up before I burst with envy.'

After this conversation, Isobel found Lilian less dominating and much more lovable.

Eily was on the wing. Briskly she stitched up the koala she had promised for Gladys's baby, then announced that she was off.

Sister Connor debated this decision at length and with energy.

'You don't give yourself a proper chance, Eily. It's always the same story. You're too impatient.'

'They can't keep me here if I'm not positive. I haven't thrown a positive for months.'

'That's not the whole story and you know it.'

Eily shook her head.

'Sorry. I'm off.'

'Can you be trusted to look after yourself?'

'Yeah. I'll take it easy.' She grinned. 'Cross my heart.'

'Well, I suppose you know your own business best. Though you've shown no sign of it yet.'

Eily remained obstinate.

On rounds, Doctor Stannard said, 'Give it a bit longer, Eily.'

He smiled in vain. He sighed and said, 'Well, try to stay away this time.'

'I'll do my best.'

It seemed that Doctor Stannard and Sister Connor shared some saddening knowledge about Eily and the life to which she was returning.

Isobel got an inkling of it when Eily, dazzling in a suit of beige linen and a shirt of coffee-coloured silk, came along the verandah to say goodbye. Her handbag and the matching shoes were of the same colour as the shirt and of the same impressive quality.

Sister Connor at the door of Room 2 said angrily, 'How are you going to get to town at this hour? And what train will you catch? You'll be there all day.'

Eily looked at her coldly.

'I'm not going by train. He's sending a car to pick me up.'

She shrugged as Sister Connor turned away.

Eily came into the room.

'Well, goodbye, kiddo.' She paused, then added, 'Will you take a piece of advice?'

'Sure.'

264

'Don't stay around here too long. You'll get webbed feet.'

'What a funny thing to say,' said Isobel. 'They'll put me out when the time comes, won't they? I certainly hope so. Who'd want to stay here?'

'Well, keep it in mind.'

'I'll miss you, Eily.'

'Likewise. It was nice knowing you. Cheeroh, then.'

'You too.'

Eily went away, leaving Isobel to wonder what she had meant by that quite superfluous piece of advice.

'Isobel.'

'Yes, Elsa?'

Isobel had completed the back and the front of the khaki sweater and was now working on a white cuff. She put it down in order to respond to a request from Elsa. She did this willingly, for Elsa asked for little and was most considerate.

The request, however, was unexpected.

'Tell me about yourself.'

She answered in alarm, 'You know you mustn't talk too much, Elsa.'

'I shall not talk much. I shall listen.'

'But what sort of thing do you want to know?'

'Everything. Love, work, ambitions...'

'Oh. Love as in tennis. That is, zero.'

'Why?'

'I can't answer that.'

265

'You are an attractive young woman. You must have had approaches.'

Trevor and Robbie. She thought of them with painful regret.

'Yes.'

'Were they not acceptable to you?'

'They would have been if I had been acceptable to myself, I suppose.'

'Go on.'

'I'm not a good girl. I'm not dear, sweet little Isobel. I'm a tramp. That's the truth. I go with men who despise me and treat me like dirt, but if a man comes offering... anything, affection, admiration, anything but beastly, cold sex, I go for my life.'

'Go on.'

'It all began, I think, because my mother hated me.'

'That happens oftener than people suppose. They never want to believe it. Did your parents get on together?'

'No.'

'So you had no model for sexual happiness.'

'I could not believe that love existed,' said Isobel. 'Or at least not for me.'

She began to talk, to tell the story of Frank's odyssey.

'Not that he was in love with me, no way. But he cared for me and it made me feel, I have to look at things differently, somehow, or he'll have done all that walking for nothing. I don't know if you can follow.'

'You saw yourself through the eyes of the enemy. You must learn to see yourself through the eyes of those who love you.'

266

'It's not just myself. It's like, I'm a member of the human race, and every member of the human race deserves... I don't know. Respect? If you deny that to yourself, you're damaging the fabric, somehow.'

'Love thy neighbour as thyself. First, love thyself.'

'It's a lot to ask, in the circumstances.'

Elsa after a long pause said, 'Would you like to tell me the circumstances?' She added, 'There's no harm in talking to me, you know.'

Her own circumstances at present were strangely privileged.

'Well, when I say that my mother hated me, I mean that she hated me so much that she acted out murder fantasies. My earliest memory...people ask you sometimes for your earliest memory, like a parlour game. But mine is of my mother holding me down a lavatory and pulling the chain. It wasn't so much the terror and the humiliation as the desperate desire to be rid of me, to flush me away like... oh, hell. In all my life, I've never felt that I had firm ground under my feet. I've always been...like...suspended over a void. A great, black void.'

'How old were you?'

'I suppose two. I don't really know. But it happened. I remember it.'

'Yes. It would not be easy to forget. Go on.'

Elsa's voice was calm and matter of fact. That tone, and the quiet of the room, which their subdued voices hardly interrupted, made speaking easy.

Isobel went on.

'I think it was that she had planned for a son. Fate hadn't just frustrated her. It had disobeyed her. You understand?'

'Yes. I see her clearly, I think. Were you the only child?'

'No. I have an elder sister. She was acceptable.'

'I think that is enough for today. Tomorrow you will tell me a little more.'

This was the first of many conversations—of one conversation, rather, with pauses sometimes of a day or a few hours, sometimes of two minutes or so while Elsa gathered breath or Isobel found words.

She told her life story, little by little, even to the matter she had never thought to confess.

'I used to make phone calls. To people I didn't know. Hideous phone calls, spitting out rage and hatred.'

'To men and women?'

Suddenly, Isobel began to laugh.

'Elsa, you are like a priest. Do you know the story of the man who had committed murder? He wasn't found out but he couldn't bear the burden on his conscience any longer, so he decided to kill himself. On his way to the river he passed a High Anglican church with the notice: Confessions 5 p.m. to 6 p.m. So he went in and told the minister about his horror murder, and the minister said he would go with him to the police and give him spiritual comfort as he confessed. He didn't want to go to the police, he thought he preferred the river. But further down the street he passed a Catholic church and he thought he'd give it one last try. So he went in to the confessional, knelt down and said to the

priest. "Father, I have sinned. I have committed murder."
And the priest said, "Yes, my son. How many times?"

'I tell you my worst sin and you say, "To men and
women?" Just the same tone. Well, if a man answered the
phone I said, "Sorry. I must have the wrong number," and
hung up.'

For Elsa, laughter was a dangerous indulgence. She
smiled.

'So they were the words you couldn't say to your
mother.'

Isobel was silent in astonishment.

'So they were. I never thought of that. And isn't it
obvious?'

'I should like,' said Elsa, 'to say a word or two to her
myself. Your anger is understandable. I think it is inescap-
able. And that is enough for today.'

'Isobel!'

'Yes?'

'I've been thinking about your mother and about anger.'

'For two whole days?'

'Not continuously. But I have a thought which might be
useful. I believe there is some progression here. Would you
accept that your mother suffered physical abuse as a child?'

'Yes. No doubt about that, I should say.'

'But her attacks on you, damaging as they were, were,
as you say, sham. Not real murder.'

'Poison in jest. No offence in the world,' said Isobel
with bitterness.

269

'Plenty of offence, but no murder. Infanticide does happen. It didn't happen that time. Perhaps she was learning to manage her anger a little.'

'I thought it was fear of the consequences that saved me.'

'That might have been a motive, but perhaps she was fighting her own anger. And you went a step further, into verbalising. And in a way that did as little damage as possible. After all, getting a nasty anonymous phone call isn't much to worry about. We've all had them and survived.'

'You'll be turning poison pen letters into a virtue.'

'I'm not saying that they are a virtue. Only that they are better than poison. And those letters go to a chosen target. That makes a difference. I think you handled your anger very cleverly. You made a great commotion of evil in your own mind without doing any real harm. One might say that you spent your rage on the air, the almost empty air.'

'You make it all sound very trivial,' said Isobel, mock pettish yet pettish.

'I diminish your sins. If I diminish you, it is because you identify yourself with your sins.

'Elsa, are you a psychiatrist?'

'No, my dear. A pianist.'

She spoke the word with a touch of amusement which made Isobel aware that many people would have known this.

Elsa added, 'But I have lived and sinned. Who hasn't had to cope with anger?'

She closed her eyes, which was the sign that she was too tired for speech.

*

Later, Isobel resumed the conversation.

'About anger. Sometimes it sneaks up on you, in disguise. Like tactlessness. You think, "Whatever made me say that, to her of all people?" And it's anger that's writing the script.'

She told the story of Val and her misadventures with foreign language, of her jealousy of Isobel's friendship with Wang and then of the poem read in Mandarin, at her request and under poor Val's nose.

'It was a cruel thing to do. I thought so afterwards, but I couldn't really say I didn't mean it. It was too precisely tailored to the situation.'

'Perhaps it brought enlightenment.'

'I don't think Val ever sought enlightenment.'

Elsa was now exhausted and the conversation ceased.

Mrs Kent brought with the library books a crochet book with instructions for flowers and other motifs.

'Miss Landers asked me to buy it in town. I hope this is what you want. What's it all about?'

'We are trying to shift some of that khaki wool. I'm going to crochet motifs to sew on the shoulder of a sweater.'

'Well, I wish you joy, dear. I don't think that khaki will ever move. Even the moths won't touch it.'

'It's not too bad.' Isobel fetched the completed sections of the sweater from her cabinet. 'We're experimenting with contrasting colours. Then I crochet a motif and we put it all together as a kit. This one is going to be a sample.'

Mrs Kent picked up the khaki and white sweater front and studied it.

271

'Well, perhaps you're right. It doesn't look too bad. Perhaps if one called the colour something else. Like desert gold, perhaps.'

'Don't put ideas into my head,' said Isobel glumly. 'I'm trying to make it respectable.'

'Don't be wicked, now. What a little treasure you are. I hope it doesn't make Elsa cry. Remember poor Val bursting into tears when I said I loved the grey lace?'

'She thought that knitting lacy patterns in 8-ply was positively illegal.'

Elsa whispered, 'I think it's charming.'

'How is Val, by the way? Has anyone heard?'

'Gladys had a letter. She's very well. She has to go back for a check-up at the Clinic in six months. Have you had any news of Eily?'

'You won't hear any more from Eily, dear.' Mrs Kent knew something she did not care to tell. 'Out of sight out of mind with that one.'

'That one' pronounced in a tone which suggested the less heard about Eily and her doings the better.

This saddened Isobel, who would have liked very much to keep in touch with Eily.

Sim appeared when Elsa had been in residence for a fortnight. He came in bearing a hyacinth in a pot, advanced and kissed Elsa on both cheeks, saying, 'Darling! I only just heard. I got back from Italy last week and rang Lee, who told me the news.'

'Not very good news.'

'No. Well, here I am.'

272

'Sim, this is Isobel. Isobel, Sim Frobisher, a very old friend of mine.'

'Sim short for Simon, a name I much dislike,' he said. 'My parents could never understand why I screamed so loudly at my christening. They thought it was an instinctive dislike of organised religion. There was that, too, of course. Happy to know you, Isobel.'

Isobel was now free to study Sim's appearance. He was elderly. He could never be called old; age instead of withering him seemed to have peeled him, so that the skin of his sharp-boned face shone pink. He had sharp, bright blue eyes and sparse white hair, a figure of less than medium height but neat proportions. The words 'spry' and 'dapper' seemed to have been coined for him. His pale grey suit was of excellent cut, his shirt was snowy white, his tie was of rich silk in darker shades of grey. His shoes shone. One guessed that someone else had polished them.

'My room mate. Though I am not very good company for a young woman.'

'Ah,' said Sim, observing the book Isobel had been reading. 'But a young woman who reads Kafka. I should think she would find you very good company.'

'Yes,' said Isobel. 'I'm the one who profits by the acquaintance.'

Such formal talk seemed in the circumstances to be acceptable.

Sim was pleased by it.

'That was nicely said. I have profited very much from her acquaintance, too.'

'You're a flatterer.'

273

She smiled at him as if flatterers were her favourite people.

'It is really good of you to come so far to see me. Did you drive up?'

'Yesterday. I've booked into a marvellously decadent old pub, with stained-glass transoms over the door to the loos. I do not lie. Stained glass. I'm here to stay.'

'Sim! How long?'

'Why...'

They won't mention death in front of me, thought Isobel. Like sex...not in front of the children.

'You've given me so much joy with your music, my dear. It's time for me to repay. I'll give Europe a miss next winter. I'm staying for as long as you need me. If you get tired of me, you can say so and I'll take myself off.'

'It may be years.'

'I very much hope so. We'll make them good years.'

Elsa turned her head away. Sim took her hand.

Isobel bent her head to her book, wishing she could give them the privacy they deserved.

She considered getting up and going out on the pretext of a visit to the lavatory, the only excuse for leaving her bed, but the moment had passed.

Elsa said, 'Now tell me about Italy. Talk about the landscape.'

This was subject matter to which one could listen without offence. Sim talked, and talked well, conjured up cypress trees, olive groves, hills crowned with ruined temples, until Elsa closed her eyes.

He got up to go.

'I'll be back tomorrow morning. Is there anything I can bring you?'

Elsa opened her eyes and said with astonishing energy, 'Tomatoes!'

This amused them all, Elsa included.

'Tomatoes it shall be. I suppose the food is rather dreary.'

'It's not so bad if you season it properly. Freshly ground salt and pepper make a difference.' She gestured towards the grinders and summoned a smile. 'Isobel calls them the aspersions. Casting aspersions on the food. But I'm persuading her.'

Sim looked with interest at Isobel.

'She's lucky in your company. She loves a joker. Even gives marks for trying.'

'I'll admit it wasn't much of a joke,' Isobel agreed amiably.

She was not sensitive on this subject, being aware that her own wit often outstripped her wellbeing. She was pleased to see that she had startled him.

He recovered quickly.

Indeed, one did give Sim marks for trying. His eagerness to please was reassuring.

Isobel looked back always to the first weeks of Sim's visit as a happy time. In the company of grieving Sim and dying Elsa she was happier than she had ever been. There was the physical pleasure of health returning: she knew that the illness was over and the languor which kept her quiescent was the beginning of convalescence. There was the animal satisfaction she got out of enjoying food again, eating from hunger rather than forcing food down with determination and often with fortitude.

Elsa too was growing stronger. She was conscientious in attempting the food Sim brought and sometimes managed half a portion. Doctor Stannard smiled and declared her condition stable, if not a little improved.

Isobel was living on the shore of a great, shining lake of devotion which sometimes overflowed to touch her. It made no demands of her, except the respect she gave unasked; it did not exclude her. It existed, simply, and changed the climate round her.

Sim observed the routine of the hospital. He arrived every morning during the free hour, which gave him some private time with Elsa, while Isobel joined the group on the verandah. He brought gifts of food, which Isobel shared, stayed to prepare the lunch and then drove to the restaurant on the highway for his own meal. He came back for a visit at some time in the afternoon, observing the rest period with care. He was tolerated by the staff, his devotion to Elsa being much admired.

On Friday afternoons he drove to the city for the weekend.

'I have to collect some scandal to amuse you, darling,' he said to Elsa.

He talked at her request, or they were silent in a shared peace which made Isobel feel that she was in church—not the Catholic church of her childhood but some empty church in a foreign place, a space which imposed respect though it asked no obeisance.

At these moments she wished she could offer them privacy, but they were unselfconscious, untroubled by her presence, so that she began to share their serenity.

Sim brought salads and fruit and delicacies from David Jones' food basement: anchovies, caviar, foie gras, which Isobel did not like at all but was glad to have tasted. It would be useful for future fiction to know what the rich ate.

His main mission was to persuade Elsa to eat. He searched the town for supplies of appetising food, arriving one morning in triumph, carrying two screw-top jars which he set down one on each cabinet.

'Potato salad with sour cream dressing,' he said modestly. 'I have found the most divine little delicatessen. Run by migrants, a married couple, Czech, and such charmers. And they take food seriously. We talked for half an hour about recipes. They grow their own herbs. Basil on the tomatoes. I couldn't believe it.'

Isobel, who could hardly believe that cream which had been acknowledged to be sour was considered fit for human consumption, eyed her portion with apprehension. She was determined not to betray her inexperience to these sophisticates: she attempted the first mouthful with apprehension, the second with relief, and the third with appetite.

There was food for the mind, too. Sim talked about the theatre, reporting on the plays he had seen in London, and Isobel made no pretence of absenting herself from the conversation. She had too many questions to ask, and his answers were enlightening. Indeed, she was useful, since Elsa confined herself to listening and smiling.

He did bring back scandal from the city: political scandal, literary scandal, stories of betrayal, divorce, slanderous anecdotes about the lives of people whose names were known to those who did not know them. She should not have listened to that, of course, and did pretend to be reading, but it was too entertaining to be ignored.

He brought progress reports on the foundering marriage of a pair named Paul and Marianne.

'Looked at one way, Marianne's a saint; looked at another way, she's a kind of greenhouse where the vices of others come into full and glorious bloom. As for Rachel' (who must be the villain of the piece) 'she's so suspicious of men that she has to get some other woman to try them first.'

Elsa had smiled and nodded, whispering, 'Like an emperor with his taster.'

'Precisely.'

Elsa listened to Sim's gossip with the quiet relish of one sucking on an acid drop. This was at first disconcerting to Isobel, who had expected a nobler stance. But there it came again—the illusion that suffering ennobled.

Herself, knowing one system of ethics only, she put these remarks and many others away for future use.

Sim was looking for a house in the town.

'I talked to that remarkably pretty doctor of yours. He says there'd be no objection to my taking you out for the day, so long as you feel up to it and there's not too much walking.'

'The hearty breakfast,' said Elsa.

'Now, don't let's have any naughty talk. I can move in the record collection and get a decent player so that we can have music.'

'Oh!'

Elsa closed her eyes, this time not in fatigue but in joy.

'As for the furniture, we'll simply have to avert our eyes. Such horrors as I have seen, my dear!'

He went into the matter of wicker whatnots, photo frames encrusted with shells ('like some disgusting skin disease, my dear'), flights of plaster ducks, an occasional table with sinister legs ('Darling, I thought the object was *about to walk*').

'I shall simply have to dismiss aesthetics, that's all. What do you think, darling? Could you make the effort?'

'To hear music again, yes.'

'Then I'll settle for this last place, I think. And I'll bring up the records next weekend.'

Elsa's day out was planned, as Elsa whispered with amusement, like a safari, every detail a triumph or a concession in the long struggle between Sim and Sister Connor, who made every possible objection to the scheme. Sim asked for a wheelchair to take Elsa to the main door, he would bring the car to the door, there was no need for Elsa to dress, since he would take the car to the door of the rented house, she would lie down all day, yes, on a suitable bed—would Sister Connor care to come and inspect his arrangements? There would certainly be no visitors. He would observe every rule.

To Sister Connor's objections he opposed Doctor Stannard's permission, in the light of which he had taken a

279

lease on a house. If he had known of all these restrictions he doubted that he would have taken such a step. He did not mention money, but its presence was understood.

Isobel noticed that, for all Sim's eagerness to please an audience, he could be sharp; he believed that the spending of money brought privilege and he did not care to have that belief undermined.

He had expected to take Elsa to the house whenever she felt strong enough for the excursion. That was not to be allowed.

Allowed?

Sim's astonishment amused them all.

The excursions were limited to one a week, on Thursday after rounds, with the doctor's approval.

Sister Connor did not hold that all animals were equal but some were more equal than others.

It was on the night after the second excursion that Isobel was awakened by the noise of water running full and hard in the basin.

She could not turn on a light. The lights went out at the main switch at nine o'clock. After that there was only the glare from the great torches the nurses carried on their rounds and the moonlight and starlight which prevented C Ward from ever being completely dark.

Elsa was standing at the basin.

'Elsa. Are you all right?'

'Did I wake you? It's nothing, dear. Just a bit pazzy. Those wretched tablets. I'm just getting back to bed. Go to sleep.'

*

280

Isobel however lay awake wondering at Elsa's use of the word 'pazzy', which was certainly not part of her vocabulary. She might have said 'bilious' if it had been relevant. Isobel did not think it was relevant. If the PAS tablets brought on a bilious attack, that happened infallibly before lunch.

She had come back to the hospital, withdrawn in a quiet happiness which she did not seem to wish to interrupt by eating dinner.

Sister Knox's affectionate protest, 'Darling, if you're naughty you won't be allowed out again,' had roused her only to a look of polite interest which quelled Sister Knox and made Doctor Wang particularly inscrutable.

Isobel, sure that Elsa was living in the memory of the day's music, had not wished to disturb her.

She had got up to go to the lavatory, had cleaned her teeth and washed at the basin without any sign of bodily weakness. They had retired with minimal communication for the night.

But *pazzy*?

Isobel was sure that what Elsa had been washing away at the basin had been not vomit but blood. That was what they called a haemorrhage.

She did not feel any urge to question further. That was the philosophy of the establishment. Living kills, but one may choose to prefer it to mere survival. If Elsa wished to risk her life in order to enjoy her music, the decision was hers.

Isobel was prepared to accept it calmly. After all, it couldn't have been a major haemorrhage and music was music, life was life.

*

On the following Thursday, Doctor Stannard said to Isobel, 'Time to get your boots on.'

'Am I going to D grade?'

'Yes. You have escaped the knife. Not by your own efforts, may I say?'

Isobel was too happy to resent this thrust, but with Elsa in her thoughts she repressed her delight.

Doctor Wang too was smiling. It was a moment of celebration.

'And what about that transfer, doctor?' asked Sister Connor.

'Oh, yes, of course. Isobel is to go down to Room 8 with Phyllis. A more suitable arrangement, we think.'

Isobel thought at once and with deep dismay that she would miss Sim's lunches.

Elsa's eyes had filled with tears.

'Please, please, don't move her. Don't take her away from me.'

'I'm not a nuisance. I'm not noisy,' said Isobel. 'And I can do things for Elsa.'

Doctor Stannard looked from one to the other. The tears on Elsa's face were a powerful argument.

In a voice full of pity and affection, he said, 'I think, Sister, we may leave things as they are.'

She knows all about me. I'm a dirty tramp and I've made dirty anonymous phone calls and she still wants me to stay.

Isobel's joy over this was greater than her joy over the promotion to D grade.

'If it suits them,' said Sister Connor, with a jaded look at Isobel.

No use trying to save some people from themselves.

IV
MORNINGTON D GRADE

On the following afternoon, translated in checked seer-sucker and summer sandals, Isobel set off for the lower block and took the wooden walkway which led past the men's wards in order to keep her promise to visit Lance.

Heads turned as she passed. She heard murmurs. Any new face was a break in the terrible monotony, therefore an object of interest.

However, the silence that fell as she entered G Ward seemed excessive. It made her self-conscious. Was there something odd about her appearance? She had put on weight, so that the seersucker was a little tight. Was it too tight? Was she bursting out of it? Did she look like a skinned rabbit?

To the man in the first bed, she said too abruptly, 'I'm looking for Lance. He's in here, isn't he?'

The man said, pointing, 'Over there in bed six.'

In bed six Lance was lying supine, staring at the ceiling.

'Hullo, Lance.' She pulled up a chair and sat beside him. He did not turn his face.

'Well, how's it going?'

'Don't expect a civil answer from that sulky little bastard,' said the man in the next bed. 'Wouldn't throw a word to a dog.'

Lance addressed the ceiling.

'You done this to me. You got me moved.'

'Lance, no. I did not!'

'You got Val moved down to surgery because she got on your nerves. They all say that. "Waiting for your op? Just get across that Isobel," they say. "Down to surgery in three days." Then I was next.'

'I think maybe they moved Val out because she couldn't cope with sharing, with me or anyone. I got on her nerves more than she got on mine. She was breaking down emotionally. I had nothing to do with it. Anyhow, she was ready for surgery. Lance, this is mad.'

'They moved her up the list because she got on your nerves. Everybody knows Stannard is sweet on you. He just does anything you want.'

I should be so lucky.

Isobel looked round for help to the neighbour, shaking her head in a denial that could not reach Lance.

'Don't pay any attention to him. Let him stew,' the neighbour said, looking shifty.

'Lance, we were friends.'

'If you was a friend of mine, I'd still be up there in C Ward.'

'I've never said a word against you to Doctor Stannard or to Sister Connor or to Doctor Wang. You have to admit that you fixed yourself with Doctor Wang. Even so, he would never speak against you. It was your own doing, you wouldn't stay in bed. If I was to blame for anything, it was for covering for you. And we were friends when you left. You asked me to come and see you.'

'Didn't know then what I know now. Stannard's baby, they say. Stannard's little bit of fluff. Don't cross her.'

'Who says? How can they say what isn't true? I wouldn't dare to say a word to Doctor Stannard unless he was talking to me. And I wouldn't talk about any other patient.'

This, she remembered, was not quite true in fact, though true in spirit.

'If you had wanted me to stay, I'd have stayed.'

'They were trying to do their best for you. You didn't make it easy.'

Lance continued to study the ceiling.

She turned in desperation to the neighbour.

'There's not a word of truth in it. I don't know where he got the idea. It's bad for him to be so bitter. And to believe such lies.'

'Don't worry your head about it,' the man said, but with discomfort.

For that moment, Isobel hated Mornington. There was poison in the air, like marsh gas that turned an act of kindness into a will-o'-the-wisp of evil. She did not believe the man in the next bed was innocent. If he hadn't helped to poison Lance's mind, he hadn't offered any antidote to poison, either.

She walked out and went no more to the men's ward.

Lance had known her. There was nothing she could do if he preferred the lies he heard to the truth he had experienced. But what a shame. What a rotten shame! She grieved for what he might have been.

Lance had been a burden. She wanted to be done with burdens.

She walked in the garden, astonished to discover the limit of her strength. Health was after all a long way off. Wellbeing was no guarantee.

She visited the store, run by a stout little ex-wog named Arthur, who had been given six months to live twelve years ago and had beaten the rap. He ran the post office and bank and dispensed paper, envelopes, soap, shampoo, razors, shaving cream, a few cosmetics, a few paperbacks, sweets, sewing equipment, things needed on a journey.

She thought about finishing the Robbie poem and rereading the long story which should be turned into a novel, and decided to put off serious effort for the time being.

She crocheted dahlias, carnations, raised roses and flat lilies, and stitched them onto cardboard. She spent time in the stockroom making up sweater kits, ten skeins of khaki, one motif in contrast and the rest of the contrast with a leaflet of instructions, all packed in the empty Koala boxes.

Miss Landers persuaded her to begin on some knitting for herself.

'You'll be needing new clothes when you go out, you know. What about a dress? Or,' she added hopefully, 'a dress and a jacket? That jacket Lilian is making with the mustard trim is very smart.'

Perhaps she was trapped in a fairy story where she had to dispose of a hundredweight of khaki 4-ply before she could gain her freedom. She accepted the offer of wool and began to knit a dress for the next winter. In the summer weather, the knitting went slowly, but there was plenty of time.

She wrote the news of her promotion to Olive ('Give my love to Frank') and to Tom Fenwick, and wished that she could write it to Boris.

She stayed away from Room 2 as much as possible, to leave Sim and Elsa alone together. Since the episode of the suspected haemorrhage, Elsa had become taciturn, repressing irritation with an obvious attempt at politeness. She would not give up the excursions to Sim's house, though she returned exhausted. She had protested to Stannard that the PAS tablets were upsetting her stomach too much and causing vomiting fits. Stannard listened in silence. He conferred with Sim in private. Isobel guessed the point at issue: must Elsa give up what made life worth living, in order to preserve life? Wang, who touched on the subject without mentioning names, said that a doctor had no freedom of choice in such a matter. His duty was at all times to preserve life.

'Is that also your opinion as a man?' asked Isobel.

'My opinion as a man I left behind me when I became a doctor.'

Elsa wanted to stop medication. The PAS tablets were causing all her discomfort—she never called it anything worse than discomfort.

Stannard did not ask searching questions about the attacks she complained of, but he did not give way about the medication.

At last he forbade the excursions, though that was hardly necessary. There were days when Elsa could not get out of bed. Diana arrived with the bath trolley, pulled down the blind and shut the door, as she had done long ago in Room 5 for Isobel.

On those occasions, Isobel withdrew, thinking sadly that it should be the beginning, not...

The happy days were over. They had not lasted long, but they would be long remembered. The moments of shared peace between Sim and Elsa grew longer and more frequent: Isobel guessed that these were their happiest times and she tried not to intrude on them.

She was still on streptomycin and was required to stay in bed until the injection had been given. She was required to return for rest period and to stay in bed for dinner and then till morning.

She talked with Wang and Lilian on the verandah, ate lunch in the dining room, worked in the stock room, took her book into the garden, rootless and restless, suffering in sympathy with the pair of friends.

Elsa wanted to see the ocean. Sim's house, the dwelling he had abandoned to be with her, stood on the heights above Bilgola Beach. Elsa seemed to believe, and insisted against all medical advice, that beside the ocean she would get better.

'Take me there, Sim. Please.'

'But what about your medication, love?'

'I shan't need it. I *know*. And those wretched tablets are making me sick.'

It was sad to see serene, rational Elsa peevish and unreasonable.

'I'll ask Doctor Stannard.'

Doctor Stannard said he would see about it.

Maybe at Christmas.

Christmas promised to be a bleak season.

Stannard gave way about the trip to Bilgola Beach.

Sim and Isobel were both depressed by what was implicit in his consent. The pair set off at the beginning of Christmas week, Elsa elated and Sim unusually silent.

Doctor Wang was on holiday with his wife and son.

Every patient who was fit to travel and had a home to go to went home for Christmas. Isobel felt like a child left behind at boarding school.

The Red Cross distributed parcels of Christmas gifts. Isobel received a tin of talcum powder and two embroidered handkerchiefs. She entered them on her list of things for which she must one day make a return: Red Cross, one Christmas parcel.

With a scattering of other patients she ate roast fowl and plum pudding under loops of paper chains made by volunteer patients.

In spite of the recent improvement in her prospects, she was melancholy.

In the afternoon, as Isobel lay reading on her bed, Olive arrived with her husband Terry. Isobel had imagined Terry as a downtrodden mother's boy and was relieved to find him tall and strong, handsome and cheerful.

'We thought you might be lonely, it being Christmas day. Terry's bought a car. There was nothing to stop us. We've only ourselves to please. We thought we'd take a picnic lunch and come up to see you and bring you your Christmas presents. So here we are.'

She had brought a bag full of wrapped parcels which she handed over one by one.

Chocolates from Frank, a pretty scarf from Nell and Sandra, a bottle of scent from that odd little Jenny, who loved her without knowing her, Christmas cake in a handsome tin from Olive.

Olive had one parcel left.

'I kept this till last. This'll kill you. Guess who from?'

'I couldn't possibly guess. Give me a clue.'

'Well, it's a violet vase imported from Czechoslovakia...'

'Oh, my God. You don't mean to tell me...' She unwrapped the little crystal vase and gaped at it in wonder.

'Right. Mr Walter himself. You see, you never miss the water till the well runs dry!'

They sat laughing at tyrants discomfited and pomposity brought low, but Isobel remembered Mr Walter on the day that Nick had died. Beautiful Nick had died on his motorbike, and she had been sent by Helen to break the news to Diana, that obsessed lover who had persecuted him with her passion. Helen had rung her at the office and she had screamed, 'Dead? Don't be ridiculous! How can he be dead?' And Mr Walter, hearing the rumble of the cart carrying forward, had been respectful, even solicitous, looking up maps and bringing water and aspirin. Mr Walter had heard the rumble of the cart and become humble and human.

She could not talk of that to Olive and to Terry. It would break the mood.

Terry brought a bottle of sherry and three plastic beakers out of a carrier bag.

'Is this allowed?'

'Anything is allowed today.'

Terry poured the wine and lifted his beaker.

'Here's to better days coming! For all of us.'

Isobel drank a mouthful, which made her feel rather giddy.

How I've misjudged this world, she thought. How wickedly I've misjudged it. She put the beaker down carefully.

She was feeling dangerously elated.

'I don't think I'd better have any more just now.'

'Right. Take it easy.'

'I suppose you get the message of the violet vase,' said Olive.

Terry spluttered into his wine.

'Does he want me to come back? I won't be working full time, maybe for two years. And I wouldn't want to take Jenny's job.'

'But to do the German mail?' Olive giggled. 'You are positively the only hope he has of getting rid of Mr Oskar. If old Mr Stephen knows you want your job back, that's about the only thing that will move him to sack his old pal.'

'I made a bit of a scene, remember.'

'Oh, but you were sick! They've all agreed that you were sick. That's the only way they can save face.'

'I suppose I could do that. Yes. I'm sure I could manage the mail. I'm so used to it. But I don't know how long I'll be here.'

'You said in your last letter you might be out early in the New Year.'

'It's not definite. It all depends on Doctor Stannard. He has the last word.'

'If you do take the job,' said Terry, 'just make sure that they pay you properly. Olive says that old fool gets as much for his efforts as you got full time.'

'I shouldn't tell secrets about the pay book,' said Olive.

'That's how you play into their hands,' said Terry sharply. 'Remember they're out for what they can get and they'll give nothing away.'

'Except a violet vase,' said Isobel, who had drunk another mouthful and begun to giggle.

'We mustn't tire you out. Time to go.'

Olive got up to wash the beakers at the sink. She left the rest of the wine, saying, 'You might feel like a glass later. It will put you to sleep.'

293

'I was expecting such a miserable Christmas,' said Isobel, 'and I've enjoyed it so much. Tell everyone thank you. And I hope I'll meet Jenny some day.'

'Make it soon,' said Olive and kissed her on the cheek. Terry nodded goodbye, with a smile that promised friendship.

Elsa did not return.

In the New Year, Sim came to collect her belongings.

He was snappish, even apparently resentful, as he said, 'She's better already.' He added firmly, 'Very much better. Never should have been here, of course. It was because of that operation, which was supposed to work miracles and has been nothing but a setback. And that wretched medication which did nothing but make her ill.'

As he spoke, he was folding Elsa's clothes into the small suitcase from the luggage room.

Isobel watched, tormented by anxiety.

No word for me? Is there no message for me?

Elsa had wept, saying, 'Don't take her away from me!' and that after hearing Isobel's confessions. Her tears had made nothing of Isobel's transgressions, had convinced Isobel that she was after all an acceptable person.

But had she wept only for fear of worse? Was it only because Isobel was quiet, read books, spoke Elsa's language a little?

She prolonged the conversation, hoping the message would come. Perhaps Elsa had sent it and Sim had forgotten it.

'What does Doctor Stannard think?'

Sim shrugged.

'She has her own man in the city. He gave me a letter for Stannard. Whatever happens, she's not coming back.' About to shut the suitcase, he looked about for trifles he might have overlooked.

There on Elsa's cabinet were the small salt and pepper grinders.

He picked them up and handed them over.

'You're to have these. She said to tell you...wait a minute. You are to continue to cast aspersions. Those were her words.'

'Oh, thank you. Thank you so much. And tell her I appreciate the thought.'

Sim laughed at her enthusiasm.

'It isn't a very rich gift, after all.'

And that's all you know, thought Isobel.

Now it was Isobel's chance to move into the bed by the window. She did not have the heart to claim it.

After lunch, needing occupation, she went to work in the stock room. When she got back to Room 2, she found the bed occupied by a small, scrawny girl of about seventeen, pale-haired and pale-faced, who stared at Isobel with small, frightened eyes.

'Hullo. Who are you?' asked Isobel, sounding bright and reassuring.

The girl whispered, 'Cheryl.' She tried again and gave it more voice. 'Me name's Cheryl.'

'How long have you known?' asked Isobel.

'About a month.'

'Gives you a shock, doesn't it?'

'You're dead right there. I just about passed out. You're Isobel, aren't you? The nurse said you'll show me the ropes. Tell me anything I want to know, like? That's what she said. What's it like here?'

'Not bad. Not bad at all.'

'She said, that nurse said, it can happen to anyone. The lady in the bed before me, she was a real famous person, a pianist. Is that right?'

'Yes, that's right.'

Cheryl uttered a small, nervous giggle.

'Well, you gonna find me a bit of a change.'

Isobel grinned at her with instant affection.

'Perhaps I was due for a change.'

She was now becalmed.

This was the time to take out the long story which Fenwick had returned and to reread it, at least.

She considered that idea and dismissed it. She thought, not yet.

She did take out Robbie's poem, added a line or two, decided it was all too difficult and put it away.

Wang said that this was a normal state, that she must not let mind and conscience impose on her body, which had its own timetable.

The literary discussions had lapsed since Lilian had gone down to surgery. Isobel did not miss them. She did not want to make the effort even to read poetry. She swallowed detective stories whole. They were smoothly written, intended for easy consumption. She visited the library and helped herself.

She worked on the dress of khaki wool which she was to wear next winter in the outside world, which seemed far away, unreal, in spite of letters from Olive and magazines from Tom Fenwick. She found the magazines a burden, a test of intellect.

Cheryl watched her knitting and said, 'Do you get the wool for nothing?'

'Indeed you do.'

'Will you show me how to do it? I could make a jumper for Mum.'

Isobel was delighted.

Mothering Cheryl was the liveliest element in her present existence.

Cheryl loved Mum. She and Mum clung together, supporting each other in a life of hardship.

Dad had cleared out and good riddance to him. Mum worked at a sewing machine in a factory, making shirts. Mum said to make the best of it, you was being looked after and getting the best attention, you might be worse off. Mum would be delighted that Cheryl was learning to knit. She wasn't to be told. The jumper was to be a surprise. Mum said, any chance you get to better yourself, take it. They don't come your way that often.

Mum and Cheryl were very poor indeed. It was the rent. If you had a roof, you had a great start, but there it was.

The Red Cross had donated Cheryl's pyjamas, two pair for summer and two pair for winter, and a dressing gown, the first she had ever owned.

Isobel said that she had never owned a dressing gown either. Hers had been given to her at a hospital.

'We just put our coats on. They were on the bed anyhow, as blankets.'

'Funny. I'd have thought you was one of the other lot. You know.'

'No. We were poor, all right. I know all about stuffing my shoes with newspaper when there's a hole in the sole.

And water that soaked in turned paper into papier-mâché one could mould with one's toes. One of the innocent pleasures of childhood.

She heard her mother saying, in cultivated tones, 'We have a good holiday every year.' Poverty and pretension were a very unfortunate combination.

'It's brains that does it,' said Cheryl. 'I was no good at school. Did my best. Mum used to say, that's all anyone can ask. Mind you, I'd have done better if they hadn't gone so fast. Just when I was getting the hang of it, they'd be off onto something else.'

Isobel helped Cheryl with the spelling of her letters to Mum and did not think Cheryl so poor when she observed the open and trusting love she expressed in them. Was this how daughters spoke to mothers, then? 'My own darling Mumma', 'your loving Bubba'?

Cheryl's way to self-improvement must be through reading. She had brought in her suitcase a surprising number of grubby and battered paperbacks, their colourful covers bearing pictures of blonde young women and dark, muscular young men, the young women rarely completely dressed and the young men apparently up to a considerable amount of no good of a sadistic or amorous kind.

This, thought Isobel, is what is called an avid reader, as she watched Cheryl clutching her book, as much with her eyes as with her hands. We all read for escape; Cheryl read with the speed and the desperation of a prisoner digging under the wall of her cell.

Mrs Kent winced at the sight of *The Price of Passion*, eased the loved book out of Cheryl's hands and substituted Daphne du Maurier.

Cheryl clung to her paperback. Mrs Kent left *Rebecca* on Cheryl's cabinet and with a glance commended it to Isobel's attention.

'Well, I like her nerve,' said Cheryl resentfully. 'Nearly tore it away from me. Me own book, isn't it?'

'Read it when she isn't around. And you can read *Rebecca* too, to keep her quiet. You'll like it, I promise. You can manage both of them. There's nothing wrong with your reading speed.'

Rebecca had hard covers. Books with hard covers were full of words Cheryl didn't understand.

'You can look them up in the dictionary,' said Isobel, understanding a moment too late that dictionaries, which were to her the disregarded furniture of even the poorest life, were alien objects to Cheryl. Not unknown, but alien.

'If I got you a dictionary, you could look up the new words. That would be bettering yourself, the way your Mum wants you to.'

Cheryl reflected.

'Okay. If you show me how to use it.'

Isobel wrote to Tom Fenwick, described Cheryl and her situation and asked him to scrounge a dictionary, 'nothing elaborate, something like a *Pocket Oxford* that a student has outgrown.'

She felt no embarrassment about this. Scrounging in a good cause had become a respectable occupation. She was simply a little annoyed at Tom Fenwick's tactlessness when the dictionary arrived—a brand new *Pocket Oxford* inscribed 'To Cheryl, with best wishes, Tom Fenwick.'

Cheryl stared at the inscription and said, without grace, 'Do you mean I'm supposed to keep it?'

Isobel did not answer.

'Hey, what's the matter with you? What's the blub for?'

She was not there. She was nine years old. It was her ninth birthday and she was staring at a parcel on a table in a lakeside boarding house. The parcel was small, wrapped in pink paper and tied with gold string. There was no name on it. Could she dare to suppose that it was meant for her?

She had said in a surly tone, 'Is that thing mine?'

She had been beaten later for ingratitude. Ingratitude!

She shook her head, dislodging the single tear which had settled on each cheekbone.

She could be sure at least that Cheryl had never been told to keep her birthday secret, for fear of embarrassing the family.

'Nothing. I just thought of something. He's just trying to be kind, that's all. Now the next time you see a word you don't know, we'll look for it in the dictionary.'

'Do I have to write and thank him?'

'Not if you don't want to. I'll do that for you.'

*

Mrs Kent was delighted with the dictionary.

'What a wonderful idea! You can be enriching your vocabulary while you read. It's so sad to see a young person wasting time, getting nothing out of the experience. I wish there were more like you, darling.'

Seduced by approval and dazed at the notion that she owned a vocabulary, Cheryl spent more time with *Rebecca* and less with her paperbacks.

She paused over the title of *Love's Minion*.

'Hey, Isobel. What's a minion?'

Isobel paused.

'I'm not too sure. I think it means "darling" and I think it means "servant". Give me the dictionary, will you?'

Cheryl handed the dictionary over. Isobel found the place and read, '"Minion: favourite child, servant, animal etc., slave." I think this time it means "slave".'

Cheryl had listened in deep silence.

'I thought you knew all the words.'

'Good Heavens, no! There are thousands of words I don't know. I just keep on learning them.'

Cheryl's words emerged from that long silence.

'Do you mean that anybody can?'

'Sure, anybody can. I do it all the time.'

Still thoughtful, Cheryl opened her book.

Isobel picked up her knitting.

Cheryl broke the silence with a giggle.

'Isobel?'

'Yes?'

'Are you Doctor Stannard's minion?'

'*What?*'

'Well, you're his favourite child.'

'What makes you say that?'

'Oh, just the way he looks. And his voice goes different when he talks to you, like you both had some joke you weren't telling.'

'That doesn't make me his minion. I'm not a servant or a dog. I wouldn't want to be anybody's minion. Neither would you. It isn't a good thing to be. You'd better read your book and find out.'

She had spoken with unnecessary force.

'Well, don't get off your bike. It was just a thought.'

Minion, indeed! Isobel was never going to be anybody's minion.

That dictionary had been a very good idea. Cheryl, with the means of learning in her hands and under her control, applied herself to the study of English. Isobel explained 'archaic' and 'derogatory', a definition which made Cheryl giggle again.

'You mean like "poofter" and "shit"?'

'And "mug" and "no-hoper".'

Miss Landers contributed a notebook and a pencil. Cheryl listed new words for the edification of Mrs Kent. Isobel helped with emotional support and occasional explanations.

Cheryl was on the way to a higher standard of literacy, and, perhaps, the office job which was Mum's ambition for her.

Isobel tried not to be too proud of this. She hadn't, she reminded herself, had much success with Lance. Anyone

302

with Cheryl's passion for reading even lurid paperbacks must be sensitive to language.

Mum's jumper grew quickly.

Only Cheryl's X-ray showed no change.

One day in February, Sister Connor said to Isobel, without enthusiasm, 'Doctor Stannard wants to see you. Two o'clock today in his office.'

Isobel grimaced at the undertone of disapproval.

'What's this about?'

'Search me.'

But, as so often, Sister Connor knew more than she told. No use asking.

At two o'clock she knocked at the door of the superintendent's office trying not to feel guilty. Damn it, she hadn't done anything wrong. It was just that atmosphere of the headmaster's office that made one apprehensive.

He called, 'Come in, Isobel.'

He smiled at her encouragingly. 'Take a seat. I think it's time we had a talk about your future. Do you feel up to a bit more activity?'

'I've been helping Miss Landers with the occupational therapy.'

It would not do to mention her gratifying success with the sweater kits: six placed, one khaki and turquoise, two khaki and white and three khaki and beige. They would be able to place another if Mrs Kent could find turquoise wool in the town.

'I'm sure you've been a great help to her.'

Politely he repressed amusement.

Perhaps it's more important than you suppose, thought Isobel.

'What I was thinking of was helping Chris in the office. Just start with an hour a day for now, till we see how you go.'

'I'm used to office work. I think I could manage it.'

He smiled again.

'That's not quite what I meant. It's your health I was thinking of.'

He rubbed a knuckle against the corner of his mouth, a sign of hesitation.

'You've made a very good recovery, but at one stage...'

'It was touch and go?'

'Well, there was some cause for concern. We want you to take it slowly, and if you start work here, we can monitor your progress. In fact...'

She waited.

'How do you feel about staying with us for a while? Chris could train you in the office work. We need extra help in the office, particularly someone with shorthand who can help me with the correspondence. It wouldn't be a paid job just yet, but you could have one of the chalets and get your meals here, of course, which would help with the pension. Then when you begin real working hours, we make up the pension to award wages.'

Isobel did not know what to say. She did not know what to think.

'Well, there's no hurry. Think it over and let me know.'

Still too astonished to speak, she got up, nodded and went away.

Sister Connor was blunt.

'You do know that Doctor Stannard is married, don't you?'

Isobel gaped in shock and indignation.

'Of course I know he's married. He's married to Doctor Bennett, who works at the Clinic. And just what has that to do with me?'

'Just thought I'd mention it.'

Isobel spoke with righteous anger.

'And why did you think it necessary to mention it? He has offered me a job, that's all.'

'And what a job. Filling in record cards, typing up case histories.'

'Well, it has to be done, I suppose!'

'It doesn't have to be you. There are plenty of people who can do that job. You should aim a bit higher.'

Isobel said, less certainly, 'It's a contribution. I owe something, don't I? And if that's what's wanted, well... how can I say no?'

'Try it sometime. It gets easier with practice.'

'You wouldn't be getting personal, would you?'

Isobel hoped that she was not blushing.

'If the cap fits, wear it. But that's by the way. There's nothing to be said against Doctor Stannard's morals. Just watch yourself, that's all.'

Nothing against his sexual morals. He's just a careless, amoral bastard who eats little girls like you for breakfast and doesn't even know he's doing it.

Sister Connor tried again, saying dryly, 'And, of course, it's cold out there.'

'Now that's not fair! I'm not afraid of going out.' She wondered as she spoke if that was quite true. It was a shaming memory that the day Stannard had said, 'I think we can stop the medication,' she had felt, not the expected relief, but a serious stab of fear. 'I have somewhere to go and a good chance of a part-time job. That's not the issue.' She added, 'It wouldn't be for life. Maybe a year.'

'That's what you think.' Sister Connor spoke urgently. 'You think you'll stay a year, then some crisis will come and you'll put it off till that's over, and another year will go by. You say you're not scared. Perhaps you're not scared now, but you will be. Life outside will seem tougher and tougher. You'll lose touch with your friends. They'll forget you. This place will seem like home and you'll forget about leaving. Believe me, I've seen this before. Take my advice and go while you can.'

She looked despondently at Isobel, wondering how a young woman could be such a fool as to take a job with an authority figure who traded on charm and looked like the Sheikh of Araby, a man who had paid her too much attention already. She knew she had better not tackle that subject again, yet she tried an indirect approach.

'Would you feel so grateful if Matron offered you a job in the wards?'

Isobel felt that a lie was justified.

'Yes, I would! And I wouldn't have to put up with those beastly insinuations! How did they start? Where do they come from? That talk in the wards…How did it ever start?'

306

'In the wards they will say anything to pass the time. But if they do talk, it's a sign that you shouldn't take a job like that. It just isn't sensible.'

'Well, it makes me think I ought to take the job, just to prove them wrong. And I'm sorry you should have such a poor opinion of my character.'

It's not your character I'm thinking of, my dear.

'Oh, go away. I'm too busy to waste my time talking to you. Just get lost, will you.'

Which was the opposite of what she meant.

On the verandah Isobel said to Doctor Wang, 'But I thought you'd be pleased.'

'I think you have more important things to do than fill in record cards and type case histories.'

'That's what Sister Connor thinks.'

'And I agree. Selfishly, I should be pleased. You would be an ornament to our social circle. Our very limited social circle,' he added bitterly.

'Aren't you happy here, then?'

'I have my wife and my son and this has to be my work. A tubercular doctor has something special to give here, and little to give anywhere else.'

It had not occurred to Isobel that Doctor Wang might have preferred some other specialist field.

'I don't have special skills to offer, of course,' she said snappishly, 'but I thought I could do something for the young people. Boys like Garry and Lance. It's terrible to see Lance lying there in the men's ward like a mummy. There's more to him than that. If one gave him some hope for the

307

future, some sort of vocational training. I think I could talk to the Red Cross. Miss Landers thinks I could. That's something I could do.'

Doctor Wang, who had not forgotten the incident of the joke teeth, said coldly, 'One day Lance will make a decision, whether it is worthwhile to fight to be cured. Nothing you do will influence that decision. Indeed, anything you did to make his life here more tolerable might be to his disadvantage.'

'Yes. I see.'

'There is something you have not learnt from your English poets. It is better to love those who give rather than those who take.'

Isobel said crossly, 'Who's talking about love? You're as bad as Sister Connor. Just plain vulgar, she was, asking me if I knew Doctor Stannard was married. What do you all think of me? I'm grateful to him. So I ought to be.'

'Sexual love is not the only form of love.'

Like Sister Connor, he believed that she was bound for disaster. 'You do have special skills, my dear. They belong elsewhere.'

'I shouldn't give up writing. I can write in the evenings.'

'And what would you write about? APs and lobectomies? Idealists can be very dangerous to people like you and me. Well, I must not try to play the god. You must do what you think best.'

'I don't know what to think.'

It was Doctor Hook who decided her. It was astonishing for Doctor Hook to show any interest in a patient and that made her more inclined to listen to him.

Overtaking her in the corridor, he grasped her by the upper arm and spun her around to face him.

'Listen to me.' His voice was as cold and contemptuous as usual. 'Tuberculosis is an episode, not a way of life. Why don't you get out of here and grow up?'

He then released her arm and walked on, leaving those words resounding behind him.

Grow up. Grow up.

She thought of Katie, talking to the dear little girl in the mirror, Katie crouching under her blankets refusing health.

She thought of the unlined faces of Chris, whom she'd taken to be twenty-five though she was forty. Of Ron, of Max, of Diana, all youthful, all cheerful, forever young. The other category: those who stayed.

This is wog world, where everyone walks a little aslant and everything is a little askew. Everything is a substitute for something else; medical attention for love, doctors and sisters for parents, their approval a substitute for achievement, a hospital for a home and safety for real life and its chances. Had she really been puffed up with pride over the success of a knitted sweater? Yes, she had. And the joy of being chosen by him? Chosen for what? To fill in forms and type up case histories.

She knocked on the door of Doctor Stannard's office and obeyed the call to come in.

'I came to thank you for the offer of a job, but...I want to leave. If that's all right.'

'Oh. I see.' He was silent for a moment. 'I would have liked to keep my eye on you for a while longer, but if you feel confident…very well. When would you like to leave?'

'When I've finished the work I'm doing for Miss Landers. That will be a couple of weeks.'

'Do you have any plans for the future? The Red Cross will give some help with accommodation and employment if you need it. I'd be happier if I knew you had some place to go.'

I am going, thought Isobel, to a rented room, to part-time jobs, chance encounters, rejection slips and maybe some successes. My typewriter will be my only security. My only real fear, the failure of inspiration.

A pompous declaration. Lucky she did not need to speak it aloud.

She said instead, 'Yes. A friend is giving me a room while I look around.'

It was understood that one did not give Mornington as one's last address.

'Right. We'll send your records down to the Clinic and make an appointment for you to report there. You'll need to report every six weeks for a while. Then, if everything goes well, it will be every three months…but they'll tell you all that at the Clinic. And Isobel…'

'Yes, Doctor?'

'No more trips to that corner shop, if you please.'

This time his smile was full-blown and, she had to admit, enchanting.

She smiled back, then both smiles turned to laughter.

310

They had shared a secret and now were sharing a sunlit moment.

'I'll see to it.'

She thought, You may be a selfish, exploitative bastard, but in one corner of my mind, I'm going to love you all my life.

She got up and went through the door, closing it gently and firmly behind her.

Text Classics

textclassics.com.au